'As well a girl with spirit as one with only milk and water in her veins,' Jack murmured softly.

'I shall be honest with you, Charlotte. Left to myself, I would not bother with marriage at all, for I have no great opinion of it, but my grandfather needs me to provide him with an heir. I am very fond of him and minded to oblige him. You need a fortune to clear your father's debts and give your brother a good start in life—why not mine as well as any other's?'

Charlotte digested this in silence for a moment, then looked at him hard. He had brought the curricle to a halt and was looking at her expectantly. He knew the truth, for she had hidden nothing, yet she still felt that he could not have considered fully.

Honesty made her speak out. 'But surely... there must be a girl more suited to the honour of being your wife and the future Marchioness. Why me?'

'Since I am being honest, I have no idea— but I think it is because you amuse me.'

AUTHOR NOTE

This is an adventurous story of a brave girl and an outwardly cool and aloof hero. Jack Delsey can be charming, but can any woman really touch his heart or is it too thickly encased in ice? Charlotte is reckless, but brave, and determined to save her brother from shame. Her escapade leads her straight into the arms of a man whom she knows to be a rake. No sensible girl would give her heart to such a man, but Jack is looking for a lady to be the mother of his heirs, and Charlotte is in danger of being exposed to scandal and ruin…

My readers will know that I like to combine adventure with passionate love stories, and this book has one or two other characters begging for books of their own. I hope to oblige them and my readers by giving them exciting stories. I very much enjoy writing these tales of a bygone time when ladies ought to be fragile creatures but never are, and gentlemen are both heroes and rascals. My hope is that my readers will find these stories well worth reading.

You may contact me at: www.lindasole.co.uk

Look out for the next book
in Anne Herries's trilogy

Regency Brides of Convenience

Coming soon

RESCUED
BY THE VISCOUNT

Anne Herries

First published in Great Britain 2014
by Mills & Boon, an imprint of Harlequin (UK) Limited,
Large Print edition 2015
Harlequin (UK) Limited, Eton House, 18-24 Paradise Road,
Richmond, Surrey TW9 1SR

© 2014 Anne Herries

ISBN: 978-0-263-25533-1

Harlequin (UK) Limited's policy is to use papers that are natural, renewable and recyclable products and made from wood grown in sustainable forests. The logging and manufacturing processes conform to the legal environmental regulations of the country of origin.

Printed and bound in Great Britain
by CPI Antony Rowe, Chippenham, Wiltshire

Anne Herries lives in Cambridgeshire, where she is fond of watching wildlife and spoils the birds and squirrels that are frequent visitors to her garden. Anne loves to write about the beauty of nature, and sometimes puts a little into her books, although they are mostly about love and romance. She writes for her own enjoyment, and to give pleasure to her readers. Anne is a winner of the Romantic Novelists' Association Romance Prize. She invites readers to contact her on her website: www.lindasole.co.uk

Previous novels by the same author:

THE RAKE'S REBELLIOUS LADY
A COUNTRY MISS IN HANOVER SQUARE*
AN INNOCENT DEBUTANTE IN HANOVER SQUARE*
THE MISTRESS OF HANOVER SQUARE*
THE PIRATE'S WILLING CAPTIVE
FORBIDDEN LADY†
THE LORD'S FORCED BRIDE†
HER DARK AND DANGEROUS LORD†
FUGITIVE COUNTESS†
BOUGHT FOR THE HAREM
HOSTAGE BRIDE
THE DISAPPEARING DUCHESS**
THE MYSTERIOUS LORD MARLOWE**
THE SCANDALOUS LORD LANCHESTER**
SECRET HEIRESS
BARTERED BRIDE
CAPTAIN MOORCROFT'S CHRISTMAS BRIDE
   (part of *Candlelit Christmas Kisses*)
A STRANGER'S TOUCH†
HIS UNUSUAL GOVERNESS
PROMISED TO THE CRUSADER
COURTED BY THE CAPTAIN††
PROTECTED BY THE MAJOR††
DRAWN TO LORD RAVENSCAR††
THE REBEL CAPTAIN'S ROYALIST BRIDE†

A Season in Town
†*The Melford Dynasty*
***Secrets and Scandals*
††*Officers and Gentlemen*

DEDICATION

I dedicate this book to my husband,
without whose love and understanding none
of my books could ever have been written.

Prologue

'No, Mama,' Charlotte Stevens cried in dismay. 'Please do not expect such a thing of me—to marry without love for the sake of a fortune...' She stared at her mother, tears welling, but too proud to let them fall. Charlotte was a pretty girl, diminutive, being no more than five feet and three inches, but her large expressive eyes and her unquenchable spirit made up for her lack of height. 'How could you ask it of me?'

'Because there is little choice left to me,' Lady Stevens said. 'Your father is close to ruin and if you do not oblige us by making a splendid marriage, we shall lose everything.'

'Yes, I see...' Charlotte banished her desire to scream and shout, because she loved Papa dearly and could not bear to think he was in so much trouble. 'Who have you selected for me to marry?' She lifted her head, determined to be brave and face whatever terrible fate awaited her.

'It is not that desperate just yet,' Mama told her with a determined smile. 'Fortunately, I have some money put by for you to have a Season in town. You are very lovely, Charlotte. I am convinced that more than one gentleman will be prompted to offer for you—and you may choose for yourself, provided that your choice is in a position to assist your family.'

'Yes, I see,' Charlotte said, her spirits lifting a little. At least she was to be given a little freedom before she was thrown to the lions! 'Well, Mama, I see that there is no choice and I promise that I shall do my best to oblige you.'

'If only your aunt had not sold her best jewels and replaced them with fakes,' Mama said wistfully. 'Your uncle was so kind as to leave them to you, but I'm sure he had no idea that the best diamonds and the rubies, to say nothing of the emeralds and sapphires…all fakes, and only a few paltry trinkets left that are worth little more than a few pounds…'

'I would gladly sell them if they would help Papa.'

'Unfortunately, his debts run to at least twenty

thousand pounds,' Mama said, a note of distress in her voice. 'Even if you sold everything, you could raise no more than a thousand or so. I see nothing else for it, my love—you must marry a fortune.'

Charlotte turned away to look out of the parlour window at the gardens behind her father's house. Mama loved her home and it would break her heart to be forced to leave it—and Matt would have little chance of marrying well if they were ruined. Her love for her father, brother and Mama was too strong for Charlotte to think of rebelling. She knew that she must do her duty. All she could hope was that she would find a rich man who was not too fat or too old, whom she could respect, even if she could not love him.

Sighing, she turned to Mama with a smile. 'I shall do my best to oblige you and Papa, but I cannot promise that anyone will fall in love with me enough to ask for my hand.'

'Some gentlemen do not look for love in marriage,' Mama said. 'They wish for a comfortable arrangement with a girl of good family that will provide children—and, once the heir is secure, they take their pleasures elsewhere. After you have given your husband at least one son, but preferably two—it is always wise to have a spare, you know—he will no doubt leave you to do much as you please.'

'Do all men behave in that manner, Mama?' Charlotte asked innocently. 'Are they never faithful? I thought perhaps if one loved one's husband...'

'Perhaps there are some that remain faithful,' Mama allowed. 'Indeed, I hope that you will find such a man—but you must not look for it, Charlotte. The most you can expect is a comfortable home and a life spent enjoying your children and entertaining your friends.'

'Oh, I see.' Charlotte turned back to gazing out of the window. It seemed that all her dreams of love and romance were a girl's foolishness and nothing more.

'Well, I can only hope you will be sensible,' Mama said. 'I have been honest with you, Charlotte. Papa has taken a house in Berkeley Square. It is very expensive, even for just a few weeks, my love, so you must make the most of your chances—because if you fail...' A little shudder ran through Lady Stevens. 'Well, we shall not consider that eventuality. I have always thought you a remarkable girl and I am certain you will not let us down.'

Charlotte crossed her fingers behind her back. She could only hope that her mother's faith in her was not misplaced. Somehow she must forget her dreams of the tall dark stranger, who would sweep her off her feet and fall desperately in love with her, and make up her mind to accept someone with whom she might make a comfortable life.

Chapter One

'Well, sir, what have you to say for yourself?' The Marquis of Ellington's thick grey brows met in a ferocious scowl that would throw fear into the hearts of most men, but merely brought a smile to his grandson's mouth. 'Damn it, Jack, can you never be serious? This is important. You know you will have to step into my shoes one day, boy. You should consider setting up your nursery.'

'Certainly, sir.' Captain Viscount Delsey's smile flashed out at him. A handsome man, tall, strongly built with good shoulders and legs, dark hair and deep-grey eyes, he had been more or less master of his own fortune since his father died when he was but seventeen, leaving him to the care of his mother, Lady Daisy, and his grandfather. 'I am willing to consider whatever you wish—but you know my opinion on marriage...'

'How many times must I tell you that marriage is a duty that need not interfere with your pleasures? A girl properly brought up and from a decent family will give you the heirs you require without any fuss and bother about love or fidelity. She will understand that a man has his own concerns and confine herself to caring for her children and her home.'

'How perfectly awful for the young woman in question,' Jack murmured softly, but his grandfather's hearing was as acute as ever.

'A lady understands these things,' the marquis growled. 'If your sense of what is right is so nice, then you must find a young lady who will fulfill all your needs.'

'Ah, but where is such a lady to be found?' Jack teased. 'Where is the beauty that can tame the rake's heart and make it hers? I will make you a promise, Grandfather. If I ever find such a young woman, I will marry her whatever walk of life she comes from—and then I shall settle down and be the family man you all want me to be.'

The marquis sighed and shook his head, a scowl settling on his noble brow. 'You will be the death of me, sir. I forbid you to bring a woman of ill repute into this family.'

'How can you think that I would do such a thing?' Jack pulled a mocking face of dismay. 'Do you imagine I spend all my time with such barques of frailty?'

'From what the gossips say you have been through a string of opera dancers and the like in the past year or so! It is time you thought about your family—about me. I have done my best for you, in all conscience—could you not give some thought to the idea of finding a wife?'

'You should not listen to Mama, sir,' Jack said. 'She spends too much time with Aunt Seraphina, and *she* has the gossip from my cousin Reginald. Now honestly—would you wish me to be like your nephew Reginald?'

'No, I should not. The man is a prosy fool.' The marquis exploded with wrath. 'Jack, why will you tease me so? You know I think the world of you, boy. I am proud of you—of what you achieved in the army, even though I did not wish you to go to war—but I cannot live for ever and it means a great deal to me to see your first son: my heir. God forbid that Reginald should have a son to inherit the estate.'

'Yes, that would be very bad,' Jack said thoughtfully. 'I should not like to think of Reginald stepping into your shoes—though I must say I have no intention of dying for many years yet.'

'Your father's accident was sudden and unexpected.' A look of sudden deep and hurtful sadness flashed into the old man's eyes.

Jack's mirth was sobered instantly. 'Yes, sir, forgive me. I do not mean to upset you.'

'Then…to please me?'

'You want me to visit Mama's cousin Lord Sopworth and inspect his daughter Celia?' Jack's brows met in a frown and at that moment the likeness between the two men was very marked. 'Very well, sir. I shall accept Uncle Gerald's invitation, but I make no promises. I dare say the young lady is all that you promise—but marriage without love, or at least a deep affection and respect, leads only to unhappiness. You have only to remember what it was like for my father and mother.'

'That was unfortunate,' his grandfather admitted. 'Your father was a selfish man—he inherited that trait from his mother—and I fear he made your dear mama suffer. I am very fond of Lady Daisy. I thank God that you have her sweet nature, though you also get your stubbornness from me.'

'I shall pay my uncle a visit,' Jack acquiesced, 'but I do not promise to make Celia an offer, unless she suits me. Now, if there is nothing more, sir, I am committed to some friends for this evening. I must go home and change.'

'I had hoped you might dine with us?'

'Not this evening, sir. Perhaps tomorrow, before you return to the country.'

'Very well. And when will you leave for Cambridgeshire?'

'At the end of next week. I have engagements until then—and I must give my uncle time to prepare.'

'I shall see you tomorrow, then, Jack.'

'I shall look forward to it.'

Leaving his grandfather's study, Jack walked in leisurely fashion from the house, stopping in the magnificent hall to exchange a few words first with the marquis's valet and then with Pearson, the butler who had served at Ellington House for as long as he could recall. His grandfather's servants had been eager to tell him that the marquis had called the doctor on two separate occasions recently. Indeed, it was the reason he had come to London for a few weeks' stay, preferring his home deep in the Sussex countryside to the bustle of town.

'I know the master would never dream of troubling you,' Pearson told him, 'but he is not as well as I should like, Captain Delsey, and that is the truth.'

'Do you know what the trouble was?' he asked of the valet.

'It's his heart, sir. Nothing too serious yet, I understand, but he's been warned to cut down on his port and cigars—and to take things more easily.'

Jack thanked them both for confiding in him. His grandfather had said nothing of the doctor's visits, but it explained why he had been summoned and lectured on the subject of marriage once more. However, the valet and butler had alarmed him with their tales, for Jack was sincerely fond of his grandfather and did not wish to distress him more than need be.

The marquis had never interfered unnecessarily in Jack's life. When he'd left college, Ellington had introduced him into society, put him up for his clubs and given him the name of his tailor. After that, he'd pretty much left him to his own devices, merely asking him to consider carefully when he announced that he was taking up a commission in the army. War had been looming at that time and Jack spent some years away fighting under Wellington's command. The friendships he'd made then formed the basis of his circle now, and consisted of some six gentlemen he felt bound to as brothers, though he had countless acquaintances for he was a popular man—both with the gentlemen and the ladies, which accounted for the gossip concerning his affairs.

The viscount was a catch and more than one pretty young woman had tried to enchant him, but although he was happy to indulge them with a dance or a light flirtation, none could say that he gave them reason to hope. He spent more time flirting with the matrons than their daughters, and more than one thought of Jack Delsey as she lay next to a snoring husband and wished that the young viscount was in her bed rather than the man lying next to her.

Jack had been home from the war for more than a year now, spending his time much as every other wealthy young man of fashion, visiting his clubs, placing bets at Tattersall's or Newmarket and taking pride in his stables. His pistols came from Manton's; he wore coats made by Scott or Weston, and his boots shone like silk. Jack's cravats were always neat and freshly starched, but he wore them in a simple fashion rather than in the complicated folds and frills of the dandy set. He was happiest when exercising his horses or fencing with friends, or popping a hit over the guard of Gentleman George, a pugilist whose salon he visited now and then to keep in shape. In short, he was what society was pleased to call a Corinthian and idolised by most of the young bloods. To call him a rake was unfair, though if all the fluttering one direct glance from those compelling eyes aroused in a myriad of female breasts was taken into account, his reputation was deserved to a point. Without meaning to, his careless dalliance had sent more than one lady into a swoon, leaving a trail of wounded hearts when his casual flirting came to naught.

His grandfather had, though, exaggerated the number of mistresses Jack had kept over the past few years. During his service in the army, he had found some of the beautiful Spanish girls much to his taste. Like his friends, he had taken his pleasure where he could, knowing that each day might be his last, but the camp followers had been girls of a lower class and none of them had ever touched Jack's heart.

There had been three ladies with whom he had shared intimate relations since then, one of them a married lady whose husband was thirty years her senior and more interested in his port than his wife, the other two opera dancers. Jack's current light o' love was very beautiful, but also very greedy, and he suspected unfaithful. He believed she had other lovers despite their arrangement, and it was in his mind that he would tell Lucy it was over before he went down to the country.

Jack supposed that he ought to think seriously of marriage. He was seven and twenty and he'd been his own master for ten years, for though his fortune had been in trust for four years the allowance was so generous that he had never been in danger of finding himself in debt. Since coming into his capital, he'd made several improvements to his estate and to the investment of his funds. His fortune was sufficient to support a family with no alteration to his way of life, other than on a personal level. Indeed, some jealous folk had been known to complain that he had far more money than was good for him.

The trouble was that he enjoyed his life and saw

no reason to change it. As a single man he need consider no one else's feelings very much. The obligatory visit to his mama and his grandfather in the country every few weeks or so cost him little and he was free to take off to stay with a friend, visit Newmarket or Bath, or attend a mill at the drop of a hat. Some would say that marriage need change very little in his life, but Jack could recall seeing his mama in tears when she was left alone in the country with a small son and her husband was off enjoying himself in town. He imagined that his dislike of the idea of marriage had grown in him over the years, triggered by an incident when he was seventeen, and as yet he had not met a lady who was beautiful or generous enough to overcome that dislike.

His father had indeed been a selfish man. Jack wondered if he had inherited the trait, for he was rather inclined to go off without informing his family that he would be out of town and unreachable for a few days. He knew that Mama sometimes worried about him, though the marquis said she was a fusspot, and perhaps she was. It would have been much better had Jack not been an only child, but for some reason there had been no more babies in that unfortunate marriage.

Sighing, Jack put his troubled thoughts to rest. He was engaged with friends for the evening and it would not do to be caught up by a problem he was not sure he could solve.

Marriage to a woman he could not like or admire would be worse than a living death. Perhaps it was not strictly necessary to fall in love, but as yet he had not met a young lady that made him want to see her every day, let alone protect her and cherish her for the rest of his life.

'Have you seen the latest heiress?' Lieutenant Peter Phipps asked of Jack when they met at the club, where they were engaged to dine with three of their friends. 'Cynthia Langton has everything—beauty, wit and money.'

'Really? A veritable goddess,' Jack quizzed, one brow arched in mockery. 'Going to have a tilt at her, Phipps old fellow? Run aground again?'

Phipps shook his head, a wry smile on his mouth. 'Not yet, Jack. I had a run of luck last month and I'm just managing to hold my head above water. Not that she would look at me even if I had hopes in that direction. She may be beautiful and rich, but she's like an iceberg—so proud and cold. I imagine she's after a marquis or an earl at least…'

'A bit above your touch, then, and mine,' Jack quipped. 'Never mind, there's always the Dumpling. If you really fall into the suds, she would have you like a shot.'

'Cruel, and unworthy of you,' Phipps said. 'I rather like Miss Amanda, she's got a warm heart, even if she is a little on the dumpy side.'

'Well, then, your problem is solved,' Jack murmured wickedly. 'You have only to crook your little finger and she will fall into your arms—if they are strong enough to catch her.'

'Really Jack, that's a bit strong,' his friend said and frowned. 'She cannot help being short and she likes sweet things…which I do myself, but I never seem to put on weight.'

'You are a regular lanky boy. You should wed her because you're all bones while she is an armful of delicious flesh… Oh, I'm merely jesting,' Jack replied as he saw that Phipps was annoyed. 'I think Amanda Hamilton is a pleasant young woman and will no doubt make a loving wife. Just the sort of young lady my grandfather thinks would suit me if his hints this afternoon are anything to go by.'

'So that's why you're in a bad mood this evening.' Phipps smiled, clapping him on the shoulder. 'I know how you feel, old chap. Pater had a go at me last time I went down to the estate—told me that he had bailed me out for the final time and it was up to me to find an heiress.'

'Duty calls us both, it seems, but do not let it spoil our evening. Here come the others.'

Jack turned to greet the three young men with a smile and a handshake. They had all five of them served on Wellington's staff and, though two of them had recently become engaged, they were all still single and could enjoy a night at the club drinking and playing cards.

'How are you, Jack?' Malcolm Seers asked, shaking his hand with a firm grip. 'This is my last evening in town before I go down to the country. Please congratulate me, I have just become engaged to Miss Willow.'

'Jane Willow?' Jack asked and grinned, only half-mocking, because Miss Willow was one of the few young ladies in society that he actually liked. 'So she accepted you at last? I thought it would not be long...'

'She couldn't make up her mind, but in the end

I wore her down.' Malcolm looked pleased with himself. 'I'm the happiest man alive.'

'Then I do congratulate you. I shall miss you when you disappear into the mists of matrimony, but I'm pleased for you.'

'Oh, Jane wants to spend as much time as possible in town and you're a favourite with her, Jack. We shall expect you to visit often when we are in the country.'

Jack murmured something appropriate, but knew it would not be the same once his friend married. Malcolm was a serious man and had been a dedicated soldier—and he would be as dedicated to his wife and family. They would still be friends, but things would be different...

Jack had a hunted feeling, as if he were being driven in a direction he did not wish to go. His grandfather had pushed him towards marriage and his friends were succumbing one by one to its lure—how long could Jack resist?

It was barely three in the morning when the friends parted at the club, three of them going to their homes and leaving only Jack and Phipps to consider where to go next.

'The night is young,' Jack murmured. 'We

should find a gambling hell and indulge ourselves for an hour or so.'

'Not for me, old fellow,' Phipps declined. 'I've sworn off gambling for the next month at least, otherwise I shall be in hot water with my father. I'll come home with you for a drink if you like, otherwise I think I'll call a cab and go home.'

'I think I'll pay Lucy a visit,' Jack decided and laughed. 'I'll see you at Markham's affair tomorrow?'

'Yes, certainly,' his friend agreed. 'You will be certain to meet Miss Langton there.'

'Oh, I'll leave her for you, my friend,' Jack said and gave him a friendly punch in the arm.

They parted on the best of terms, Jack sauntering through the streets as if he had not a care in the world, while Phipps summoned a cab to take him home. A smile touched Jack's sensuous mouth, for if he were not mistaken Phipps was a little the worse for wear, while he had drunk only enough to feel mildly pleased with the world. A visit to his mistress would round the evening off nicely and stop him falling into the melancholy that more serious thoughts of marriage looked likely to bring about.

* * *

He had been walking for perhaps five minutes when he heard the screams. Someone—a girl, he thought—was screaming for help. Jack's chivalrous instincts were instantly aroused and he looked for the source of the sound, which seemed to come from the park across the street. Even as he hesitated, he saw a small figure run from that direction followed by two very drunken gentlemen, who lurched unsteadily in the youth's wake.

'Hounds, hounds to me,' one of them called and made a loud noise that was supposed to sound like a hunting cry. 'We'll catch the little vixen yet!'

The second gentleman lurched after his comrade even as the diminutive figure bolted across the road. Jack moved like lightning, grabbing the figure and noting it was a young gentleman with delicate, rather female features, before pushing him behind him against the wall and turning to confront the pursuing gentlemen.

'That's the spirit, old fellow,' the first cried gleefully. 'Hand the vixen over and we'll finish our business with her.'

'And what might that be?' Jack asked in a pleasant but cool voice. 'I believe you are a little the

worse for wear, sir. Pray let me recommend you
to the comfort of your bed.'

'Damn you, sir! What business is it of yours
what I choose to do? Pray stand aside and let us
at the—'

'I asked you to take yourselves off nicely.'
Jack's voice carried a hint of steel. 'Now I'm
telling you. Get off where you belong before I
teach you some manners.'

'Think you'll have the bitch for yourself, do
you?' the man snarled. 'I'll show you!' He threw
a wild swing at Jack and found himself on the
receiving end of a heavy punch. It floored him
and he lay moaning on the ground. 'She's a whore
and a thief,' he muttered.

'Come on, Patterson.' His friend, in slightly
steadier condition, bent down to help him rise.
'You don't know she's a thief, even if we did see
her climb out of that window.'

Patterson muttered something vile, but accepted his friend's help. He glared at Jack, holding his friend's arm as they reeled away.

'Good riddance to her,' he muttered and then
laughed and pointed a finger. 'Look at her go.
She's got away from us all.'

Glancing over his shoulder, Jack saw the diminutive figure disappearing round the corner. He was conscious of regret for he would have liked to discover whether the young person was a youth or the girl in disguise that the drunken gentlemen seemed to imagine. He had not even had a chance to discover if she—or he—was harmed, but at least he had prevented further harm.

He stood his ground, watching as the two men lurched off down the street in the opposite direction to the one the fugitive was heading. Only when he was certain that the young escapee must be out of sight did he resume his journey. He was vaguely aware that the knuckles of his right hand were bruised, but he dismissed that as a worthwhile consequence of his interference in what might have been a very unfortunate outcome for the young person.

Jack found that his mood had changed. He was amused by what he'd seen of the fugitive's behaviour, catching the merest glimpse of an elfin face in the streetlights. If the inebriated men were to be believed, the young person was a thief and a whore—but the clothes the fugitive had been wearing were good quality, the property of a young gentleman of perhaps thirteen or so. That did not bring the words thief or whore to Jack's mind, but something more innocent like a very young gentleman escaping from his home for a lark. Unless it had been a girl in borrowed clothing, which was an intriguing idea.

Jack arrived outside the small but exclusive house he had purchased for his mistress's use. The windows were in darkness, as he might have supposed, had he given a thought to the hour. He considered climbing over the gate and going round to the back of the house; he could throw stones at the window and get Lucy to come down and let him in without waking the servants.

Suddenly, he realised that the desire to see his mistress had left him. He laughed ruefully and turned away just as a light came on in the hall upstairs. Hesitating, Jack was still wondering whether to call on Lucy just for a drink and a chat when the door opened and a gentleman came out.

He recognised the man as Lord Harding—a man he particularly disliked as a hardened gambler, and, if Jack were right, a particularly nasty cheat. He was the kind of man who fastened on young men just out on the town, introducing them to sleazy gambling hells and all kinds of dissolute activities.

There could be only one reason why he would

be leaving Lucy's house at this hour of night and the realisation turned Jack's stomach. Any desire he'd had to see his mistress was banished. He would finish the affair tomorrow by sending a farewell gift and a letter that would leave her in no doubt of his disgust at her behaviour. He had no desire to follow Harding in her bed!

Had it been almost any other gentleman, Jack would have taken the discovery with a laugh, for he'd guessed she was not the sort to be faithful for long—but Harding was a man he really disliked.

Jack walked the length of the street before hailing a cab to take him home. He had a bad taste in his mouth and was angry that he'd allowed himself to be duped so long. Well, he would make sure that when he next took a lover she was at least honest enough to entertain only one protector at a time. Why was it that so many women thought it necessary to lie to get their own way? If there was one thing Jack could not stand, it was a liar or a cheat.

Having arrived in the pleasant square where he lived, he was just paying the cab driver his fare when he looked across the pleasant gardens to his left and saw a diminutive figure clamber over a wrought-iron railing and disappear down the steps leading to the servants' quarters.

Jack hesitated, because although he was friendly with Lord Bathurst, the owner of the house, he knew that it had recently been let to a family, with whom he was not yet acquainted. He did not feel able to knock on the door at this hour in the morning and tell them they might have an intruder—especially as he could not be sure the youth he'd seen earlier and the figure climbing the gate were one and the same.

Indeed, he was not sure of anything. However, he could not allow a neighbour to be robbed—if the girl was a thief, if she was even a girl...

Cursing, Jack sprinted across the square himself and tried the gate, which was locked, as he might have known. He climbed the railing easily, feeling guilty though his intention was quite innocent. Peering down the narrow stone steps, he was just in time to see the flicker of a candle as a door opened and his quarry disappeared inside.

It shut before he could reach it, but not before he'd seen a taller young man come and look about, as if to make sure that no one was there.

Jack stood uncertainly. The taller youth was also wearing the clothes of a gentleman. Whoever he was, Jack did not think that he was in collusion with his quarry to rob an unsuspecting family. No, his first impression was probably correct and the diminutive youth was just kicking up a lark, aided and abetted, it seemed, by an older brother.

Laughing softly to himself, Jack climbed back over the railing and stood on the pavement, glancing about before re-crossing the square and knocking on his own front door. His man answered almost immediately and Jack nodded as he was admitted.

'A good evening, sir?'

'Yes, I think so,' Jack said. 'Go to bed now, Cummings. I'll see to myself this evening.'

'I'll just lock up, my lord,' his valet answered with quiet dignity. 'Mr Jenkins has only just retired. I took it upon myself to sit up this evening—and I should be failing in my duty if I didn't attend you, sir.'

'I do not imagine the world will end if I remove my own boots for once, Cummings.'

Jack sauntered past him and up the stairs, lost in thoughts that were mildly intriguing. Just who was the young imp who had got himself into trouble that evening?

Well, he had been remiss in making the acquaintance of his new neighbours, so he would give himself the pleasure of remedying that later in the day.

Chapter Two

'Charlie!' Mr Matthew Stevens cried and grabbed his sister's shoulders, giving her a little shake. 'Thank goodness you're back. You've been so long and I was terrified that you'd been caught!'

'Oh, do stop fussing, Matt.' Charlotte dimpled mischievously up at her brother. 'I told you I could do it. It was a simple climb up the wisteria into his bedchamber. He'd left the window open, as we knew he always does, and the stupid thing was lying on his dressing chest. I grabbed it and climbed down again, in no more than a few minutes. He will never guess it was I—no one could possibly know. I shall just have to make sure never to wear the necklace in town, because if he saw it he might recognise it.'

'I was sick with worry the whole time. You

were so long. If it was as simple as that, why were you so long?'

'Getting the necklace back was easy enough,' Charlotte said and bit her bottom lip. 'It was when I climbed *out* of the window and then over the railings into the street that I got into a bit of bother…'

'What happened? Damn it, Charlie. Mother will kill me if I've ruined your chances. I should never have let you talk me into letting you risk yourself.'

'You didn't, you just stood there and lectured me about my morals—which is more than rich when it was you who stole the damned thing in the first place.'

'I didn't intend to steal from you, Charlie,' Matt said, torn between remorse and reproach. 'He is just such a brute…to be honest, I'm scared of him. He said if I didn't pay the gambling debt he would approach Father and I couldn't let that happen.'

'No, it would have been dreadful,' his fond sister said and smiled her forgiveness. 'I don't care about the wretched necklace, but if you'd asked I would have given you what is left of my allowance, and I could have told you that those diamonds were fakes.'

'How was I to know? They're damned good, Charlie. I thought they were real.'

'Uncle Ben left me all his wife's jewellery in good faith. I'm sure he didn't know that Aunt Isobel had replaced most of it with fakes.'

'Why do you think she did it?' Matt asked, puzzled. 'Surely her allowance was enough without doing such a thing to family heirlooms?'

'I think she was a secret gambler,' Charlotte said, wrinkling her smooth brow. She sighed and shook out her long dark hair, which had been jammed under one of her brother's old school caps with the badge removed. They were in her private sitting room, which led into her bedchamber, and she was tired, the shock of having narrowly escaped being roughly abused coming home to her now that she was safe. 'Mama said something about it when we had the jewels valued and realised some were fake.'

'I feel awful about having Uncle Ben's money now. He might have left some of it to you if he'd guessed about the jewels.'

'That money is to buy you a commission in the army and to keep you as a gentleman should be able to live. Besides, you won't come into it for another year and it isn't so very much after all.'

'No.' He looked rueful. 'Harding thought I was the heir to a large fortune, which is why he fastened his claws into me—but ten thousand and a small country estate is hardly a huge fortune, Charlie, and I can't touch a penny for ages. If I'd had my own money I wouldn't have taken your necklace. I was going to pay you back when I could afford it, and I knew you didn't like that necklace anyway.'

'It is old-fashioned,' Charlotte replied. 'Had it been real I should have had it remodelled for me, but Mama says it isn't worth it. She says I can wear her diamonds if I have occasion.'

'Why did you go to all that trouble to get it back then?'

'Because if Lord Harding realised you'd given him a fake necklace to settle your debt to him, he would have labelled you a cheat and a thief—can you imagine what the gossips would make of that? My chances of making a good marriage would be lost, as would yours of joining a decent regiment.'

'Yes…' Matt looked gloomy. 'I've been such a damned fool, Charlie. If it hadn't been for you…'

'It's over and no one ever needs to know anything about it,' Charlotte said. She thought about the man who had grabbed at her as she was passing through the park. His hands had soon discovered her secret and the thought of him touching her breasts made her feel sick, but it had been dark there in the park and she was fairly certain that he would not recognise her if they met in society. Both he and his companion had been drunk—but the man who had saved her was another matter. Charlotte knew him by sight, for she'd seen him leaving his house across the square earlier that evening, and a couple of times he'd driven by her as she was returning to their house, but they had never met in a formal way. She knew that for a moment he'd had the opportunity to look at her face in the streetlight—but had he seen enough to know her when she was dressed as a young lady of fashion? She could only hope that he had not taken much notice.

'I hope no one will find out, for both our sakes,' Matt said. 'If Harding guessed it was my sister that took the necklace…he might kill me. Yet, you're right, Charlie. He can't know. No one can if we keep it to ourselves.'

'I'm not about to tell anyone.' She dimpled

wickedly up at him, her eyes wide and innocent,
but filled with mischief. 'It's over now, Matt. Go
to bed and let me get some sleep. It's that big ball
tomorrow and I want to look my best. Unless I
can find a husband poor Papa is going to lose
everything.'

'Why did he have to invest his money un-
wisely?' Matt bemoaned the situation. 'We were
happy enough with what we had—but he thought
that venture in the East would bring in a fortune
for silks and spices, only the ship sank and all
its cargo with it.'

'And he didn't think to insure it,' Charlotte said.
'Thankfully, Mama had some funds put by for
my come out—and if I can find a rich husband
he will settle Papa's debts and all will be well.'

'What about you?' her brother asked, looking at
her with dark brown eyes that were very like her
own, except that hers were flecked with gold and
his were simply dark. 'Will you be happy taking
a man just for his money? He may be years older
and not at all handsome.'

'Beggars cannot always choose,' Charlotte said,
sighing despite herself, because she had once
dreamed of being swept off her feet by a tall
dark prince who would carry her off to his castle

and lavish her with love and gifts. 'I shall hope for the best. And not all rich men are old and fat.'

'No, I suppose there are a few eligible young men around, if you can find one. A man would be a fool not to marry you if he were rich and single.'

'You are my brother and prejudiced in my favour.' She gave a gurgle of laughter and then darted at him, giving him a peck on the cheek before pushing him towards the door. 'Go, before we wake everyone and they come to see what's going on. I want to get out of these things before anyone but you has the chance to see me.'

Locking the door behind him, Charlotte went into her bedroom and glanced at herself in the long cheval mirror. A mischievous grin curved her mouth as she saw that she made a fetching youth. No one would know she was a girl unless they happened to touch her in the wrong places, which one of those horrid men had done. They hadn't seemed to care whether she was a girl or a youth, but were intent on having their way with her in the park either way. And would have done had she not kneed one of them in his privates, leaving him yelling in anger and pain as she made it as far as the gates. However, they would probably have caught her again had it not been for the viscount—Captain Jack Delsey.

Charlotte had known the name of the gentleman who came to her rescue almost from the first day they took up residence in the pleasant garden square. Her mama had been given a list of the residents of the square so that she might leave calling cards, however, she could not do so until they called on her for she was the newcomer. Papa might call if he so wished on the single gentlemen, of which there were two in residence at the moment. One was a widower with three children on a rare visit to town, the children left in the country with their maternal grandmother, and the other was the viscount. Papa had not yet called on either, though the widower had left his card and therefore Mama was preparing to invite him to a small card party she was arranging with her acquaintance in town. The viscount, meanwhile, was the grandson of the Marquis of Ellington and one of the best prizes on the matrimonial market. However, Mama had warned Charlotte not to set her hopes too high.

'Captain Viscount Delsey is rather too far above us, dearest,' she'd told Charlotte when they'd seen him drive up in a spanking rig of the first order. 'Quite charming I understand—but elusive. Some of the most beautiful girls in society have cast their lures at him, but he ignores them all. He is a rake, my love, and flirts with all the pretty girls, but never forms an attachment—or only clandestine ones. He would merely break your heart. Now Mr Harold Cavendish is another matter. He is in his early forties, still attractive and wealthy—and Mrs Featherstone told me that he is looking for a wife to care for his poor motherless children.'

'A widower with three children, Mama?' Charlotte pulled a face. 'I think I would prefer someone who had not been previously married—we are not desperate just yet, are we?'

'No, dearest, of course not. I do not wish to push you into anything that distresses you. Indeed, I wish this had not been necessary at all— but poor Papa is at his wits' end, and if you do not marry to oblige us...'

'But I shall, Mama,' Charlotte assured her. 'Please do not worry. There will be someone who is both rich and agreeable to me. I promise you, it will all come right in the end.'

'My poor dear child,' her mama said. 'Had your aunt not sold those jewels we might have avoided this. You could have sold them to pay a part of Papa's debt.'

'I would gladly have done so,' Charlotte assured her. 'But they are worth very little. I must marry to advantage. I have made up my mind to it—and I shall not let you down.'

Undressing and hiding the youth's clothing at the bottom of one of her drawers, Charlotte reflected on that evening's episode. Had she been caught and abused…it did not bear thinking about! If she'd been unmasked and her wicked act had been revealed, she would have been ruined and her family with her. It was no wonder that Matt had been terrified. He'd begged her not to consider such a mad escapade, but she'd overruled him, as she always had in the past. Her brother might be three years older, but she had the stronger will. It was she who ought to have been a boy for very little frightened her. Even the near-escape she'd had had not truly bothered her, only the fear of what might have happened.

But it hadn't and she refused to worry about what might have been. She'd recovered the fake necklace. Lord Harding could only blame himself for leaving the necklace on his dressing table before going off for the evening. Besides, he deserved no sympathy. Matt was certain he'd been cheated and was determined never to play cards with the man again.

Charlotte was just going to forget all about it.

Mama had decided to leave cards at the homes of her acquaintances in town and wanted Charlotte to accompany her.

'We shall not stay anywhere, but merely leave cards,' Mama had told her. 'On the way home we will visit the mantua maker and collect some rather lovely shawls I ordered from Madame Rousseau.'

However, Mama's plans did not go entirely as she anticipated, for at the first house they called, they encountered Lady Rushmore just as she was leaving and she begged them to come in and take some refreshment with her.

'It is such an age since we met and I was going to call on you this afternoon,' the lady said, insisting on sending for coffee and little almond cakes in the front parlour.

They were soon joined by the lady's son and daughter, who had come down to see why their mama had not gone shopping as she planned. Miss Amelia was a pretty, fair girl with a lisp and pouting lips, her hair hanging in ringlets about a heart-shaped face. Her brother Robert was tall, well built and dressed in the height of fashion, with shirt points so high he could scarcely turn his head. He seemed to spend most of his time preening before one of the gilt-framed mirrors, and when he did speak his conversation was of horses and his new phaeton.

Miss Amelia laughed a lot and talked endlessly of her new clothes, which she was purchasing for her trousseau. She had recently become engaged and was interested in little but her wedding and clothes. Accustomed to talking of poetry and music with her brother, and of listening to Papa speaking in an entertaining way of the gentlemen he met and dined with at his clubs, Charlotte found herself longing to go home after just half an hour.

However, just as she thought they might be ready to leave, a gentleman was announced as Sir Percival Redding. He was a man of perhaps five and thirty, brother to Lady Rushmore and of a florid complexion. His dark hair curled in a manner intended to be casual and his clothes were as elegant as his nephew's, though slightly more wearable for his shirt points were not above average, and his coats were cut to allow for ease of movement. However, he had a pleasant manner and regaled the ladies with his tales of society.

Somehow he ousted Amelia from her seat beside Charlotte and sat down to tell her the story of how he had recently dined with the Prince Regent at Brighton in the Pavilion.

''Pon my word, Miss Stevens, it must have been nigh on a hundred degrees. I felt I was melting and poor dear Lady Melrose fainted twice.'

Charlotte had heard that the Regent liked his rooms over-warm, but was interested in all the details of the Pavilion, with its Chinese decoration and the towers that gave it the look of an Eastern Palace.

It was as Mama stood up to pull on her gloves some twenty minutes later, clearly intending to leave, that Sir Percival stood and bowed to Charlotte, as she too rose from the small sofa. His neck was a little pink as he bent over her hand and asked if she was going to Markham's ball that evening.

'Yes, we have been invited. It is my first ball in town, though I have been to the assemblies in Bath several times.'

'I too shall be there,' he said, smiling down at her. 'May I hope that you will save me two dances, Miss Stevens? I prefer the country dances for I am not enamoured of the waltz—though I see no harm in it for others.'

'Thank you, sir,' Charlotte replied easily. She quite liked the gentleman, for he was friendly and more entertaining than his relatives and she was grateful to know that she would not sit out at least two of the dances that evening. 'I shall be very happy to reserve the first of the evening and the last country dance before supper.'

'I shall now look forward to the evening,' he promised, looking a little like the cat that had stolen the cream. 'And if I may I shall claim you for supper.'

Charlotte inclined her head and followed her mama from the house. It was only when they were inside the carriage that Mama turned to her with an approving look.

'I am proud of you, Charlotte. Sir Percival was very taken with you. I saw it at once. I do not say it will lead to an offer immediately, but he would be a good choice. He was in the army for many years, my love, and never married, but Lady Rushmore told me she believes he is at last thinking of settling down. Would it not be a fine thing if you were married to the brother of one of my oldest friends? He is comfortable, you know. Perhaps not as rich as...'

Charlotte's mind drifted away as she glanced out of the window, watching the fashionable ladies and gentlemen promenading in the busy streets. The morning had flown and they would have time only to collect their shawls before returning home for nuncheon.

Mama was still droning on about how fortunate it was that they should mcct her friend, as she was driving away, and Charlotte managed to stifle her sigh. She supposed that Mama must review every gentleman they encountered as a possible husband for her daughter, but she wished she would not jump to the idea of marriage so swiftly. It was not that she disliked Sir Percival. Indeed, she would prefer him to the father of three motherless children, but Charlotte was still hoping for more. Surely she was entitled to a little romance before she settled for marriage?

When they were set down outside their lodgings in the fashionable square, she shook out the folds of her gown and walked into the house a little ahead of her mother. She stopped abruptly as she saw her father; he was bidding farewell to a gentleman, who had clearly been visiting while they were out.

Charlotte's heart caught with a mixture of shock and pleasure, for it was the viscount, and mixed with the relief that he had at last called on them was the fear that he might recognise her from the previous night.

'Ah, Charlotte my dear.' Her father's warm deep voice reached out to her. 'You have returned just in time to meet Captain Viscount Delsey— he lives in the house opposite, just across the square, and kindly called on me this morning to invite us all to a dinner and cards one evening next week. Sir, this is my daughter, Charlotte.'

Charlotte took off her bonnet and shook out her long dark ringlets, extending her hand towards their visitor as she dipped gracefully. 'I am delighted to meet you, sir, and sorry we were out all morning.'

'No matter,' he murmured, lifting her hand to drop an air kiss just fractionally above the soft leather glove. 'I was happy to meet your father— and your charming brother. Matthew is to attend a card party with me another evening, but I believe we are all promised to Lord Markham this evening.'

'Yes, we are looking forward to it,' she said, her heart fluttering as he gave her an intent look before releasing her hand. She glanced down, her long lashes hiding the fluttering emotions inside her. Could he possibly have recognised her from that brief glance the previous night—or was it just her guilt that made her think his gaze narrowed in speculation?

'As am I,' he replied gallantly. 'Will you grant me the privilege of a dance for this evening— preferably a waltz? I trust you do waltz, Miss Stevens?'

'Yes, Captain Delsey, I do and I shall,' she replied, demurely. 'I have waltzed in Bath several times, and in town, with the approval of Lady Jersey, who is a great friend of Mama's and granted me vouchers for Almack's. I am older than I look, you see.'

She saw an answering gleam of humour in his eyes, his brows rising to tease her. 'I would hazard a guess at eighteen?'

'I am more than nineteen,' she murmured in a soft voice. 'It is my size, you understand. People think because I am petite I must be younger.'

'Ah, such a great age,' he murmured. 'One would think you hardly above fourteen if one saw you briefly from a distance…' His eyes held a look of mocking amusement that made her heart thud rapidly.

Was he hinting that he had recognised the urchin of the previous evening? Her gaze fell away in confusion for she was unsure how to reply.

Fortunately, her mama had entered the house, and, after taking off her shawls, bonnet and gloves, looked expectantly towards the viscount. The introductions were made and Charlotte was able to move on towards the stairs. She was about to climb them, when she heard herself addressed and turned once more to see that the viscount had spoken directly to her.

'I was wondering if you and Lady Stevens would like to drive to Richmond with me on Friday, Miss Stevens? My sister, Lady Sally Harrison, has got up a picnic to watch a balloon ascension and she asked me to bring some friends with me. I have invited two gentlemen, who will ride—but there is room in my curricle for both of you.'

'We should enjoy that very much,' Mama answered for her. 'It is kind of you, sir—and your cousin. We are not yet acquainted with Lady Harrison.'

'Then I shall remedy that this evening,' he promised, bowed deeply to her and sent Charlotte a knowing smile before leaving.

'Well, what a charming young man,' Lady Stevens said as she followed her daughter to the landing above. 'I hardly dared to hope that he would call on us. I expected we might meet in company, but to call on your father shows true consideration, my dear.'

'So you approve of him now, Mama,' Charlotte said, struggling not to laugh. 'Why, only the other day you called him a hardened rake— I'm sure you did.'

'I did not think then that he would pay you the least attention,' her mother said sharply. 'You are a pretty girl, Charlotte. No one could deny that, but you have little fortune to recommend you and I do not expect every gentleman we meet to fall at your feet. That is why you must make the most of your chances…not that I am suggesting the viscount is a chance for you. Charming as he may be, I do not expect an offer from him.'

Charlotte turned away without answering. She suspected that Captain Viscount Delsey had called this morning to discover whether his sus-picions concerning her were correct. Had he seen her prior to that escapade last night? Or had he somehow seen her return to her home in the early hours of the morning?

She had not dared to hire a cab, walking swiftly through the streets and keeping to the shadows as much as possible. However, if he had done so, he might have arrived at the same time as she did, if perhaps he'd delayed his return for some min-utes before taking the cab. Charlotte was almost sure he knew the young urchin he'd rescued had been her in disguise, but she would deny it if he asked. It would be too risky to admit where she'd been and what she'd done that evening.

He had seemed to be amused. She could only hope that he would not betray her secret, as it could ruin her family.

Alone in her room, Charlotte glanced in the mirror. There was a sparkle in her eyes that she did not think had been there earlier. She sensed a challenge ahead and a hint of danger, for the viscount was a flirt and a rake and she had done something that might make him think she was careless of her reputation.

Supposing he tried to take advantage of his knowledge? Her stomach clenched with nerves, because she knew that one hint of what she'd done the previous night would ruin her.

Surely, Captain Delsey was too much the man of honour to tell anyone else what he knew?

Perhaps if she had a chance that evening, she could appeal to his sense of chivalry. But what excuse could she give? To tell him that she'd stolen back a necklace given by her brother in payment of a debt was shameful and would destroy any lingering good opinion he had of her and her dearest Matt. Yet what else could she tell him?

Try as she might, Charlotte could not think of an excuse that would not make her seem either wanton or dishonest. All she could do was to hope that he would keep her secret without being asked.

It was a long afternoon for Charlotte. Mama insisted that she spend most of it resting, and, though she had taken a book to her room, for some reason her mind would not follow the story of romance and adventure in pages of Fanny Burney's novel. Instead, she found herself reliving the moment when Captain Delsey had saved her from the drunken gentlemen. His quick action had been decisive and she would have liked to thank him at once, but had felt the best course for her to follow was to disappear as swiftly as she could. Thankfully, the remainder of her journey home had been uneventful. She'd hoped it could all be forgotten, but now the hideous thought that one careless word from Delsey could destroy her chances of a good marriage lay heavy on her conscience.

Mama was relying on Charlotte to ease her father's burden of debt. For that she must marry a man of consequence and wealth, but most of the aristocracy were rather starchy as regards reputation and behaviour; the merest hint of scandal attached to a young lady's name would ruin her chances of a good marriage. What Charlotte had done was so outrageous that, if it were discovered, she would be an outcast from society.

Matt had warned her against her mad escapade, but nothing would have persuaded her. It was not her brother's fault, though if he had not confessed to her she might not have discovered the necklace had gone for weeks. He had not been able to live with the guilt of stealing from his own sister, and, when told that the necklace was fake, confessed the whole. Charlotte had been determined to save her family from the scandal that would have resulted from such a fraud and her headstrong courage had led her to act without truly thinking of the consequences.

As a tiny child she'd followed wherever her brother led, climbing trees, swimming in the shallows of the river near their home wearing only her drawers and petticoat, and being beaten for her wickedness more than once. She'd ridden well from the age of three, joining the hunt when she was thirteen, and successfully ridden any horse her brother could master, throwing her heart over as she cleared fences three times her height. Matt told everyone she was fearless and their wild pranks were often at her instigation as they grew into their teenage years. Mama had taken her in hand when she was sixteen, insisting that she must behave like a lady if she wanted a Season in town, and so she had given up her tomboy behaviour—until the previous night when she'd climbed into a man's bedchamber and retrieved the fake necklace.

Only now did Charlotte understand that this

was not one of the childish pranks she'd shared with her brother. She was a thief. Even though the necklace was her own, Matt had pledged it in settlement of a debt. A gambling debt, and one that might have been incurred as a result of her brother being cheated, was not like a proper debt to a tradesman, Charlotte told herself, to ease her guilt. Lord Harding was known to be a hard gambler; some whispered he fleeced young gentlemen who were not up to all the tricks played on them by card sharps who treated them as plump pigeons, ripe for the plucking.

If Matt was right and he'd been cheated the night he fell so deeply in debt that he'd been driven to take her necklace, then Lord Harding deserved to be robbed of his ill-gotten gains. And yet she could not help feeling that she had done something shameful.

There was no point in thinking about it, she could not give the necklace back, but must be careful never to wear it anywhere it might be seen by a man who might recognise it as his property.

Charlotte pushed the worrying thoughts out of her mind. She'd been seen climbing from the window after retrieving that necklace, but only by a couple of very inebriated gentlemen—and one possibly sober one who had looked into her face for the merest second. She could only hope that Delsey would not put two and two together and make five.

Chapter Three

So what had Miss Charlotte Stevens been up to the previous night? Had she been trying to pull the wool over his eyes by telling him she was more than nineteen years of age? Her manner had been demure enough, but something in the lift of her head told him that she was full of spirit and very likely to have been out late at night on some mad prank dressed in her brother's outgrown clothes. If indeed it had been she, he was inclined to be amused and to like her for it. Jack was wary of the kind of female that swooned at every convenient moment and tried to trap a man into marriage, as he had reason enough to be. He had been relentlessly pursued since his first appearance on the town.

Jack pondered the puzzle as he dressed for the evening in a coat of blue superfine made by

Weston that fitted his shoulders like a second skin. For riding Jack liked a little more room in his coats, but for evening it was imperative that the cut should be superb and his valet must naturally help him into it. His pantaloons of cream fitted perfectly, his cravat was expertly tied by his own hand, though it would not rival the intricacy of those who had mastered Mr Brummell's excellence in the art, but the pin was a diamond of the first water. On the little finger of his right hand he wore a magnificent diamond set in heavy gold.

Satisfied with his appearance, Jack thanked his valet, advised him not to sit up, knowing full well that Cummings would ignore the order if he gave it. He walked down the stairs just as the door opened to admit his Aunt Seraphina and her daughter Julia.

'Ah, we are in time,' Aunt Seraphina said, looking pleased with herself. 'Jack, I must beg a favour of you. You will escort your cousin to the ball this evening, will you not? I must return home at once for your uncle is down with a chill and no one but I can handle him when he is ill.'

'Aunt…' Jack protested, thrown off balance by the unexpected change to his plans. 'My uncle could surely spare you for a few hours—and Julia really should not go without her mama.'

'Please credit me with a little intelligence.' His aunt fixed him with a beady eye. 'If you promise to look after your cousin and make sure she doesn't dance too often with any particular gentleman—or with an undesirable acquaintance—I can look after your poor Uncle David. If this chill goes to his chest...'

'If my uncle is truly ill, then you must stay with him, but surely Julia would be best at home with you and her father.'

'Don't be so mean,' Julia wailed, her pretty face screwing into an awful pout. 'What trouble can it be to you to escort me this evening? Mama's best friend, Lady Meadows, will be there and I may join her party once we are there, but I cannot turn up without an escort.'

Jack sighed inwardly, knowing that his own plans for the evening must be shelved. Julia would do well enough with Lady Meadows and her bevy of three rather plump daughters, but she would need an escort home, which meant his plans to leave early with friends and go on to a gambling club would be ended.

'Very well,' he said. 'I suppose I must take you, brat, but do not expect me to dance with you all evening.'

'You must dance with me once,' Julia said, but she was smiling now, having gained her way. 'Thank you, dearest Jack.' She took his arm and hugged him, bringing a frown from her mama.

'Remember your decorum, Julia,' she warned. 'Jack, I rely on you to look after this child for me.'

'Yes, Aunt,' Jack said. 'I suppose Cousin Reginald was unable to oblige?'

'Your cousin has his duties in the House, which he takes very seriously—and he may be late for they are sitting over an important bill this evening.'

'Of course.' Jack smothered his desire to retort that his cousin took both himself and his duties too seriously. Reginald was the personal secretary to the Prime Minister and one would think from his weighty manner and the way he gave his opinions on matters of State that he was himself meant for high office. 'Go home and take care of my uncle, Seraphina. Julia will come to no harm with me.'

'Thank you, dear Jack,' Julia said and hugged

his arm once more as her mama disappeared in a whirl of satin skirts and lace petticoats. 'You are a darling.'

Seraphina was his Uncle David's second wife, at least twenty years his junior and still an attractive woman. Her daughter, Julia, was their only child, for she had lost two other babies, and since there was already an heir to Lord Handley's estate in Reginald, they had given up trying for more. Jack knew that his uncle's constitution was far from robust and could therefore understand why his wife fussed over a mere chill.

'Behave yourself this evening,' Jack said, but the smile in his eyes denied the brusque tone of his voice as he added, 'And stop ruining the sleeve of my coat. I'll have you know it took ten minutes to get me into it and I'm not going to change because of your childish behaviour.'

Julia's eyes took fire and she sparked with wrath as she removed her hand from his arm. 'I'll have you know I'm eighteen next week—and I've had three proposals of marriage this month.'

'Only three?' He quirked an eyebrow at her. 'Does my aunt know?'

'Of course not. You are not to tell her, Jack!'

'What do you take me for?' he drawled. 'If I were your brother I would put you over my knee and spank you...'

'But you're only my cousin and it wouldn't be proper, so you can't,' she crowed and laughed, realising that he was teasing her. Her eyes sparked with laughter. 'It's such fun, Jack. At least two of them were fortune hunters. Not that my fortune is so very large, but I suppose twenty thousand pounds and the estate Aunt Tilly left me is a great deal if you are in the suds...anything to keep them out of debtors' gaol, I imagine.'

'Where did you get such ideas?' Jack asked. 'Your tongue will lead you astray if you're not careful.'

Julia gave a trill of laughter. 'Only with you, Jack dearest. I can say what I like to you. Naturally, I would not say such a thing in society— but it's fun leading them on, knowing that they only want my money.'

'You are a cruel minx,' he retorted. 'Just make sure you don't go too far. Some gentlemen are not really very nice if you scratch the surface. Be careful, Julia. Lead some of them on and you might end up getting hurt. Besides, you will get yourself a reputation as a flirt and then the right sort of gentleman—the kind you truly want—will not look at you as the proper material for marriage.'

Julia pouted at him as the footman opened the door of his carriage and Jack handed her in and then climbed in beside her. She waited until he had settled before turning to look at him.

'I only let them go so far, Jack. I wouldn't do anything foolish—but when they try to take advantage of a young girl, well, I think they deserve to look foolish. I would never hurt anyone I liked.'

'You are an innocent.' Jack looked at her seriously. 'But just be careful. I would not want to see you hurt.'

'Yes, I know what you mean. I am careful…but if a gentleman tries to persuade me to meet him in the gardens later at night and will not take no for an answer, it seems good to me to leave him waiting.'

Jack laughed shortly. 'In that case, I would agree, but take care whom you tease, cousin. There are some that might try to take a nasty revenge.'

'I shall,' she said. 'You mustn't worry about me,

Jack. If ever I think someone is really threatening me, I shall come and tell my big strong cousin all about it.'

Charlotte looked at her dance card and felt a tiny thrill of excitement. They had arrived twenty minutes earlier and already more than half of the spaces on her dance card were taken and the music had just started for the first set of country dances. She moved towards the ballroom itself and was greeted on the threshold by Sir Percival, who had come in search of her.

'I saw you earlier,' he greeted her with a smile, 'but you were surrounded by eager young men. I trust you have not forgotten our dances, Miss Stevens?'

'Certainly not,' Charlotte said, laughing up at him. 'I never forget a promise, sir. You also have the last country dance before supper.'

'I think I was fortunate to secure them this morning,' he said and took her hand, leading her towards a group of young people making up the sets for the first dance. 'I believe you will be much in demand this evening, Miss Stevens.'

Charlotte accepted her place in the line just as the music began and they all joined hands for the first few steps, before forming into two lines, the gentleman on one side, his partner on the other and another lady beside him. The lines came together in the middle, then broke apart, the promised couples taking each other's hands to promenade down the line and rejoin it. A similar movement was performed and this time a gentleman crossed to the next lady on the line and the promenade was resumed. It meant that everyone eventually had a chance to dance with everyone else and was the first of a lively set of three dances before the music stopped and the lady's original partner escorted her from the floor.

Charlotte returned to her mama and a group of young ladies and matrons. Some people refreshed themselves with a drink or a cooling ice before dancing again, but the next was a waltz and Charlotte's partner was prompt in claiming her.

'Our dance, I believe, Miss Stevens?'

'Yes, thank you.' She glanced up at the handsome face of a young officer wearing his dress uniform. He'd told her his name was Christopher Young, and he was a captain of the Royal Dragoons. 'Where are you stationed just now, Captain?'

'In London for a few weeks,' he replied, bowed and placed his hand correctly just above her waist before sweeping her into the magical dance. 'My regiment is home after some service overseas.'

It was as she was swept away across the floor that she chanced to see Captain Viscount Delsey enter the ballroom with a beautiful young woman on his arm. She was dressed in a gown of white lace and tulle embroidered with what looked like diamonds, her long fair hair piled on her head in curls that fell into one artistic ringlet over her right shoulder—and she was laughing up at her escort in a manner that spoke of intimacy.

Feeling a sharp pang of what Charlotte honestly named envy, she lifted her head and smiled up at her partner. Captain Young was a wonderful dancer and she had no reason to be jealous of the lovely woman who was now dancing with Captain Delsey. She banished the unworthy feelings and gave herself up to the enjoyment of a waltz with a truly talented partner.

'Thank you, sir, you dance divinely,' she murmured when their waltz came to an end, much too soon for Charlotte's liking. 'I do not think I have ever enjoyed a dance more.'

He clicked his heels, eyes dancing with mischief as he said, 'I was lucky enough to be one of Wellington's staff for a few months before the war ended. It is a requirement that we should waltz divinely.'

'And you certainly do, sir. I could wish a few more gentlemen had learned in your school.'

'What a very honest young lady you are, Miss Stevens,' he said. 'If you would like, I shall send some of my friends to beg for a waltz, for you also dance it divinely—and not everyone does.'

'I should be delighted to waltz with any of your friends.'

He bowed his head and left her to the company of her companions.

Charlotte was soon claimed for another dance and it was not until she had pledged all but two of her waltzes that she discovered herself looking up into the unsmiling face of Captain Delsey.

'I saw you had a queue of eager partners, most of them old comrades of mine,' Jack said, one eyebrow arched. 'May I hope that you have saved a waltz for me?'

'Yes, sir. I pencilled in the one before supper and the one after, you may choose which you prefer.'

'I am committed to Miss Julia Handley for

much of the evening,' Jack replied, 'but I shall be greedy and ask for both those waltzes, if I may?'

'Yes, if you truly wish it.' Charlotte looked at him a little uncertainly.

'Miss Handley is my cousin,' Jack said, a gleam of devilry in his eyes. 'May I bring her to you, Miss Stevens? Her mama was unable to accompany us this evening and I am duty bound to see that she is in good company—and to look after her.'

'Ah, I see,' Charlotte said, lifting her hand as her next partner arrived. 'Excuse me, sir. I am engaged for this next...' She turned to offer her hand to the good looking but rather pompous young man who had introduced himself as Lord Johnston and secured a set of country dances with her.

'Johnston.' Jack inclined his head. 'Glad to see you up and about again, sir.'

'Ah, Delsey.' Charlotte's partner looked slightly red about his neck. 'Nice to see you. Yes, I am quite recovered from the, ah...accident now.'

Charlotte threw a puzzled glanced at Delsey as she allowed her new partner to draw her into the group of people forming the sets. Something was a little odd in the way the two gentlemen had greeted each other, but she could not quite fathom it, and her partner had no intention of enlightening her. He proceeded to talk about his estate in Norfolk, where he had a very special herd of Jersey cows, and his hopes of breeding from them in the future.

'It is the quality of the milk, you see,' he explained kindly, as Charlotte struggled to follow his flow. 'They give so much more cream—and that's where the money is. I have every intention of owning the biggest and best herd in the country.'

Charlotte murmured something that seemed to please him, though since his conversation, though turned from cows, was all of a rather bucolic nature, she was relieved when their dances ended and she rejoined her mama.

'Ah, here you are, my love,' Lady Stevens said. 'You must be very warm. Will you not take a moment to eat one of these ices your brother has just procured for us?'

'Oh, that would be nice, Mama,' Charlotte said but even as she reached for a lemon ice, Viscount Delsey brought his companion to her and bowed before them.

'Lady Stevens, Miss Stevens—may I present

you to my cousin Julia Handley. I have explained that her mama entrusted Julia to my care this evening. She has friends here, but I thought she might keep company with you for a while? I was about to procure some champagne…if I could tempt you, Lady Stevens?'

'Thank you, but we have these ices for the moment and more than enough for all. Will you not partake, Miss Handley? It is rather warm and they have already started to melt a little.'

'I could fetch some fresh ices, if Miss Handley would care for it,' Matt said, his expression, his sister thought, one of a man struck by lightning.

'Oh, no, one of these would be delightful,' Julia said and accepted a strawberry-flavoured ice from his hand.

Jack moved closer to Charlotte, murmuring in her ear, 'You seemed puzzled just now by my reference to Lord Johnston's health?'

'I thought he looked quite fit and well.'

'The matter of a little disagreement that ended with a duel,' Jack said. 'I stood his second since he could find no other willing to undertake it— and I fear he came off worse. The other fellow's ball grazed his arm, but his own ball was way off the mark. He should never have been such a

fool as to challenge Lord Harding over the matter of a dropped card.'

'Lord Harding?' Charlotte was chilled, a trickle
of alarm sliding down her spine. 'What makes
you say Lord Johnston should not have challenged him?'

'The card dropped to the floor from Lord Harding's hand. Johnston swore it had come from his
sleeve and Harding denied it—since it could not
be proved, Johnston should have apologised, but
he is rather stiff-necked and would not. Therefore, it was impossible to prevent the duel. I asked
both if they would withdraw but…' He shook his
head and his eyes held an unfathomable gleam.
'I have told you a secret no gentleman would dis-
close to a lady. Have I sunk beyond reproach in
your eyes?'

'Not at all,' Charlotte replied seriously. 'I hate
it when gentlemen tell me that something I want
to know is not suitable for a lady's ears—as if we
were children or too delicate to know the truth.'

'Precisely,' Jack said and smiled at her. 'I believe I see a rather determined young man approaching. Your next partner, I imagine. I shall
come to claim you later.'

Charlotte was duly claimed and once again

found herself being whisked around the floor by a polished performer, another of Wellington's former staff, she was reliably informed, though she thought him not quite as perfect a partner as Captain Young.

Glancing across the room, she saw Matt dancing with Julia Handley. They seemed to like each other well and were enjoying the dance, Julia looking very lovely as her eyes sparkled up at her partner.

Charlotte suspected that Delsey's cousin might be a bit of a flirt and hoped that her brother would not fall too deeply in love with her too swiftly. However, next time she herself was dancing, she saw that Julia was once again dancing with her cousin and seemed to be enjoying herself just as much. Matt, too, had another partner, a quietly pretty young girl whom Charlotte only knew slightly. She saw Sir Percival dancing with Amelia Rushmore and Mr Rushmore was standing with a group of other young men watching the dancing with a brooding expression that might have been boredom.

As soon as Charlotte returned to her friends she was, once again, claimed by Sir Percival for the last set of country dances before supper. She found him good company and they parted with a smile and promises of meeting again quite soon.

'I shall pay an afternoon call and perhaps you will drive out with me in the park one morning, Miss Stevens?'

Charlotte agreed to it, then turned as Captain Viscount Delsey approached her. She took his hand and was led to the dance floor just as the music struck up once more. He placed his hand firmly just above her waist and took her hand, drawing her into the swirl of dancing. A tingling sensation pervaded Charlotte's body and she felt as if she were dancing on air, seeming light as a feather as he whirled her across the floor, appearing to carve a swathe through the other dancers as if he had some divine right. She had thought that Captain Young danced beautifully, but this feeling was exquisite, like nothing she'd ever experienced before. In that moment Charlotte wished that she might stay in the viscount's arms for ever.

There were no words to describe the wonderful sensations that flooded through her, no way that she could understand why she seemed unable to breathe and yet could dance and dance for ever. Something inside her seemed to join with him, to become a part of her partner and lift her beyond the room and everyone in it. She felt as if she floated on a cloud in an otherwise clear blue sky…drifting away to a world where there was always sun and pleasant warmth.

When the music stopped and he released her hand it was such a shock that she almost fell. For a moment her mind refused to come back from wherever it had been and she could neither speak nor move.

'Are you faint?' he asked, looking at her anxiously. 'Perhaps some air?'

'No, no thank you, I shall be fine in a moment. I must find Mama and go into supper.'

'I have reserved a table. Let me take you there and your mama and my cousin will join us. I mentioned it earlier.'

'Did you?' Charlotte could not trust herself to say more. She felt the touch of his hand on her arm as he guided her through the press of people to a table near an open window. She could feel the coolness of the air calming her heated skin and with the coolness some semblance of normality returned. 'Oh, that is pleasant. I think I must have become a little heated.'

'It is very warm in here,' Jack murmured close

to her ear, his breath warm on her exposed skin. 'I felt it, too.'

Charlotte shivered with what she could only think was sensual delight, though she had never experienced anything like it before. There was something in his tone and his look that made her feel special, as if she were the focus of his attention, of his world. The thought made her feel quite giddy with pleasure and she wished that she might be alone with him somewhere private, somewhere they might make love.

What was she thinking? Charlotte came to herself with a shock. She was allowing herself to be seduced by a man's smile, by the caress in his voice and the stroking of those compelling eyes... She was reacting like a foolish girl of twelve, instead of a young woman of more than nineteen. Viscount Captain Delsey was a practised flirt and a rake; he thought nothing of breaking hearts and she had no intention of offering hers up as a sacrifice.

His eyes met hers with a quizzical look, as if he sensed her thoughts. 'Please, make yourself comfortable, Miss Stevens. I see your mama making her way here with the others and I must speak to the waiter.'

Charlotte inclined her head, not quite trusting herself to speak. The viscount was undoubtedly a charming man, but also a heartless flirt, if the gossips were to be believed. She knew that he was regarded as one of the best catches on the matrimonial market, but he was unlikely to cast his hat in her direction. Indeed, most of the matchmaking mamas had given up hope of him. So if he seemed bent on capturing her interest it probably meant that he thought there might be a chance of seducing her into a clandestine flirtation…as he might well think if he'd seen her wearing her brother's cast-off clothing.

It seemed likely that he'd recognised her as the urchin that he'd helped escape from unwelcome attention in the street—and a girl who would brave the streets at night dressed as a youth might be capable of anything. Indeed, she might so far forget herself as to be willing to indulge in something more than flirtation, might allow herself to be seduced. The thought sent waves of heat rushing through her once more and she struggled to compose herself. She must think of something else…a cool stream trickling through a sunset meadow…

Still feeling a little uncomfortable as her mama

joined her, Charlotte decided that she must be careful in future. It would not do to become too intimate with the handsome viscount. Not only could he break her heart, he could ruin her reputation.

Yet when he returned with a trio of waiters, bringing a selection of all the choicest treats and two bottles of chilled champagne, Captain Delsey devoted himself to her mama and engaged her brother for a game of cards, before engaging his cousin for a drive to the park the next day. Since he paid Charlotte no more than polite attention, she was able to school her wayward thoughts, and, by the time he claimed his next dance, she had recovered her composure.

Try as she might, Charlotte could not hold back once he swept her away across the floor, her whole being given over to the joy of the music and the feeling of floating as she immersed herself in the dance. However, she did not let her thoughts drift to the desires that had formed during the first dance and was able to breathe easily and to thank her partner when the dance ended.

'You dance like an angel,' Delsey murmured in her ear. 'I shall wait impatiently for the next time, Miss Charlotte.'

The sound of her name on his lips was like a caress. Such tactics were calculated to make foolish girls fall at his feet, but Charlotte was made of sterner stuff. She must and would resist the spells he wove—she had to for her family's sake.

'Thank you, sir. I must always be pleased to dance with such a delightful partner.'

She made him a deep curtsy and then walked away to join her mother, her back very straight, her head high, though every nerve in her body felt as if it were being torn apart by the loss of him. This was ridiculous! She hardly knew the man and she would be foolish beyond anything to let herself be drawn into his net, simply because when she was in his arms she was ready to cast aside the world for his sake. No, no, she would keep a guard between her and the charming viscount in future. She must remember who she was and what Mama expected of her rather than allowing herself to dream of passionate love in the arms of a man who fulfilled all her girlish hopes.

Three dances later the room began to thin of company and Lady Stevens told her daughter that they should be thinking of leaving.

'I have promised that we shall take Miss Handley home for it is on our way, Charlotte. Julia is a very pleasant young lady and I have invited her and her mama to dine with us as soon as it may be arranged. She says she would like it if you would walk with her in the park tomorrow afternoon, and I thought you would so she will call for you at two.'

'Oh…yes, of course, Mama,' Charlotte agreed, though she seemed to recall that Delsey had made some sort of arrangement with his cousin for the following day. Yet she had not been paying attention and perhaps that had been for another day.

Because both young ladies had danced all evening they had had little time to become acquainted, but sitting in Mama's comfortable carriage on the way home, Julia told Charlotte that she was looking forward to becoming better acquainted.

'Mama has many friends in town,' Julia confided, 'but some of their daughters are so…well, to be kind, they are silly and have not a sensible thought in their heads. I think you are different, Charlotte. I should like it if we could be friends— and I know Jack likes you.'

Charlotte's cheeks felt warm and she was glad

that it was too dark in the carriage for Mama to notice. 'What makes you say that?'

'He seldom dances with very young ladies, but he danced twice with you—and he stood talking with you on every occasion you were not dancing.'

'I dare say that was so that you might be comfortable with us,' Charlotte murmured softly. 'I think your cousin is an accomplished flirt, Miss Handley.'

'Please, call me Julia. I hope I may call you Charlotte?' Julia lowered her voice. 'Jack has a terrible reputation, but he isn't very wicked. I am sure he would never seduce an innocent young girl as some unscrupulous gentlemen do, but he cannot help it if the foolish ones break their hearts over him. If he takes a mistress now and then…well, all men do it, you know, at least until they marry.'

'Who told you that?' Charlotte asked in a whisper with a quick glance at her mother to make sure she was not listening.

'Mama.' Julia's eyes sparkled. 'She said it was quite the thing for young men and better than picking up…ladies of the night from the street. But of course, it should stop when the man gets married, though she confessed that it doesn't always do so. My father has been faithful to her for ever, but she says she is lucky—and told me to make sure that I choose a man who will love only me.'

'What are you two girls whispering about?' Mama asked. 'I believe we have arrived, Miss Handley. Pray tell your mama I should be happy if she will call and then we may all be comfortable together.'

'Mama will be grateful to you for taking care of me this evening,' Julia said. 'She was worried for my papa or she would not have let me go alone with Jack—and he did not truly wish for it, but he's such a dear that he could not refuse her.'

'In future your mama may send you with us, should she be unable to attend a function to which we are invited.'

'You are so kind,' Julia said, thanking her again as the carriage stopped and a groom came to open the door for her, after first knocking at her house so that her footman had the front door open and waiting for her. 'Goodnight, Charlotte. I shall see you tomorrow.'

'Yes. I shall look forward to it.'

Charlotte sat back against the squabs after

Julia had gone and closed her eyes, thinking of the evening she had enjoyed—and the partners who had given her the most pleasure. Captain Young and Captain Viscount Delsey—both of them were excellent dancers, but very different in other respects. Of the two, only Jack Delsey had made her lose control of her senses for a short time, though Christopher Young had come to her between dances and asked if he might take her driving one day.

'I know we are not much acquainted,' he'd said, 'but I feel as if I have known you all my life— and I should like to know you better, if you would like it?'

'Thank you. Yes, I should be happy to drive out with you one day,' Charlotte had said, smiling up into his blue eyes. 'You must call on Papa, sir. I am sure he would invite you to dine with us one evening.'

'You did very well this evening.' Mama's voice interrupted her train of thought and Charlotte opened her eyes. 'Sir Percival seemed quite taken with you—and I believe you danced every dance, my dear.'

'Yes, Mama, I did,' she agreed. 'It was the most enjoyable evening.'

'Did you know that Captain Young is the heir of Lord Sampson?'

'No, Mama, I did not realise that,' Charlotte said. Lord Sampson was a neighbour of Papa's in the country, but the estates were some fifteen miles distant and Charlotte saw little of the elderly gentleman, who was something of a recluse.

'Neither did I until Papa told me,' her mama said with a look of satisfaction. 'Lord Sampson is quite comfortably off, Charlotte—wealthy, in fact. His heir will be in possession of a large fortune in the future…but I do not imagine that he personally has the funds to settle Papa's debts. Sir Percival is not as wealthy as one might like, but at least his fortune is his own. Not every gentleman is as fortunate, my love.'

'No, I imagine not.' Charlotte realised what her mother was telling her. The charming officer had prospects, but if her marriage was to ease her father's burden of debt, she needed someone already in possession of a fortune: such as Sir Percival.

Turning her face aside, Charlotte swallowed the little lump that had formed in her throat. She had liked Captain Young very much…almost as much as Captain Delsey, but while the one might perhaps offer her marriage she was fairly certain that it was far from the mind of the other. Sir Percival was a pleasant gentleman, but he had not made her flesh tingle when he held her as they danced.

Tears stung her eyes for a moment as she wished that her father had not wasted his fortune and obliged her to think of such things. She longed to be free to follow her heart, but knew that in the end she might have to settle for less than she wanted.

Chapter Four

Jack yawned over his brandy as he relaxed in his boldly patterned silk dressing gown, his feet stretched out before him, his head back against the soft leather of the comfortable wing chair in his private sitting room. What he had expected to be a tedious evening in the company of his cousin, of whom he was fond but not in the least enamoured, had turned out to be more promising than he'd imagined.

He had no idea what had made him flirt so outrageously with a certain young lady. Jack's aversion to becoming emotionally involved with a beautiful girl ran deep and was of some years' duration. Normally, he reserved his flirting for older—married, or widowed—ladies, who understood that nothing serious was meant or offered. After all, even if he was considering a marriage of convenience, he had no intention of ever allowing a woman to take over his heart and mind, to inflict the kind of pain that he knew could result from loving too much. He knew from experience how disastrous that could be, for he had learned it when very young and seen two people dear to him nearly destroyed by a love that was too powerful.

However, Miss Charlotte Stevens was a revelation. He'd known from the first that she was a bold minx, because of that escapade when she had narrowly escaped being abused by a pair of rogues. Though, in fairness, what was a man to think when a young woman went about dressed as a youth—and, according to one of the men, had been seen climbing out of a window?

Whose window might that be? Jack pondered the mystery, a half-smile on his mouth. Had she been visiting her lover—or was there more behind her reckless behaviour?

Having spent some time in her brother's company, Jack was inclined to think that her mission might have been in some way related to him, simply because he was not the kind of young man to acquiesce to his sister behaving loosely. Indeed, Jack had seen him frown when Charlotte danced with a man who was known to have questionable morals. He'd been waiting to let her into the servants' quarters that night, so he must have known where she'd been—but surely he could not condone his sister going out alone in the guise of a youth? It was far too dangerous!

Jack had seen enough of the girl at their first meeting to be intrigued, for she had a mischievous twinkle in her eyes and a way of laughing that caught one's interest. There had been nothing in her behaviour then, or that evening, to suggest that she was wayward or indeed wanton. Yet in his arms she had seemed to become a different girl. Light and nimble, she moved with him instinctively and he did not recall having felt so swept away by passion while dancing ever before. When their waltz ended and she seemed a little dazed, he'd known an overwhelming urge to sweep her up in his arms and run away to somewhere quiet where they would not be disturbed. His arousal had been almost painful and he'd wanted to shower her with hot kisses and feel the satin softness of her skin as they lay together...but he'd known that he could not treat her in such a fashion. She was the daughter of a gentleman...but was she a lady?

Jack frowned, because the need to question made him angry. He did not wish to think ill of her—but what lady would act as she had? What could possibly have driven her to such reckless behaviour?

He could not bring anything to mind. Surely Matthew Stevens was not so careless of his sister's safety that he would allow her to go wandering about alone at night…and why had she climbed out of a window? Had she also climbed into the window of a house across the park?

Jack frowned over it as he tried to remember who lived in the houses at the other side of St James's Park. But of course, he couldn't be sure how far those rogues had chased her before she ran from the park gates.

Shaking his head, he finished his brandy and thought about pouring another, but decided against it.

He was no nearer to solving the puzzle of Miss Charlotte Stevens, but he had no intention of letting the matter drop. Jack would make it his business to discover more about the family and their circumstances. They were newcomers to the social scene in London. Though they had presumably come to give their daughter a Season, their background might bear more investigation. The best way to discover what he needed to know was to cultivate Matt Stevens's acquaintance; a few card evenings and a drinking session at the club should prove enlightening, for he believed that the young man would be easy enough to pump for information.

Jack did not consider what his interest in the girl might be when he discovered what he needed to know; it was merely a mystery to be unravelled, which amused him, and a mild flirtation with a pretty girl was never a waste of time, though where it might lead was another matter.

Next day, Jack saw the two girls walking arm-in-arm through the park and smiled inwardly, as he noted that Julia's maid was walking some distance behind, as no doubt she'd been warned to do by her mistress. He'd wondered why she'd insisted that she would not drive with him, but would meet him if he chose to walk through Hyde Park that afternoon. Now what mischief was she up to?

He doffed his beaver hat to the ladies, one eyebrow quirked as he saw Julia's wicked smile.

'How pleasant to meet you, cousin…Miss Stevens.'

'Yes, what a surprise,' Julia said, a challenging smile in her eyes. 'We are getting to know one another, Jack dearest. You must know that Charlotte is to be my best friend. I love her already and you must be nice to her or I shall never speak to you again.'

'I am almost tempted to do her some mischief,' Jack murmured so softly that only the ladies closest to him might hear. 'Yet I fear she does not deserve it and, worse, you would not keep your word.'

'You wretch!' Julia cried and gave him a little punch on his arm. 'Did you hear him, Charlie? I declare he is not worthy of our notice. We shall walk on alone.'

'I believe your cousin merely means to tease you,' Charlotte said and laughed.

'He is clearly in an odd humour,' Julia accused. 'We shall ignore him. Oh, look, here comes your brother. It seems everyone is walking in the park today.'

'More of my cousin's plotting, I dare say,' Jack murmured as he matched his pace to Charlotte's and his cousin walked a few steps ahead to take Matt's arm. 'Somehow I do not think these chance meetings—do you?'

'It would seem unlikely,' Charlotte admitted. Her head lifted as she met his eyes. 'Is your cousin a flirt, my lord?'

'Oh, most definitely. You should warn your brother not to lose his heart to her. I shall certainly put him on his guard.'

'I believe Matt can take care of himself,' Charlotte replied. 'Julia is a delightful companion, but I imagine her parents intend her to marry well?'

'Naturally, she is the heir to a sizeable, though not huge, fortune, left to her by her godmother.'

'As I thought,' Charlotte said, meeting his enquiring gaze honestly. 'Matt has a small estate and some capital, though by no means a fortune.'

'He is surely your father's heir?'

'Yes, of course, but Papa...Papa has some unfortunate debts,' Charlotte said honestly. 'Whether he will have an estate to leave to my brother is not certain. I have a little money of my own, but we are neither of us a good prospect—unless money is no object. In matters of the heart it does not always matter what one has, does it?'

'You are very straight, Miss Stevens. Is that wise, do you think?'

'I see no reason to lie, sir. My mother hopes that I shall make a good match and perhaps be able to help Papa a little, but I would not deceive anyone in the matter of our circumstances.'

'Some would say you would do better to keep the information to yourself, at least until a proposal is made.'

'Yes, indeed. I do not shout it from the rooftops, but I have confided in Julia and she is bound to mention it to you, I think.'

'Julia has few secrets from me. We've always been almost as brother and sister.'

'Yes, she told me as much, which is why I thought it safe to confide in you. Obviously, we do not wish it generally known, for it might spoil my chances, but I do not accuse you of being a gossip, sir.'

Jack looked at her intently, trying to discover why she had been so open with him and his cousin. Was she telling him that she did not consider him a likely suitor, therefore felt it did not matter what he thought of her? Or was she putting him on his mettle, challenging him?

She intrigued him more each time they met and he felt his hunting instincts rise, as if scenting exciting prey. It might be that Miss Charlotte would be interested in becoming the mistress of a man who was prepared to free her father of debt and advance her brother's prospects…or was he misjudging her? After all, he could not know what had led her to the mad escapade that had so nearly been her undoing.

Hearing a little sound of alarm from Charlotte, he glanced at her face and saw the colour had left her cheeks. She was staring at a couple of men walking towards them and he noticed that her hand trembled on his arm.

One of the gentlemen was Lord Harding and he halted as he saw Matt, lifting his hat. The other man was one of the two rogues who had been pursuing the young woman at his side the other evening, though Jack did not know his name.

'Stevens, well met,' Lord Harding said. 'Patterson and I were arranging a little trip to a new gambling hell of which I am a member—for this evening. I think you would enjoy it, we dine at my house at seven.'

'No! I can't,' Matt blurted out, his eyes staring like a hunted rabbit and a hot tide of colour sweeping his neck. 'I am engaged to…'

'Matt is engaged to me this evening for cards and dinner,' Jack supplied easily. 'Forgive us,

Harding, but we have somewhere to be. Mr Patterson...'

He tipped his hat slightly, but did not remove it. 'Excuse us, please, I do not care to keep the ladies standing. The air here, you understand, is not fitting.'

His tone was cutting and he saw the anger rush into Harding's face, turning it puce. The man had a choleric temper and would end by having a fit if he were not careful. Jack's insult had been deliberate and yet veiled so that although Harding knew perfectly well what was intended, he could not make anything of it, but would no doubt find a way to retaliate another time.

Once they were safely past, Jack looked at his companion. She was still a little pale, but had recovered her composure.

'You do not like that gentleman?'

'He...he led Matt into bad ways and my brother lost money he could not afford. What capital he has is in trust, you see, and he has only an allowance from Papa.'

'Yes, I understand. Do not fear, I shall not allow your brother to gamble for large stakes at my house. We play for amusement only.' Jack spoke the lie easily. As a rule there was no limit set, but he would make certain that the young man stayed within his means; there were innocuous games of chance that could be played for a few guineas. Some of Jack's friends might think he'd run mad, but since they were content to drink his fine wine, eat the excellent food his chef prepared and simply talk, they would be happy enough to indulge themselves while he played for shilling points with his protégé.

'Oh, I dare say he can afford to lose a few guineas, but not thousands,' Charlotte said ruefully. 'That was how he came to lose—' She broke off suddenly, a flush in her cheeks. 'I am looking forward to the drive to Richmond and the balloon ascension, sir. It was so kind of your cousin to extend the invitation to me.'

'Ah, yes, she is always obliging,' he murmured, surprised at the sudden change of direction, though he wondered if perhaps her impulsive remarks were more revealing than he yet understood.

Matt had seemed almost frightened by Harding's invitation and his sister was clearly protective of him. She had looked as if she might faint when Harding and his friend came up to them—

of course she might have worried that Patterson would recognise her. Jack did not think it likely; the cheeky urchin who had fled through the night looked very different to the young lady of fashion on his arm, but it was natural that she should be anxious.

However, he sensed there was more beneath the surface that he did not yet suspect. Although he was not a friend of Lord Harding—indeed, he despised him and others of his ilk, knowing them for what they were, greedy predators that made fortunes from the young pigeons they plucked before they were aware of what was happening—it might be an idea to seek the man out at one of his haunts. He would not ask questions outright for he did not wish Harding to know his interest in Charlotte Stevens and her brother, but he would watch and listen, and discover what he could by subtler means.

'Did you enjoy the ball last evening?' Charlotte asked and Jack indulged her by talking of the event. It was clear to him that the key to the mystery of her escapade was her brother. Once he had gained Matt's confidence and trust, he would discover her secret soon enough.

* * *

They walked for some half an hour in the warmth of the spring sunshine, then arrived at the park gates, where the girls took their leave and returned to Charlotte's house, where they would take tea together.

'I shall see you on Friday,' Jack said and pressed her hand, adding impulsively, 'If there is anything troubling you, I am your friend, Miss Charlotte. I would help in any way I could, any way at all.'

She looked up at him in surprise, doubtful and then dimpling with mischief. 'How kind you are, sir, but be careful what you promise—that is a wide scope.'

'I mean it, none the less,' he replied earnestly. 'If anyone…threatens you, tell me.'

Charlotte stared up at him for a moment, her gaze steady and serious now. 'I believe you mean that, sir,' she said, 'and I thank you for it, though I am not in any trouble for the moment.'

'I hope that is true,' he said and turned away, touching Matt on the arm. 'Do you go to your club? Or will you do me the honour of dining at mine this evening?'

Matt looked pleased and agreed instantly. 'I

was thinking of dining at home, but I should like to meet you later after I've changed for the evening.'

'No need, we do not bother if we dine informally. Come back with me now and I'll introduce you to some friends of mine. It is a small intimate group and we meet a few times a month to discuss sport and horses.'

'Well, that all went off very well,' Julia said as the two girls strolled towards their destination at a leisurely pace. 'I wasn't certain that Jack would come and it would have been awkward if he hadn't.'

'Did you arrange it with them both?' Charlotte asked, a smile on her lips.

'Yes, of course. It is so easy to arrange some time alone with a young man if one plans it carefully,' she said and gurgled with laughter as Charlotte arched an eyebrow. 'Mama would never allow me to go walking alone with your brother, at least not until she knows him well enough to be sure of his intentions, but if Jack was there, she could make no objection. Is it not the same in your case?'

'Yes, perhaps,' Charlotte replied. 'Will you

make it sound as if they were together when we met them?'

'Only if necessary.' Julia's eyes sparked with mischief. 'I do not lie precisely, but how would I ever get a chance to talk to someone I like if I did not arrange things? One cannot talk properly at balls and musical evenings.'

'No, that is very true,' Charlotte agreed. 'I was glad they were with us. Had we been alone when…Lord Harding and Mr Patterson encountered us…' She gave a little shiver. 'I do not like those gentlemen.'

'I should think not,' Julia agreed instantly. 'They are neither of them pleasant gentlemen. Mama would not invite either to one of her parties and I have been warned to have nothing to do with Lord Harding. He asked me to dance once, but I refused and he did not ask again.'

'He introduced my brother to a gambling hell and poor Matt lost a considerable sum to him, but at least he learned his lesson. He will not gamble with him again.'

'I do not see what gentlemen get from gambling large sums, for it causes so much misery and pain when they lose.' Julia frowned. 'One of Mama's uncles got into debt that way and was nearly ruined. He only recovered when he married an heiress. I never gamble more than a guinea at loo and I do not really care for it at all. Mama will only play cards for points at her parties. I do not see why it is not always so. It is just as much fun to win merely for the pleasure of showing one's skill—but of course, men do not see it that way. Jack gambles thousands, but then, he always wins.'

'I thought perhaps he was not a gambler?' Charlotte frowned over it, because he had told her that Matt would not get into trouble in his company.

Julia laughed and shook her head. 'He is not reckless but he plays for high stakes quite often and always wins. Oh, I suppose he must lose sometimes, but if he does he can afford it and he seems to win most of the time, at whatever he does.'

'What do you mean?'

Julia shrugged her shoulders and wrinkled her brow as she answered, 'I'm not sure what I mean, except that if Jack sets out to get something or somebody, he always has his way. If he takes a bet that he'll win a horse race he does, and he won a duel last year—and there was that girl, seemingly so beautiful and cold, and all the men wanted her, but she threw herself at Jack and he could have had her for the asking, but he didn't want her.'

'What happened to her?'

'Oh, in the end she married an earl, but he was old enough to be her grandfather and he had bad breath…' Julia hesitated, looking a little strange. 'Someone said Mariette had to marry quickly because she was having a baby, but she only looked at Jack.' Charlotte gasped and Julia shook her head. 'No, I'm sure it was just a nasty rumour because she upset so many girls who were jealous of her success. Jack wouldn't seduce an innocent girl. I know he wouldn't.'

'I'm sure he wouldn't,' Charlotte agreed, but she remembered the way she'd felt as they danced their first waltz and knew that she for one might surrender to the handsome viscount if he set out to seduce her. When a man's touch could make you feel that way, how was it possible to remember your mama's warnings?

'I really am certain he wouldn't. I don't know why I told you—please do not hold it against him, Charlie. I think Jack likes you a lot and we all want him to settle down. He's been on the town for ages and all the matchmaking mamas have tried to catch him, but he never gets caught. He has a mistress, I know, but it isn't like having a wife, is it? He ought to have a settled home with a wife and children… He's wonderful with children. I've seen him with cousins and the children of his friends.'

'I dare say he will make up his mind when he's ready.'

'Yes, I expect so. Mama has hinted that we might suit, but Jack and I agree that we shouldn't—and she is only thinking of the fortune that will be added to his own when the old marquis dies.'

'Captain Delsey is the heir?'

'Oh, yes, he'll be the Marquis of Ellington one day. Did you not know?'

'I knew he was a viscount, but I didn't know he was the heir to another title and a fortune.' Charlotte's heart sank, for the charming captain was even less likely to be interested in a girl like her than she'd thought. 'Is his father dead?'

'Oh, years ago. There was a dreadful accident when Jack was seventeen. His father had been up north to their estates in Yorkshire and the carriage was crossing a mountain road when a wheel came off the carriage and it went over the side of a ravine. He was instantly killed, the coachman and groom, too. The servants following in the baggage coach several miles behind retrieved the bodies later and took them home.'

'How tragic,' Charlotte said. 'What caused the wheel to come loose?'

'No one has ever been sure, but they think that there may have been an obstacle in the road and the coachman pulled up sharp, which caused the carriage to lurch and then the broken wheel tipped the whole thing over the edge.'

'That is so tragic,' Charlotte said, her throat catching with pity. 'Your cousin must have been devastated—to lose his father in such a way when he was still very young.'

'Yes, I think it was a shock to him, though he is devoted to his grandfather—and they say—' Julia broke off, shaking her head. 'Well, I suppose you will not repeat this, but I've heard his father was a selfish man and not always to be relied on.'

'Oh, I see,' Charlotte nodded. 'But Lady Delsey—she is still alive?'

'Yes. She lives with the marquis most of the time— though she has her own house in Bath—

but she is a little…well, *silly* is an unkind word, but she is delicate and faints if something distresses her…that kind of thing.'

'Ah, I see.' Charlotte smiled. 'The fluttery kind of lady who needs looking after whenever a gentleman is around, but is perfectly capable when in the company of other ladies.'

'Yes, exactly.' Julia beamed at her. 'I knew you and I would understand each other, Charlie. I think she plays on Jack, tries to make him feel sorry for her—and Mama says in truth she is as fit as you or me.'

Charlotte laughed. 'Mama has no patience with women of that kind, but I suppose they must need attention or they would not play up to their family in that manner.'

'Well, I call it unfair,' Julia said. 'It is no wonder to me that Jack cannot contemplate marriage, for he must imagine that all ladies are likely to become prone to a fit of vapours in their later years.'

'Oh, surely not?' Charlotte laughed as Julia pouted at her. She had realised that her new friend was outspoken with strong opinions of her own, and though she might not agree with all of them she could understand Julia's point of view. 'We do not know what she may have suffered in the past—if her husband was inclined to be selfish...'

'Indeed, I had not taken that into account, but I suppose it may be the reason that she clings to Jack so much.'

'I dare say he may be fond of his mother and, if he is kind to her, as he should be, no doubt she finds comfort in his attentions.'

'You are more considerate than I.' Julia laughed and let the subject drop. 'I wish I were going to this picnic with you on Friday.'

'I do not see why you should not come along,' Charlotte said. 'Matt would be delighted to accompany you and you could take your own picnic and sit close to us so that we may talk.'

'Yes, why not? Will you ask your brother for me—and if you could let Jack know...? I am not sure whether I shall see him before then...and I believe he is engaged to dine with you soon?'

'He is dining with us tomorrow evening,' Charlotte said. 'I shall tell him that you wish to join our party and I'm sure he will speak to his cousin so that you may join us on the day.'

'Yes, of course—that will be perfect.'

* * *

In complete accordance, the girls had walked on until they reached the house. When they entered, it was to find that several people had called and were taking tea in the drawing room with Lady Sybil and Sir Mordred Stevens. Seeing that Sir Percival was one of them, Charlotte went up to him, extending her hand and apologising that she was not at home to greet him.

'No matter, I have but this minute arrived,' he said and kissed her hand. 'Your walk in the park has been enjoyable? You have a glow of the fresh air about you, Miss Stevens.'

'Thank you,' Charlotte said and dimpled up at him. 'It was very pleasant out. There were many others enjoying the afternoon. We met my brother and Captain Delsey.'

'Ah, I wish I had known, I should have liked to stroll through the park with you, but perhaps you will permit me to take you for a drive tomorrow?'

'That would be delightful,' Charlotte said politely. 'You are good to think of it, sir. Julia and I have been talking of the balloon ascension in Richmond on Friday, to which I am invited and she is determined to come.'

'Ah, yes, I am committed to my sister and her

friends for that,' Sir Percival said and brightened. 'We may see you there—it will be an opportunity for you to meet Lady Peters. I came today to deliver an invitation to her soirée next week, which your mama says will fit with her plans.'

'Your sister is kind to invite us, sir.'

'Henrietta is very fond of me, she always wishes to oblige me,' Sir Percival said in a low voice meant for her ears alone.

Charlotte could not mistake his meaning. She breathed deeply, keeping her expression of mild interest in place, but underneath her heart was jumping all over the place. Sir Percival was pleasant company and undeniably a presentable gentleman, being neither old nor overweight nor yet pompous, nor even the father of several hopeful children. If he were to come to the point and was prepared to ease the worst of Papa's debts, she ought to take him for the sake of her family.

The thought settled like a hard lump in her chest that became an ache as the ritual of tea progressed and Sir Percival's attentions were marked. She could not have hoped for more when they first came to town, but now…now her heart had a mind of its own and all she could think of was a pair of challenging eyes and a mouth that made her long to feel it pressed close to hers.

Oh, she was such a fool! The viscount might offer her his services, he might take her driving or on a picnic with his cousin, but he would never offer her marriage. If she set her heart on him, she would be doomed to disappointment.

Charlotte knew her duty. Mama was relying on her to marry a gentleman of independent means who would be prepared to assist her father with his difficulties. She was being offered a chance and it would be foolish of her not to respond... even though the thought of wedding anyone but a certain viscount was a little painful.

With a pang of regret, Charlotte realised that it was already too late. Somehow in the last couple of days she'd given her heart to a man who would never give her his in return.

Chapter Five

Jack spent a pleasant evening in the company of his friends, reserving the right to play piquet with his new protégé, after a lavish dinner of lobster soup, baked sea bass, braised kidneys in wine, capon, lamb cutlets and side dishes of peas, creamed potatoes and asparagus, followed by cheese tarts, apples and dates. All of it washed down with quantities of fine wine, the vintage brandy and cigars that kept them lingering, leaving everyone in a mellow mood.

There were four others besides Matt and Jack in the company that evening, all of them close friends, and not one of them had complained when he suggested that they keep the stakes to a maximum of five guineas. Harry Brockley—known as Brock to his friends—had raised his brows, but seeing Jack's warning look made no protest. He suggested that the winners of each individual game threw dice for it at the end of the evening, and the eventual winner should treat all the others to a day at Newmarket races with dinner at an inn on the way home.

'Just to add a touch of spice to the game,' he said, raising his right eyebrow. A murmur of agreement and shared laughter greeted his suggestion, and they split into three pairs.

Quantities of wine were consumed during the evening and Jack noted with approval that Charlotte's brother drank no more than was sensible, playing his cards with skill and some flair and eventually winning two of the five hands. Honours were almost even and Jack was the eventual winner of fifteen guineas, which his young friend had no hesitation in handing over. Phipps had won his games four to one and Harry the third pairing. They threw the dice for it and Phipps won, declaring good-naturedly that he would be delighted to arrange a trip to Newmarket for the big meeting the next month. An arrangement was made and the company dispersed, Phipps offering to share a cab with two others and Matt departing to walk across the square. Brock lingered for a last brandy with his friend.

'Why the limits this evening? Been badly dipped at the races?'

'It was for the benefit of my young neighbour. He has had rough treatment at Harding's hand so I promised his sister I would see he came to no harm. Did it irk you to play for such paltry stakes? I will make it up to you another time, Brock.'

'Damn you, Jack. I am not such a fool.' Brock glared at him. 'I'll keep an eye out for him, a pleasant enough young fellow. If he was burned at Harding's hand I dare say he has learned his lesson…' His eyebrows arched. 'But tell me more of the sister, if you please. What made you take an interest in the girl—or is it the whole family?'

Seeing the mockery in the other's eyes, Jack laughed. 'Do not go marrying me off, Brock. I find the girl intriguing, that's all.'

Brock made a wry face. 'Intriguing! That is worse than if you found her a diamond of the first water or an angel. Rather too serious for me, old fellow. Please do not join the rest of them in their headlong flight into matrimonial chains.'

Jack frowned over his friend's warning. Yet even if he had toyed with the idea of making an offer for Charlotte, it would be merely a marriage of convenience. He was determined never to give his heart to a woman, because he had seen the consequences of love and the pain it could cause. Jack's father had met an early death and he believed the underlying reasons for that tragedy to be laid at a woman's door. He looked intently at his friend, arching his right brow.

'No hope of you making a match yet, then?'

'None whatsoever.' Brock was decisive. 'However, I am curious to see this intriguing young lady—will you introduce me?'

'Why not come to my sister's picnic on Friday? Charlotte will be there and Matt, too, he told me, though not as my sister's guest. He has been roped into bringing Julia.'

'Ah, the irresistible force,' Brock said and smiled. 'I have felt that myself and it takes a man of steel to resist.'

'Our wager still stands?' Jack asked, a gleam in his eyes. Six months earlier they had made a wager that neither of them would be wed before Christmas and the loser would pay the other a fine of five thousand guineas.

'Of course,' Brock murmured silkily. 'I believe I shall win after all.'

Jack yawned, as if the subject bored him. 'Do

you have a home to go to, old fellow, or are you planning to sleep on my sofa?'

'I think I shall visit my mistress,' Brock said. 'You keep early hours these days, Jack.'

His gibe went wide, Jack merely grinning as his friend took his leave. However, although he was more than ready for his bed, he did not immediately retire, but sat nursing his brandy glass for half an hour or so before making a move.

Brock seemed a confirmed bachelor, the only one of his friends who truly was not interested in marriage and content to go on as he had for the past ten years or more. Jack was no longer entirely sure of his own mind. Marriage might be bearable with the right companion, but he would hate to make a mistake and then be trapped, as his father had been, in a loveless marriage.

Jack was fond of his mama, but knew that he would hate to be married to a woman who wept so easily and clung at every opportunity. His father had told him once that it was the worst mistake of his life.

'She doesn't deserve the treatment I hand out,' he'd said when in his cups one evening, shortly before his death. 'I married on the rebound and it was stupid. Lillian was so different. Her temper was like quicksilver and when she was angry… she was magnificent. I fell in love with her the first time I saw her.'

'Why didn't you marry her, then?'

'Because she wouldn't have me,' his father admitted. 'Told me to my face that I was a selfish brute and she wouldn't have me if I were the last man on earth. But she didn't mean it…' A sobbing laugh broke from him. 'She loved me, Jack, and she had more passion in her little finger than your mother has in her whole body. I shouldn't tell you such things…but don't make my mistake. Never marry a milk-and-water miss—you're too much like me. You need a woman that can match you, in bed and out of it.'

'What did you do that made Lillian so angry?'

'I ruined a man at cards. It wasn't intentional, but he was drunk and kept throwing IOUs into the pot. How was I supposed to know that he was pledging money he didn't have? He lost his estate to me that night—and then the poor fellow blew his brains out before I could speak to him. I would have let him keep, it Jack—but he didn't wait for me to get in touch.'

'Why did Lillian turn against you for that?'

'Because her younger sister was engaged to

marry the fellow and the foolish girl went into a decline…'

'Ah, I see. So Lillian turned against you—and you married my mother.'

'She was lovely, then, and her father gave her an excellent dowry—but I regretted it the minute my ring was on her finger. I never stopped loving Lillian and she always loved me. Though she married a marquis— he was a cousin of Lord Harding. Rockingham, his name was…Alistair Rockingham.'

'How do you know she still loved you?'

'We had an affair years later—just a brief one—and then she died, in a riding accident. I wasn't told until days later, through an insertion in the newspapers. It broke my heart.'

'And when was this?'

'Just a few months ago.'

The seventeen-year-old Jack had found it difficult to comprehend that the man who seemed to be advancing in years to him could still be so passionately in love with a woman he had lost at least eighteen years earlier. Although, it seemed that they had found each other again…

Since then Jack had come to realise that a man's feelings might continue to be strong about things he felt deeply for his life long and he'd understood how his father must feel having lost the woman he'd loved with such passion. But they'd never talked again so frankly, for the next morning his father had set out on his ill-fated journey to his estates in the north.

Jack shook his head, dismissing the nagging suspicion that still lingered even after all these years. Somehow he'd never been able to accept that his father's death had been the result of a simple accident, yet there had never been any proof that he could discover that it was anything else. After all, who would want him dead—unless…Lillian's husband, who also had estates in the north? If his father had been murdered because of that affair…

No, it was a ridiculous thought. The Marquis of Rockingham was an older man, even then not a well man…surely he could not have had anything to do with either his wife's death or her lover's?

Jack dismissed the thought. Rockingham had passed away a year ago; he was unlikely to discover the truth of it now.

He yawned and rose from the deep armchair that had him lazing by the dying embers of a fire, lit to take the chill from a cool spring evening, and walked up the stairs to his bedchamber, where Cummings had laid out his night things. He'd sent his valet to bed hours ago, and after struggling with his boots for a while abandoned the effort and stretched out on the bed fully clothed. Closing his eyes, he drifted into a troubled sleep…seeing a lonely stretch of road and a coach suddenly coming to an abrupt halt as a man sprang out in front of it. Even as the horses reared in fright at the gunshot and the coach went tumbling over into the ravine, taking all its passengers with it, Jack saw that there was no blockage of any kind on the road.

He sat up and cried out, staring into the darkness for a moment before realising that he was in his own bedroom. Telling himself he was a fool, he lay down again, puzzling over what he'd seen. But dreams were distorted by one's thoughts. All the reports said that there had been an obstruction on the road.

He was a damned fool to dwell on such thoughts. At the time, he'd employed agents to make enquiries and everyone told him the same story—it was just his foolish imagination…he must stop torturing himself and go to sleep.

* * *

'We played for a few guineas,' Matt told Charlotte the next morning. 'I won two games and lost three, so in actual fact I lost no more than five guineas. Yet it was a marvellous evening and I made some good friends. I'm engaged to dine with Phipps at his club next Monday.'

'I am glad you enjoyed yourself,' Charlotte said and smiled. She was pleased that Captain Delsey had kept his word to her. 'You can afford to lose a few guineas now and then, Matt—but don't let that dreadful man entice you into a game with him again.'

'Phipps warned me not to play too deep anywhere. He says that one can have a pleasant evening playing for small stakes as we did last night, or simply hazarding a few guineas against the dice. As long as you know when to stop—and of course, many gentlemen just go to watch the play and drink, or place a small bet on a sporting wager.'

Charlotte nodded, relieved that her brother seemed to have learned his lesson. She hoped that they had brushed through the affair pretty well and that nothing more would be heard of it, but it was not long before her hopes were dashed.

* * *

That evening when Captain Delsey arrived as her father's guest, the talk at the table was of a spectacular jewel theft.

'Harding swears the necklace was worth five thousand pounds,' Mr Cavendish said importantly. Charlotte heard the note of glee in his voice and wondered why the widower should so dislike Lord Harding. 'Of course, only a fool would leave the thing lying on his dressing chest when he went out for the evening.'

'It does seem careless,' Sir Mordred said. 'Yet it makes one uncomfortable to think there are such wicked rogues abroad in London—after all, one should be able to leave one's possessions without fear of them being stolen.'

'Whoever took it must have been a bold piece,' Mr Cavendish went on and now the note of glee intensified. 'They say the thief climbed a drainpipe at the side of the house—and the footprints beneath it were small, which makes Patterson's claim that he saw the thief climb out of the window and chased her through the park until she escaped more believable.'

'She? Are you saying the thief was a woman?'

Lady Stevens was shocked. 'Surely he was mistaken? A woman could not have done such a thing.'

The censure in her father's voice, and the horror in her mother's, made Charlotte squirm with embarrassment. She did not dare to look at her brother or at Captain Delsey, for fear that she might give herself away with a sign that she was the guilty party. Her mother's friend Mrs Kent and her daughter, Anne, made noises that showed they also thought it outrageous that anyone could suspect a woman of doing such a thing.

Charlotte kept her silence. She had been inclined to think of her act of defiance as a mad prank to rescue her brother, but now she realised how wicked she had been and what everyone would think of her if they ever guessed the truth.

'I do not doubt that Patterson was in his cups,' Captain Delsey said, twirling his glass as if to look at the ruby liquid inside it. 'A small youth is my guess…thieves choose a young boy to climb through open windows, as a rule, and some of them may look a little feminine before they reach puberty.'

'Yes, that sounds more reasonable,' Charlotte's

mother agreed. 'I am sure it could not have been a young girl.'

'If a girl was responsible, it will be one of those wretches from the slums.' Matt spoke jerkily, as if half-afraid to open his mouth. 'I think Delsey is right and it was a youth.'

Charlotte glanced at her brother and away. He looked tense and a little pale and she did not want to catch his eye lest he give himself and her away. Turning her gaze towards Captain Delsey, she saw that he was looking at her oddly and her heart caught. She tried to meet his gaze, but her cheeks felt hot and she was obliged to look away. He believed it was she who had climbed into Lord Harding's house and must suspect that it was also she who had taken the necklace.

How he must despise her! Charlotte felt ashamed, even though she knew that she'd had little choice. If she had not acted promptly, her brother would have been labelled a cheat and a fraud—and yet she had made herself a thief and she did not much enjoy the feeling now that she had seen her parents' reaction to the news.

Ought she to have tried to purchase the necklace instead of stealing it? Yet Matt swore he'd been cheated—and Charlotte had no means of paying his debt, for the sale of all her jewels would not raise the huge sum of four thousand pounds.

She raised her head defiantly, looking at Captain Delsey. Perhaps what she'd done was wrong, but there had been no other option open to her. She refused to feel guilty for rescuing Matt from certain scandal and disgrace.

'I trust you are looking forward to the picnic on Friday, Miss Stevens?' Captain Delsey said, his stern expression softening. 'My sister is certainly looking forward to meeting you—and Julia has invited herself to the affair so you will have a friend to keep you company.'

Charlotte felt grateful for the change of subject and answered him with a smile. 'Yes, she was certain your sister would not mind, sir. Matt is to drive her there and they will sit with us. Miss Handley called here this morning to make certain we knew of the arrangement, though we spoke of it previously.'

It was the signal for the conversation to turn and various functions were discussed until the ladies withdrew and the gentlemen lingered over their port.

* * *

Charlotte was kept busy serving tea and coffee, and by the time the gentlemen joined them, she was perfectly composed. However, when she took a seat by the window, her heart jumped as Captain Delsey approached and asked permission to sit beside her.

'May I take you driving tomorrow, Miss Stevens?' he asked, but the look in his eyes told her that it was more an instruction than a question.

'I am engaged to your cousin for tea,' she informed him in a voice that was slightly above a whisper. 'If the morning would suit…?'

'Yes, that will do perfectly,' he said. 'We should talk, Miss Stevens.'

'Yes…' She gave him a look of appeal. 'I know we must.'

'Tomorrow, then.' He rose to his feet. 'Matt, would you do me the honour of walking across the green? I thought we might have a game of billiards…if it should please you?'

'I should be pleased to,' Matt said, shooting a glance at his sister that told her he was hoping for a word alone with her later.

Charlotte watched the two gentlemen leave together. It was not long after that Mr Cavendish came to her and asked if he might sit with her for a moment. She inclined her head, watching as he rather fussily perched beside her on the edge of the sofa.

'I had wondered if I might steal a few words with you, Miss Stevens? I should like to take you driving one day, if you are willing?'

'How kind of you, sir,' Charlotte said. 'I am engaged for the next few days, but perhaps one day next week?'

'Yes, of course. I shall ask you again,' he said. 'How are you enjoying your stay in London?'

'Very well thus far,' she replied. 'We seem to have engagements for most evenings now and several during the day.'

'Yes, I am certain, though your papa has promised that you will attend my little affair next week. Just a soirée, you understand?'

'How lovely,' Charlotte said, gave her hand to be kissed as he stood to take his leave, and then rose and went over to her mother. 'I shall go to bed now, Mama.'

'Yes, for Anne and her mama are leaving now,' Lady Stevens said. 'I shall not be long after you. I shall come in to say goodnight, my dear.'

Charlotte nodded, wondering what her mother

would have to say that could not wait for the morning. Quite possibly a further warning not to like Captain Delsey too much, she thought.

Mama had no idea that the gentleman in question could not possibly have any respect for her and was likely to cool the connection as soon as he could do so politely.

'I do not wish to spoil your pleasure, dearest,' Mama said when she entered the bedroom to say goodnight. 'I am not too old to remember that it is flattering to be noticed by a gentleman such as Captain Delsey—but please remember that he is by reputation a flirt and unlikely to make you an offer. He is also a viscount and heir to the marquis, and will look higher for his wife.'

'I have not forgotten your warning, Mama,' Charlotte replied dutifully. 'But surely it is better not to seem too particular towards any gentleman until one of them makes me an offer.'

'Yes, of course.' Mama sighed and patted her arm. 'How I wish that none of this was necessary, my love. You should be at liberty to follow your heart, although you would be unwise to give it to a man who may treat your gift with contempt.'

'I do not think you need worry, Mama. I believe I shall receive an offer I can accept before too long.'

'I must admit that I am counting on it. Otherwise your poor papa may find himself having to sell most of the land and almost certainly the house—and then I have no idea how we shall live.'

Charlotte blinked hard as her mother left the room, blocking the ridiculous tears. She felt so guilty, because of her reckless behaviour everything that Mama had striven for could so easily be lost.

She shrugged on her dressing robe and went into her own little sitting room, waiting for Matt's knock, but though she waited for two hours he did not come and she decided to go to bed, feeling too tired to sit up any longer. She'd been so certain he wanted to talk to her, but he must have forgotten and gone off to bed. Feeling a little annoyed with her brother, she went through to her bedroom and tumbled into bed.

Charlotte drifted away into a deep sleep, though once during the night she had a troubling dream that woke her. When she was awake she could not recall what had disturbed her—except that she thought someone had been threatening her.

It was her guilty conscience, of course. She closed her eyes, deciding to think of her drive in the park with Captain Delsey and was soon drifting into a peaceful sleep.

In the morning she felt a little tired and would have liked to snuggle down for longer, but her maid had been asked to wake her and, confronted with a pot of hot chocolate and some soft rolls and honey, Charlotte made a good breakfast.

Her situation was an uneasy one, for as a young unmarried girl any hint of scandal attached to her name might be the end of her chances of a good marriage. What that would do to her family was unthinkable.

Charlotte supposed that she must do as her mama expected of her and accept the first proposal made to her, which seemed likely to come from Sir Percival. A deep sigh escaped her, because although she did not dislike him, he had not touched her heart.

Putting away her troubled thoughts, Charlotte summoned her maid and proceeded to wash and dress for the day. At least this morning she could enjoy a drive to the park...or could she?

It depended on how much of her story Captain Delsey had guessed.

By the time that Captain Delsey's knock came at the door, Charlotte was downstairs and dressed in a pretty gown of heavy old-gold silk and a pelisse of white. Her straw bonnet was trimmed with white ribbons and she wore dark-blue jean boots and white lace gloves. In her hands she carried a delicate parasol of white lace with an ivory handle. The look in the captain's eyes told her that he appreciated the picture of angelic innocence that she presented and the quirk of his brow hinted that he was rigorously controlling his amusement. He himself looked the picture of sartorial elegance in tight-fitting buckskins and a jacket that showed off his fine shoulders, his linen pristine.

'How prompt of you, Miss Stevens,' he said. 'Most young ladies keep one waiting at least ten minutes.'

'I am not most young ladies.'

'Indeed, you are not,' he replied and bowed over her hand before assisting her into his curricle. Once he had the reins in his hands he dismissed his groom, giving her a brief glance. 'I believe we may dispense with Fred's services. I am not likely to seduce you on a sedate drive to the park and back.'

'Even had you a mind to, it would not be practical,' she answered in the same mocking tone he'd used.

'Oh, I have a mind to,' he murmured. 'You are bold, Miss Stevens, but still a lady and I do not seduce girls of good family who are hardly out of the schoolroom—even if they are provoking.'

'How disappointing,' Charlotte answered rashly, goaded into an unwise reply by his challenge. 'One had heard so much of your reputation—but of course, people exaggerate these things.'

'A hit,' he acknowledged with a laugh. 'My reputation is not undeserved, Miss Stevens, at least in so far as it touches the fact that I have broken hearts. It was never my intention, but it seems even a smile will encourage some foolish girls to think of marriage.'

'Then they bring their heartache on themselves,' she replied. 'I for one would need more than a smile to break my heart—however enchanting it might be.'

'That's given me my own,' he replied and she could see a tiny pulse flicking at his temple, as for a few moments he guided his horses through the press of traffic. After leaving the quiet square behind, they had met vehicles of all kinds, including a wagon loaded with sacks that had shed some of its load, causing congestion. Omnibuses, carriages, wagons and costers' barrows crowded the roads for a while and during this time Charlotte was left to admire the way the captain handled his horses and to reflect on the wisdom or otherwise of challenging him.

When at last he was at leisure to engage her in conversation again, she said, 'Did my brother keep you late last evening, sir? I thought he wished to speak with me, but he did not come to my sitting room, as he usually does if we wish to be private.'

'He refrained from disturbing you under my instruction.'

'Your instruction?' Charlotte turned her gaze on him in instant indignation. 'May I ask what right you have to offer Matt advice, let alone instruction?'

'Only what he gave me,' Captain Delsey replied. 'We had a frank talk, you see, Charlotte, and Matt confessed that your little escapade was his fault—but he also told me that he had begged you not to act so rashly. Apparently, you never mind him...have not done so since you were nine.'

'He had no right to tell you anything.'

'I had guessed most of it,' he said. 'Therefore he had little choice but to tell me the whole—and, once I had given him a set down for allowing his sister to behave so foolishly, he quite saw that he must accept my help in the matter.'

'You are not to be my judge!' Charlotte glared at him. 'Pray take me home at once.'

'I fear I cannot turn my horses here. We shall take a little trot about the park and then I shall of course return you to your mama.'

'I want to get down. I refuse to be spoken to in this manner.'

'Please do not make a scene,' he advised patiently. 'For my sake, if not your own. I do not care to be the subject of more scandal.'

'You are impossible.' She hunched her shoulder at him, but sat decorously enough as he turned into the park and let his horses slow to a gentle walk.

'Now we may be comfortable,' he said and seized the chance to glance at her. 'Why are you so angry with me? Because I persuaded Matt to confess his part in the affair? You knew I had guessed it. Come, admit it, Charlotte. From the beginning I suspected that you were in it together. I saw Matt admit you to the house that night.'

'I did not give you permission to use my name.'

'You did not, but it is foolish to stand on ceremony, especially as I have promised to give Matt his heart's dearest wish.'

'What do you mean?'

'Does you brother not hanker after a commission in the cavalry—one of the best regiments?'

'Yes, a commission in the army is his dream, but it would be expensive, for now we are not at war the officers are on half-pay. At the moment, Papa could barely afford to buy the colours, let alone give him a sufficient allowance to live comfortably. He wants Matt to enter the church, for there will be a vacant living at my uncle's estate...what? Why do you look at me that way?'

'Can you imagine your brother being happy as a parson?'

'No, I think it a foolish idea of Papa's—but what else is there for him? He must find work of some kind...unless he marries well.'

'Yes, and when he leaves the army in a few years I shall help him find work as an estate manager or some such thing, but he may find a way of making his fortune. I believe he hopes to serve in India.'

'But Papa cannot afford—' Charlotte gasped. 'No, you cannot...why should you? Papa would never accept charity.'

'Who mentioned charity? Besides, I believe your father may agree that it would suit Matt down to the ground, when I have had the chance to speak to him at length.'

'How could he? You are not related to us by any chance?'

'Not to my knowledge...but I do not see that as a drawback. Indeed, it might be awkward, since I intend to become a part of your family through marriage.'

Charlotte gaped at him, her mouth falling open. 'You will sanction Julia's marriage to my brother? I am not at all sure that she truly wishes it...'

'And her parents would never agree. No, Charlotte. I am intending to make your father an offer for you.'

'No!' The refusal sprang to her lips. 'No, I won't—I cannot… Why should you want to marry me? After what I've done— If it ever came out…' His expression made her gasp and pause, waiting for his answer. There was amusement in his eyes, but also something more, a command that took from her the power of speech.

'Of course, it must not become common knowledge, which is why Matt is leaving almost immediately. Harding is the sort that will not let go once he has his claws into a man. Matt will go down to my estate for a visit until I have purchased his colours. Indeed, I have to visit relatives myself quite soon—next week, I think—and we shall travel together. I shall insert a notice of our engagement in *The Times* before I leave.'

'How dare you? I have not agreed and Papa will not… We hardly know you.' She stared at him in bewilderment. 'I cannot believe this is happening. I thought you might cut the connection—politely, of course—but you cannot want to marry a girl like me. Why should you?'

'As well a girl with spirit as one with only milk and water in her veins,' Jack murmured softly. 'I

shall be honest with you, Charlotte. Left to myself, I would not bother with marriage at all, for
I have no great opinion of it, but my grandfather
needs me to provide him with an heir. I am very
fond of him and minded to oblige him. You need
a fortune to clear your father's debts and give
your brother a good start in life—why not mine
as well as another's?'

Charlotte digested this in silence for a moment,
then looked at him hard. He had brought the curricle to a halt and was looking at her expectantly.
He knew the truth, for she had hidden nothing,
yet she still felt that he could not have considered fully.

Honesty made her speak out, 'But surely...there
must be a girl more suited to the honour of being
your wife and the future marchioness. Why me?'

'Since I am being honest, I have no idea, but I
think it is because you amuse me. If I married my
cousin—not Julia, but another I'm being asked
to inspect—or indeed any other society miss, I
should be bored within a couple of weeks.'

'How do you know it wouldn't be the same
married to me?'

'Of course I don't,' he admitted but there was
a gleam of mischief in his eyes now. 'However,

none of the very correct girls I've met would dream of climbing into a house to steal a diamond necklace…nor would they have the courage.'

'It wasn't truly stealing. I had to retrieve the wretched thing before Lord Harding realised it was a fake. Just think of the scandal if it had come out—' For a moment she forgot herself as she looked at him innocently, her eyes wide and appealing to his sense of the ridiculous.

'Enough of that, you foolish girl,' he said and caught his breath. 'Did it never occur to you that it would mean a far greater scandal if you were caught?'

'I did not intend to be caught.'

'Yet you almost were.'

'Yes, and I have you to thank for it that I escaped.' Charlotte drew a shaky breath. 'I know it's wrong to steal. I am ashamed of what I did—do you think me sunk beneath reproach?'

'Not at all. Harding cheated your brother and therefore got his just deserts. However, if you ever try to steal from one of my friends, I shall put you across my knee and thrash you. You will not sit down for a month.'

'How dare you!' she cried loud enough to make

a passer-by stare at them. She felt the hot sting of colour in her cheeks and lowered her voice. 'I wouldn't. You know I wouldn't—how could you think it?'

'I don't. It was just a friendly warning.'

'I did not need such a warning.' She was smarting with indignation but there were people all around them, walking or driving in open carriages, and she dared not raise her voice again.

'Well, then, we shall not fall out over it again,' he murmured, but the challenge in his eyes made her bite her lip in frustration.

'I wish we were alone so that I might tell you just what I think of you, sir.'

'Call me Jack,' he invited and smiled at her in a way that made her catch her breath. 'After all, we are practically engaged.'

'We are not!'

'Oh, I see. You would prefer to marry Sir Percival or Mr Cavendish? I don't think either of them would understand what you did the other night.'

'You wouldn't tell them?'

'Would I not?' He arched his eyebrows at her. 'Can you be sure of that? I can be ruthless when the occasion demands.'

'Wretch!' Charlotte was forced to laugh. 'I believe it would not sit well with your notion of fair play.'

'You begin to know me,' he murmured throatily. 'So—do we have an arrangement? You marry me in order to please my grandfather and give me an heir—I for my part give your brother all the help I can to make his fortunes, and assist your papa to sort out his finances.'

'Papa owes a great deal of money.'

'Not so very much according to your brother, though he may not be privy to the whole. But I dare say it will not ruin me. Besides, there are often ways to improve a man's fortunes without recourse to paying all his debts, but this is your father's business and you do not need to know it all.'

'I still do not see why you chose me. You could have any girl you wished.'

'Then I must wish to have you, mustn't I?' he said with a mocking look. 'Do not disturb yourself, Charlotte. Once engaged to marry, I shall be free of the constant plaguing of my family and, when we marry, you will have a title, as much pin money as you can spend and everything else that goes with marriage. All I ask is that you treat

Grandfather kindly and give me the heir he so desires—can you do that?'

'I… Yes, I can do that,' Charlotte said, but avoided looking into his eyes, because she was not sure she could trust herself. This was all wrong, and yet her heart told her that she would regret it if she refused him. 'It is very good of you, sir.'

'Is it? I shall expect you to provide heirs and entertain my friends, so the obligation is not all on your side,' Jack said and shook his head at her, a question in his eyes. 'Come, you must try to look like an adoring bride you know. I have proposed marriage, not an execution.'

Charlotte was provoked into laughter. 'I am happy, sir. I think we shall be…comfortable together, but I must point out that you did not propose—you gave me an ultimatum.'

'Not quite that,' he murmured. 'Forgive me, it did not occur to me that romance would be appropriate, but it was remiss of me. I shall make it up to you another day, Charlotte.'

Averting her gaze, her cheeks burning, Charlotte wondered just what she had let herself in for. It was true that she would prefer marriage to Captain Delsey to any other gentleman she knew, but could she really be happy with the arrangement he offered?

Well, she had no choice now. She had agreed to the idea, though he'd left her little choice, but how could she draw back when it would mean so much to her family? If she had doubts for her own happiness in the future, she could conceal them. After all, she must marry to suit her family, and as well a man she liked rather more than she was comfortable with as one she disliked.

As long as she did not like him too well, for if Charlotte were unwise enough to give her whole heart to this man, she might very well find it broken in a few years.

Chapter Six

'**W**ell, that was quick work,' Julia whispered as she and Charlotte walked a little apart from the others at the balloon ascension. The girls had linked arms and gone a little closer to watch the preparations to prepare the large, brightly coloured bag and its basket to float into the air. 'I knew Jack liked you, but you could have knocked me down with a feather when he came round to tell Mama and Papa the news. My eldest brother looked most put out.'

'Oh, why? I do not think I've met Mr Handley, have I? Does he dislike the idea of Captain Delsey marrying beneath him?'

'Oh, no, it would be the same whomever Jack married—and you are not beneath him, do not be silly, Charlie. You may not have a fortune, but everyone is pleased, except Reginald, because he hoped that he might inherit the title if Jack were to die before he had an heir.'

'But surely— I thought your brother was older than Jack… He is your father's son by his first marriage, is he not?'

'Yes, and it was only that Jack enlisted and went off to war—he was always such a daredevil that we lived in fear of his being killed. At least most of us did. Reginald would have benefited, of course, because he is the next in line, through his mother, who was the marquis's eldest daughter—but I should hate it. I'm fond of my cousin.'

'Good, I'm hoping we shall see lots of each other.'

'Yes, I also…' Julia pulled a face. 'I don't know why Jack has to take your brother off to his estate. And Matt says he's going to join the army and hopes to go out to India.'

'It will be a good thing for him,' Charlotte explained. 'I know he admires you very much, Julia. I dare say he is a little in love with you, but he knows that he has no chance until he is older and has made some sort of life for himself. Your parents would never let you marry someone like Matt.'

'I might not ask them,' Julia said and threw her

a challenging smile. 'I could simply elope. I've always wanted to have adventures. I wouldn't mind being a soldier's wife.'

'But India is not good for English complexions,' Charlotte pointed out, 'and a lot of women who do follow their husbands out there die of fevers—especially if they have children. Matt's hope is that he can make his fortune and come back as a man of substance.'

'But it will take years.' Julia pulled a face at her. 'I could never wait all that time, Charlie. I'm not patient enough. Why couldn't Matt just be content to serve here or on the Continent?'

'Because in peacetime he would be paid far too little to take a wife. Don't you see, Julia—he can't ask you to marry him yet, even if it breaks his heart to leave you behind.'

Julia pouted, a look of mutiny in her eyes. 'If he loved me, he would not go and leave me—just when we are getting to know one another.'

'Would you truly wish to be a serving officer's wife? You are used to the best of everything, pretty clothes, jewels, your horses and dogs… could you give them up for his sake?'

'I wouldn't have to. I have a fortune in trust

waiting for me when I marry. Matt doesn't have to go away at all.'

Charlotte gave up the struggle and managed a look of sympathy. 'It's his pride, I suppose.'

Julia laughed and hugged her arm. 'I know I'm being selfish,' she said. 'I do like him, Charlie, but it's too soon to be sure. Are you sure you want to marry Jack?'

'Oh, yes,' Charlotte replied, though she did not meet Julia's questing look. 'It is all settled, you know. Captain Delsey asked Papa yesterday and a notice of our engagement will go into *The Times* next week. Mama will give a dance for me in two weeks and Matt will come up for that—and then he will join his unit.'

'It is all happening so fast,' Julia complained. 'When are you to be married?'

'I think September,' Charlotte replied. 'We haven't settled the exact date yet—at least I haven't been told.'

'You haven't your ring yet either.'

'Jack said he was going to give me one of the family heirlooms for the time being and will buy me something of my own when he returns to town after his visit to the country.'

'Well, I'm glad you're happy,' Julia said and sighed. 'I just wish Matt wasn't going away so soon.'

Charlotte could add nothing to what she'd already said, contenting herself by pointing out that the balloon was about to let go its anchor ropes.

'Should we return to the others?' she suggested. 'I don't know if anyone will want to follow the flight.'

'Oh, I don't,' Julia muttered. 'I've seen it before and it's always the same. You chase the silly thing for miles and then it plops down in the middle of nowhere. I came merely to be with you and Matt, and now all he can talk of is the cavalry regiment he is to join.'

Charlotte shook her head, a ready smile on her lips. 'There is no understanding men, is there?'

Glancing at the balloon once more, she became aware that two men were staring at her fixedly. A little shiver went down her spine as she realised that she knew them: Lord Harding and Mr Patterson. Mr Patterson appeared to be talking earnestly to his companion and they both looked at her intently.

Could Mr Patterson have recognised her? Surely not, she thought, trying to quell her sudden surge of fear. It had been dark in the park and even when he'd caught her briefly, before she kicked his shin and escaped, he could not have seen her clearly. He could not know that Miss Charlotte Stevens was the urchin that he'd seen climbing down from the window of his friend's house, then chased into the park and across it to the far side.

She felt herself shudder, for had she not been as quick and determined, she might have been in serious trouble that night—and she still might if the truth came out. Yet it would not, because no one but Captain Delsey had seen her arrive home that night and he would not tell.

'Are you cold?' Julia asked, looking at her oddly.

'No, not at all,' Charlotte replied. 'Someone just walked over my grave.'

'Oh, what a horrid thought,' Julia exclaimed. 'I've heard the saying, of course, but I do not like it. I am losing Matt, I cannot lose you as well.'

'I have no intention of going anywhere just yet,' Charlotte said and laughed. 'Until my marriage, of course. I do not know where we shall live then.'

'Jack hasn't said? He normally prefers living

in town, just visits the country every now and then, his grandfather's estate mostly. His mama lives there with the marquis, of course, though she has her own house in Bath. I may have told you before?'

Charlotte nodded thoughtfully. 'I believe we are to go on a visit to Ellingham when Jack returns from his trip out of town.'

'Yes, his maternal uncle invited him to visit, I believe, and he was promised to go—before he met you.' Julia looked at her in awe. 'I just cannot believe he asked you so quickly, unless it was because he was afraid he might get pushed into marrying his cousin Celia. His mama's family, you know...she is quite an heiress, though of course Jack doesn't need to consider money. He is quite rich enough already.'

'Oh, perhaps that was it,' Charlotte agreed, glancing across to where Jack sat talking with his sister, Lady Sally. His gaze was looking beyond her—at Lord Harding, she realised with a glance over her shoulder. The two men were still watching her and talking earnestly.

'Of course it wasn't that, silly.' Julia squeezed her arm again. 'He fell madly in love and was afraid you might take someone else while he was gone.'

Jack was frowning. She watched as he rose from where he'd been sitting on a rug and walked unhurriedly to meet them, her heart lurching as she looked at his face. He looked so stern. Was he wondering as she had whether Patterson had recognised her, perhaps regretting his hasty decision to ask for her in marriage?

'Would you like to follow the balloon?' he asked, as he came up to them. 'Or would you prefer to drive home?'

'Whatever you prefer,' Charlotte said, but a collective gasp from the assembled watchers made her look towards the balloon in time to see it lift off from the ground. 'Oh, how magnificent it looks. It must be wonderful to float through the sky like that...so free...'

'It is a pleasant sensation,' Jack agreed. 'I've been up a few times. The landing is sometimes uncomfortable, but while you're up there it is a good feeling.'

'I should love to try it,' Charlotte said, a wistful note in her voice, 'but I dare say it is another of those enjoyable pastimes saved for gentlemen.'

Jack smiled wryly and offered her his arm as

Julia walked to meet Matt, who had come in search of her. They strolled a little way from the company. Then Jack glanced back to where the crowd was beginning to disperse, some going after the balloon either on horseback or in carriages, others lingering to talk but at the same time preparing to leave.

'I think you noticed Mr Patterson and Lord Harding earlier,' Jack said. 'I must warn you to be careful of them, Charlotte. I wish I did not have to leave town before it is generally known that we are engaged, but my promise was given before we met. I shall be gone only a few days.'

'We have several engagements this next week, though I do not imagine I shall see much of those particular gentlemen. We are mainly invited to Mama's friends for dinner and cards or a musical evening. There is one small ball, but nothing grand until the following week, when perhaps you will be in town again?'

'I certainly intend to be,' he replied. 'I dare say there was nothing in it, but they were staring hard and Patterson had a lot to say. I know you would not go anywhere alone with either of them, but avoid them both if you can, Charlotte. If they guess what happened, they will try to force Matt to pay the value of the diamonds by blackmailing him and threatening your good name.'

'They can prove nothing,' she said, though the back of her neck prickled and she felt cold.

'Sometimes a whisper in the right places is enough to destroy a reputation,' Jack warned. 'Once Harding realises that your brother is beyond his reach, he may try threatening you.'

'I shall just pretend I know nothing of it.' She forced a smile, even though a little knot of fear had settled in the pit of her stomach.

'I shall return by the end of the week and then we shall announce our engagement to the world by giving a large ball. After that I shall take you to stay with Grandfather for a few weeks so that we can arrange the wedding.' Jack reached into his pocket and brought out a small box. 'I hope this will fit. Remember, it is only until I can buy you something better of your own.'

'Something better?' Charlotte gasped as she saw the magnificent diamond-and-ruby ring. It consisted of one large deep-red stone and two slightly smaller diamonds on either side. 'This is lovely, Jack. I like it very well and shall enjoy wearing it.'

'Allow me,' he said and slid it onto the third

finger of her left hand, where it nestled as if it had been made for her. 'Yes, that will do well enough for now.' Jack smiled as she reached up to kiss his cheek.

'Were we not being observed I would kiss you, as I wish to kiss you,' he murmured. 'I ought to have waited until we were alone, but I fear I have an engagement this evening, and tomorrow Matt and I leave for my uncle's estate. We shall call in at my own estate, where Matt will remain until I join him next week and we travel back to London for our engagement party. By then everything will be in place for his departure to join his unit.'

'I am grateful for all that you've done for him—and Papa,' Charlotte murmured shyly, unable to look at him, but he reached out and tipped her chin so that she looked up.

'You have made me happy,' he assured her. 'Never doubt that, Charlotte. I think we shall deal very well together, but do not smother me with gratitude for I cannot abide it—and believe me, as my wife, you will earn every penny of what I have spent on your family. I have not mentioned it, but Mama…my mother is not an easy person to live with. She will naturally spend some of her time with us and may try your patience now and then.'

'As she does yours?' Charlotte laughed. 'I have an aunt who drives Mama to distraction, but I have found that all she needs is a little attention and to feel wanted, needed.'

He quirked an eyebrow. 'I wish you luck with Mama,' he murmured. 'Come, I shall drive you home and take tea with you—and then I shall not see you again until we return from the country, since Matt is to stay with me this evening. We leave at six in the morning.'

Jack asked for a moment alone with Charlotte before he took his leave and was granted permission to speak with her in the small downstairs parlour. Mama had exclaimed over her ring, told her she was a fortunate young woman and kissed Jack's cheek before sending them off to make their farewells.

Jack looked as if he wanted to laugh and Charlotte scolded him.

'I will not have you laugh at Mama.'

'She is trying hard to behave as if I were the perfect husband for her precious daughter, but I see the doubts in her eyes. She believes that I shall break your heart, Charlotte. Please believe that I should never wish to harm or hurt you. I do truly believe that we shall deal well together. You are a sensible young woman, Charlotte, and I think you understand what we have agreed together?'

'Yes, of course,' she replied promptly, refusing to let the fact that he did not love her spoil her pleasure in all the advantages of marriage with a man of his standing. 'We like each other well and we both have much to gain from this marriage. I for one shall do all I can to be the kind of wife you require, to give you affection and to raise our children to respect and love their father, as well as caring for your comfort and that of your guests.'

'Not quite in the same way, of course,' he murmured huskily and reached for her, drawing her into his arms. His kiss surprised and shocked Charlotte for it was anything but passive. The heat seared through her as his lips pressed hers and his tongue flicked, seeking entrance. Instinctively, she parted her lips a little and heard his murmur of approval as his tongue moved inside her mouth, touching hers in a way that made her tremble and her body seem to melt in the heat of desire. His hand caressed the nape of her neck and he held her pressed to the length of him so that she felt the hardness of his arousal and understood what he was saying to her. This was not to be a tepid marriage, but one of passion, if not romantic love. 'There are some privileges I reserve to myself as your husband.'

Charlotte felt as if she could stay this way for hours and yet there was a part of her that cried out for more, longing to feel his hands on her flesh and the heat of his own against her skin, for something she'd never known and could not truly imagine.

'I meant only to make them welcome to our home,' she murmured softly. 'I take my marriage vows seriously, Jack. I have no intention of breaking them.'

'It would go hard with you if you did,' he said and kissed her neck. 'What is mine belongs to me, Charlotte. Never forget it.'

She shook her head, but wanted to ask if he meant to keep as rigorously to his vows of fidelity. Yet she knew she dared not. Ladies did not demand such knowledge; they pretended they did not know when their husbands took a mistress and wept only when they were alone. It was an unspoken part of their bargain: Jack would give her everything but romantic love, and in return she must be a complacent wife—and that meant not questioning where he went or who he saw.

Would Charlotte cry many bitter tears over the years? The thought teased at her, but she would not let it bother her. Jack had never pretended to love her. He had given more than she might have expected and he was the man whose company she enjoyed above all others—she must not expect more than he could give.

Jack wanted an obliging wife, one happy to indulge him in their bedroom and to give him children. She had been reared properly and was well able to accept the duties that the future would bring when he stepped into his grandfather's shoes, though she knew he hoped that would be many years ahead. He had chosen her because she had spirit and he wanted more than mere compliance from his wife. Charlotte would not always agree with him and she would stand her ground; she had an independent spirit and would expect him to accept her for what she was. If he could never love her, he must like her and respect her, otherwise he would not have asked her to wed him.

'I promise you shall have no reason to blush for me,' she said and touched his cheek as he drew away. 'I know that a man in your position must be sure that his sons are of his flesh and not that of his wife's lover.'

He nodded, looking serious, almost as if he wished to say more—much more—but he shook his head, clearly deciding that they understood each other well enough for now.

'I wish that I did not have to leave you here,' he said. 'Yet I do not wish to offer offence to my uncle and must let him down gently. I shall return as soon as I am able—but without fail before the end of next week.'

'I shall see you to the door,' she replied calmly. 'You must go home and change or you will be late for your appointment—and we have guests this evening.'

'Yes, I know,' he replied and touched her hair. 'Take care of yourself, Charlotte—and remember I shall soon be with you again.'

She smiled and accompanied him to the door, offering her hand for his to kiss under the eyes of the very correct footman who avoided looking at them directly, but opened the door at the precise moment Jack was ready to leave.

Charlotte turned and went upstairs to her bed-chamber. It was time for her to change for the evening, though for some reason she felt more like weeping than entertaining her mama's guests.

Not until she was alone in her bed that night did Charlotte have time to examine her feelings and discover why she'd felt so close to weeping after Jack had left her. She'd fought against admitting it to herself, but now understood that she was in love with him. It must have happened almost the first time they met, perhaps not in that brief instant when he'd pushed her behind him, giving her the opportunity to escape—but when he'd called the next day and the challenge in his eyes had made her want to strike out at him. At first she'd thought she was merely grateful for his intervention, but their first waltz had changed everything. The rush of sensations that had swept over her had been total and revealing, though she had still told herself it was merely the natural reaction of a young woman in the arms of a very charming and physical man.

She was to marry the man she loved with the force of her whole being, but he did not love her as she loved him. He was considerate, generous

and a gentleman, and Charlotte had no doubt that
he would treat her well. As his wife she would
have everything she could desire—apart from
his love. He would give her clothes, jewels and
beautiful homes, and she would give him children in return, but he would never give her his
heart, and perversely it was his heart that she
coveted above all else.

Could she bear it, knowing through the years
that however passionate he was in their bed, however kind and considerate in their private life,
he did not love her as she loved him? It was a
sobering thought and one that kept Charlotte
awake for some hours, but eventually she slept,
because there was no way around her dilemma.
She feared it would break her heart if she did not
wed him now—though he might well break it in
the future, slowly, piece by piece.

To walk away from him now would bring her
whole family down with her. No, she must keep
to her bargain and never ever let Jack guess that
she loved him more than her own life. If she
did, he would feel trapped, and she knew that
he needed to be free. It was the reason he'd chosen her for his wife. She had spirit and would not
be crushed by his lack of affection for her and

she would not shrink from doing her duty in his bed. Her only fear was that she might give him a revulsion of her by returning his passion too fiercely.

No, she must play her part skilfully so that he never guessed what was in her heart.

Charlotte began to play her part the next morning by entering into her mother's plans for the wedding with every show of pleasure and excitement that would be expected. She visited the seamstresses her mama favoured, standing patiently for hours as she was measured and fitted for all the new clothes she would need. Mama was insistent on providing her with an expensive trousseau, even though she would be wealthy enough to buy whatever she wanted once she was Lady Delsey.

'I cannot let you go without a decent trousseau,' Mama said. 'I have saved for this day, Charlotte, and the money is entirely my own—inherited from your great-grandfather, who left me several thousand pounds in trust. The capital will pass to your brother when I die, but the income has been mine since I married, and over the years I've put by for your wedding. You will have

Papa's gift of a diamond necklace and also some linen that belonged to my mother, but that is all we can give you, my love—apart from the small trust you know is yours.'

'It is more than enough,' Charlotte said. 'I'm not sure how much Jack has settled on me, but I know he said I shall have as much pin money as I can spend.'

'Yes, indeed. I have not seen the marriage contract, but your papa said it was generous. None the less, that does not mean you should go empty-handed, dearest.'

'I did not want you to beggar yourself for my sake, that is all,' Charlotte replied. 'Thank you for giving me this Season, Mama—and now all these lovely clothes.'

'I think you will be happy, at least at first,' her mother said anxiously. 'Marriage is never like the fairytale endings in books, Charlotte. Viscount Delsey is a gentleman and I believe he will be discreet. I think he will not deliberately hurt you, but if he goes off to stay in London or… away somewhere…at certain times, especially when you are in a delicate condition…you must not mind too much. Gentlemen need their pleasures and they do not like their wives to hang on their sleeve all the time.'

'Did Papa have a mistress?' Charlotte asked and her mama gasped, looking shocked. 'Does it distress you to speak of it? Forgive me, I did not mean to hurt you, Mama.'

'I have never spoken of these things, to your father—or to anyone, even my own mother, when she lived. It is not done, Charlotte. We guess, but as long as we do not let ourselves know, we can pretend that everything is as it should be. Your husband intends to be generous and he will be courteous and considerate. You should not expect more, unless you wish for disappointment.'

'No, I suppose not,' Charlotte agreed. 'Yet it seems a little unfair if we are expected to be faithful all our lives and they do just as they please.'

'Some ladies do not remain faithful,' Mama said. 'I was never too concerned about…what happens in the bedroom. Providing Papa was kind and did not abuse either my children or me, I had no wish to have a relationship outside my marriage. There are some ladies that do— once they have provided heirs for their husband's estates.'

'I cannot see how anyone could…' Charlotte turned up her nose at the idea. 'If you want to be happy and at peace—how can you give yourself in a clandestine affair? It must cause friction and distrust between husband and wife.'

'If you are like me, you will not consider it,' Mama said. 'It may even be a relief if your husband does not come so often to your bed…though perhaps you may take after your grandmother. Lady Bella was very different. She provided her husband with three sons that were truly his, but after that…no one was ever certain who fathered her last three children. They had red hair and her husband was dark.'

Charlotte smiled at her mother's disapproving look. She did not think she was like Mama, for she had been so aroused by Jack's kisses that, had he wished it, she might have given herself to him the night they waltzed for the first time. Indeed, when he kissed her, her body tingled and called out for much more…for the things that would happen on their wedding night.

Mama had tried to explain, but her embarrassment had prevented her from more than a muddled instruction to lie back, close her eyes and allow her husband to do whatever he wished. Charlotte had once seen her father's stallion coupling with a mare in the stableyard at home, and she'd been there when the foal was born some months later. It had given her an idea of what made babies and her brother had answered her questions more clearly than Mama.

'It's something that happens in marriage, Charlie,' he'd said awkwardly. 'A man has certain needs and his wife responds to that with love and passion. It's kissing and touching, and—coupling, like the stallion only nicer, much nicer—and the wife lies on her back, usually anyway, though there are other ways.'

'It isn't wrong or nasty, is it?' Charlotte asked him. 'Only I saw one of the footmen and a maid sort of hugging in the stairwell once, and then, some months later, she was dismissed for being wicked.'

'Yes, well, she ought to have waited for marriage,' Matt had told her. 'But it's usually nice once you get used to it—I find most ladies like it.'

Charlotte pounced instantly, 'You're not married. Why can you do it and a girl can't?'

'Because men do—it's just like going to bareknuckle fights and cock baiting. We're allowed, but ladies and females aren't—though some of the lower-class ones do. I suppose some ladies do *it,* too, but discreetly and not until they are married, because it's frowned on and they don't want to be ruined if a baby comes.'

'Yes, that's what I heard Cook say—that poor Rosie had ruined herself and the man wouldn't marry her, even though she swore the baby was his.'

'You hear and see a lot of things you shouldn't,' Matt said and frowned at her. 'Now don't go repeating any of this to Mama or I shall get a thrashing for telling you.'

Charlotte had promised and she'd been careful not to let Mama know that she was aware of what happened in marriage, but she was glad that she had some idea so that she wouldn't be afraid of anything Jack did when he came to her on their wedding night.

Mama seemed more interested in telling her how she must conduct herself as a hostess in her husband's home, who she would need to curtsy to and who would now give way to her.

'You will take precedence over ladies like me, Charlotte, but remember always to behave as if your companions are your equals when you are in society. It does not do to appear proud simply because you will be the wife of a viscount and, one day, a marquis.'

'I should not think of it, Mama. Jack prefers to be called Captain and seldom uses his title, unless it is necessary.'

'Well, he was born to it,' Mama said, 'but there will be many duties as his wife. You must entertain his friends and the important people in the county. You will be expected to take part in events that benefit the community, to care for the well being of your husband's people, and you must be aware of all your obligations as…'

Mama droned on and on about Charlotte's duties, but she'd always been reared to attend church and to help those less fortunate whenever she could. She did not see that it would be so very different from living at home, except that the duties of entertaining would fall on her shoulders instead of her mama's.

However, her mama's fussing and all the dress fittings helped her to get through the following days so that she did not have time to feel lonely or wonder if she would find it difficult to hide her feelings when Jack made love to her.

It did not stop her missing him and looking forward to the day of his return, but before that day arrived she had something more to worry her.

Chapter Seven

Only two days now until Jack returned to town. Charlotte dressed for an evening party feeling excited and nervous, because their engagement had been announced in the paper that morning and people were bound to mention it that evening. Charlotte wished that Jack had been in London so that he was by her side when she and Mama entered Lord Rosebury's drawing room and a little buzz of whispering told her that people were gossiping about her. She could feel their eyes boring into her back as she waited her turn to greet her hostess and felt her cheeks growing warm.

'Ah, Lady Stevens, and the lovely Miss Charlotte Stevens,' Lady Rosebury said, her small, narrow-set eyes going over her with interest. She gave Charlotte an arch look. 'What is this I hear,

Miss Stevens? Can it be true that you have succeeded where so many have failed?'

'I am not sure what you mean, ma'am?'

'Come, come, no false modesty. You must be
aware of how fortunate you are to have secured
an offer from the Viscount Delsey. I know of at
least three female hearts you have broken.'

'Yes, I am aware of my good fortune,' Charlotte
replied carefully, 'but not that I am the cause of
broken hearts.'

'Well, I dare say you cannot be blamed for that,
though there were a good many young ladies
with hopes in that direction. Tell me, how did
you manage to ensnare him in your toils?'

Charlotte was shocked for she sensed mal-
ice in the lady's question, but she merely shook
her head and moved on, allowing her hostess to
greet the next guest in the line. Inside, she was
aware of anger, for surely she had done nothing
to arouse dislike in Lady Rosebury's mind.

'Do not let that lady's remarks distress you,'
Mama whispered as they moved away into the
crowded rooms, where waiters circulating with
silver trays were offering champagne. 'She has a
daughter two years your senior and I dare say she
had hoped Delsey might offer for the fair Elaine.'

'I think perhaps she will not be the only one to resent me,' Charlotte replied for she'd noticed one or two cold glances being sent her way. She wished fervently that Jack had been with her, for she was certain that Lady Rosebury would not have risked making such barbed remarks if he had been there to protect her from malicious spite.

However, Mama spotted some friends of hers and they moved towards Lady Rushmore and her daughter Amelia, and from these ladies Charlotte received only warm congratulations. Amelia exclaimed over her ring and begged her to let her be bridesmaid at her wedding.

'I hope you are having the wedding in town?'

'I am not certain yet, but I think it may be at Ellingham,' Charlotte said, 'but perhaps you could come down to stay. I have thought of one other bridesmaid, but I should like it if you could be another of my attendants, Amelia.'

'Oh, I'm not sure if I shall be able to leave town before the end of the Season.'

'I believe it will be nearer September.'

'Well, perhaps,' Amelia said. 'I shall ask Mama what her plans are for that time…and I suppose

it depends on whether or not I am engaged before then.'

'Is there someone you would like to marry?'

Amelia blushed delicately, her eyes moving
across the room to where two gentlemen stood
talking animatedly. Following her gaze, Charlotte
saw two officers in dress uniform, one of them
Captain Young, who had waltzed so divinely at
her first London ball.

'Has he spoken yet?'

'No, but I have hopes he will soon. How did you
bring Captain Delsey to the point so quickly?'

'It was entirely his idea,' Charlotte said with a
little shrug. 'I was as surprised as anyone but…'
Her words tailed away as she saw two gentlemen enter the room together and for a moment
her heart jerked. Mr Patterson and Lord Harding
stood surveying the room.

She knew the instant they saw her, for Patterson whispered something and gave his companion a nudge, bringing his gaze across the room to
her. Charlotte dropped her own gaze and turned
as Julia Handley came up to her and made a big
fuss of looking at her ring and kissing her cheek.

'Oh, I love your ring,' she said. 'Is Jack back

from the country yet? I was hoping he might have brought your brother with him.'

'I believe they will be here by Saturday evening, Sunday at the latest,' Charlotte replied. 'You are coming to Mama's dance for us, aren't you?'

'How could I miss it?' Julia cried and hugged her arm. 'I told Mama that no matter what other invitations we had, I must be there for your dance.'

'And you will be a bridesmaid?' Charlotte said. 'Amelia has promised to be one of them if she is able, but I do not know whom else to ask. I have some distant cousins, but they are mostly married and their children not yet old enough to be bridesmaids, I think.'

'Do not worry, I think there are loads of young girls in our family, distant cousins, but Jack will advise you. I'm looking forward to the music this evening, aren't you? I understand Signor Morelli has a very fine tenor voice.'

Noticing that Lord Harding was advancing towards them, Charlotte linked arms with Julia and they walked through to the salon where the musicians had begun to play, taking their seats together on a small sofa. Some of the gentlemen had disappeared into the card room, where tables had been set up for their entertainment, but most of the ladies were grouping in the salon devoted to music.

Charlotte hushed Julia's whispering as the Italian tenor took up his place and then everyone waited expectantly, as the first liquid notes of a remarkable voice began to soar to the high ceiling. Absorbed in the music, Charlotte did not notice that Lord Harding had taken a seat not far from where she was sitting.

It was only when the first half of the performance had finished and she was about to follow her mama and Julia into the supper room that he made himself known to her.

'Miss Stevens,' he murmured, his hand on her arm. 'May I beg a few moments of your time?'

Charlotte started, glancing at the long white fingers resting on her arm. He wore a magnificent diamond on his little finger and a ruby of equal quality on his forefinger.

'Sir? I beg your pardon, I know we have been introduced, but I hardly think you can have anything to say to me. My mother is waiting for me.'

'Yet, I would have a few moments—alone, if possible.'

She stiffened with pride. 'No, sir. I can see no reason for that at all. Please state your business if you will and allow me to join my friends.'

'You force me to be plain. Where is your brother? He owes me a debt and I am persuaded he cannot wish to withhold payment...'

'Forgive me, I do not understand you, sir. What debt is that, pray?'

'A gambling debt...' For a moment his hand seemed to tighten on her wrist. 'I am sure you know exactly what I speak of—a debt that is yet unpaid.'

'Indeed, you are wrong, sir. I have no idea what you mean. If my brother owes you money, then you must speak with him, but I think it unlikely. He is a man of honour and would certainly pay. Now, if you will excuse me...' She tried to move away, but his hold detained her.

'The debt ought to have been paid with a diamond necklace, which mysteriously disappeared the very night I received it, while I was out...' Harding's gaze narrowed, 'But you know all about that, do you not, Miss Stevens?'

Charlotte knew that she must show neither fear nor understanding or she was ruined. Lifting her head, she met his challenge with one of her own.

'I fear I have no idea what you are talking about, sir. Now, I really must insist—or do you wish me to make a scene?'

For a moment she thought he would refuse to let her go, but Julia had noticed she was detained and was returning to fetch her. Harding saw it and his hand released her.

'This is not over,' he said in a harsh whisper. 'I shall be paid for the necklace you stole, Miss Stevens. I think your bridegroom might change his mind if he guessed that you were a thief.'

Charlotte moved away as soon as she was free, giving him what she hoped was a withering look. Her heart was beating wildly and her mouth felt dry, but she fought to keep her back straight and her head high. It was clear to her now that Patterson believed he recognised her and that was enough to make her feel sick with fear, but she refused to let her tormentor guess how close he had come to breaking her rigid composure.

'Was that awful man upsetting you?' Julia asked as she joined her. 'You look pale, Charlie.'

'No, he merely wanted to know where my brother was and seemed annoyed that I had no answer for him.'

'I suppose he feels cheated, because he can't fleece your brother of his fortune.'

'Matt has very little fortune to lose, that is the problem,' she replied and then wished she hadn't said as much for Julia stared at her in surprise. 'What he has is in trust until he's older…and that means he cannot afford to lose at the tables.'

Julia still looked a little puzzled, but they had reached the supper room and the next few minutes were spent selecting from all the delicious trifles on offer. When they had chosen tiny pastries and a syllabub, they took their plates to a table where Lady Stevens and Lady Handley were seated with several other ladies. The conversation was devoted to the excellence of the food, the delightful music and the gowns of various young women who were parading about the room in order to show them to the best advantage.

It was only as they took their seats for the second half of the musical entertainment that Julia whispered to her, 'If Matt were in trouble, you would tell me? I might be able to help.'

'He isn't, I promise you,' Charlotte whispered back. 'It is nothing to worry about, Julia. Matt has done nothing wrong.'

Strictly speaking that was perfectly true. He'd taken a necklace that belonged to his sister in good faith, believing it to be valuable, and he'd confessed the whole to Charlotte, promising to pay her back as soon as he could. It was *she* who had told him the diamonds were fakes and *she* who had decided to steal it back rather than have Matt labelled a cheat.

Lord Harding and his crony might suspect she had taken the necklace, but neither of them could know for sure. Harding had tried to bully her into admitting it, but she'd held her nerve. Charlotte was conscious of a hollow feeling inside and of shame, too, for she had cheated him in a way— even though Matt believed he'd been cheated at the card table.

Had she been able to repay the debt she might have tried to find a way of doing it, without revealing the truth, but she had no way of paying four thousand pounds to Lord Harding. Neither had Matt, even though Papa's debts were now in a way to be settled. Nothing had changed, for none of them had large sums to throw away.

No, she must just put the whole thing from her mind, Charlotte decided. There were only two more days before Jack returned. She would tell him what had happened and hope that he could see a way to prevent such an unpleasant incident happening again.

Lord Harding had threatened to tell Jack, but if he realised that her fiancé knew the truth, might he not use it to blackmail him?

The thought made her hot all over and she wished once again that she had not been so reckless that night.

Alone in her bedchamber that night, Charlotte found it difficult to sleep. She lay for hours, tossing and turning. When Jack knew that the scandal wasn't just going to go away, how would he feel about his promise to wed her? His was a proud family and Lord Harding might be vicious enough to blacken Charlotte's name just to get his revenge…

Charlotte was reluctant to keep their engagements the next day, but as they were mostly with close friends of her mother's she did not meet Lord Harding or his friend. Instead, she had a pleasant time being congratulated on her coming nuptials.

* * *

The day before Jack's return from the country, she spent the morning at the dressmakers being fitted for her new gowns. In the afternoon she took tea with Mama's best friend, Lady Rushmore, and did not return home until nearly six. Because they were going to the theatre with friends that evening, Charlotte went straight upstairs, and only after she had changed and was ready for the outing did her maid give her a letter that had been lying on the hall table.

She did not recognise the hand, but split the wax seal, a chill trickling down her spine as she realised it was from Lord Harding. He wrote plainly, demanding payment of four thousand pounds.

If I do not receive payment of your brother's debt by the end of the month, I shall inform the Marquis of Ellington that his grandson is to marry a thief and a girl of dubious morals.

Charlotte shuddered and thrust the letter into the back of a drawer where she hoped no one would find it. She would have liked to burn it, but the threat was worrying, for while Jack might have taken the news with a shrug, his grandfather would naturally demand to know the truth—and he might forbid the marriage.

Charlotte's throat stung with unshed tears and she was tormented by regret, but knew she must not let anyone see her distress. Matt had begged her not to expose herself to scandal and danger, but she had known better. She'd been so certain she could get away with it, because of Harding's habit of leaving his bedroom window open. Matt had told her that Harding had instructed his staff to let air blow through the rooms at all times, something to do with a chest complaint that was affected by a stuffy atmosphere. He'd mentioned it in company, asking the steward at the various clubs and gambling hells he frequented to open the windows if the rooms became a little stuffy.

Stealing back her necklace had seemed such a simple thing to do at the time and it would have been if two gentlemen had not just knocked at the door of Lord Harding's house, to be told he was not at home. Walking away, they had spotted Charlotte as she climbed down the overgrown wisteria at the side of the house, then ran into the park across the road. Perhaps the surprise had held them for a moment, giving her a head start, or perhaps they were a little too drunk to grab her as she darted past them, but they had recovered. For a moment in the park Patterson, as she now knew him, had grabbed her by the waist. Kicking his shin, she'd escaped, but had Jack not been there she would have been in trouble...but she'd been over this so many times in her mind and she could not change what she had done.

The shadow of disgrace and scandal loomed large in Charlotte's mind, but she did her best to forget it as she accompanied her mother and friends to the theatre. The play was a rendering of Shakespeare's *The Tempest* and one she had looked forward to seeing, but she could not follow it and was quiet as her mother enthused over the acting on the way home.

'Is something wrong, dearest? You have been quiet all evening.'

'I have a little headache,' Charlotte lied, 'but I shall be fine by morning.'

'I hope you are not sickening for anything. We have so many engagements in the next week or two—and I am sure Viscount Delsey will have more functions that he wishes us to attend.'

'It is nothing, Mama. I did not sleep well last night. I promise you I shall be fine tomorrow.'

But how could she make such a promise when things might be anything but fine in a few days' time?

Jack was relieved when he could at last set out for London. His maternal uncle had seemed disappointed that nothing would come of the suggestion he had made for the future of his daughter. Celia March was a pretty girl, but she could not hold a candle to Charlotte Stevens and Jack had no regrets when he left his uncle's estate.

Celia had certainly made no effort to attach him, but of course, her father had not told her of his hopes, which was as well in the circumstances. Even if there had been no Charlotte, Jack knew he could never have married the girl.

He joined Matt at his own estate for two days and then they set out for London together. The papers for Matt's commission were waiting at Jack's London house and he would stay only for Charlotte's dance before leaving to join his regiment.

'By the time you return to London after some years service abroad, Harding will have forgotten all about you,' he told Matt confidently. 'You've learned a valuable lesson and you will not make the same mistake again.'

'As long as it does not rebound on Charlotte.'

'Why should it? She has my protection now. I am more than a match for Harding and his like.'

'Yes, but she was chased. Supposing they recognised her?' Matt looked at him anxiously. 'I have been anxious about that—for I am to blame. I should have asked before I took her necklace and then I could have made some arrangement with Harding over the debt.'

'You would beggar yourself to pay a man who undoubtedly cheated you?'

'It was my own fault for allowing him to take me to places I knew I could not afford to play.'

'I've seen him cheat other young fools,' Jack said harshly. 'He tried it on at Watier's once and was blackballed. As yet no one has been able to prove that he cheats, but most of us suspect it. Very few of the top hostesses invite him to their homes these days. That is why he picks up younger men and introduces them to clubs where he isn't known for cheating and the play is not as strict.'

'Without proof I could not accuse him,' Matt

said. 'Had I been able I would have paid. I believed Charlie would not mind if I gave him her necklace and I intended to pay her back, but…'

'My advice is to forget it. Others have been as foolish, it is not the end of the world.' Jack smiled. 'Once she is my wife I can protect her from his kind.'

Jack was thoughtful as he reflected on the future he had chosen. His offer had been made on the spur of the moment, but he'd liked the girl from the first. She had courage and a brave spirit, and he believed they would deal well together. Of course he was not madly in love with her—he did not believe in what the poets called romantic love. Passion was real, and affection—surely a combination of the two was sufficient to make marriage worthwhile.

He'd seen passion in Charlotte on several occasions and he looked forward to initiating her into the delights of making love. There was pleasure to be had for both of them in marriage and he had forgotten that he'd once thought it a prison term for life. She would not expect him to dance after her every moment, but she would be warm and willing in his arms. She was also excellent company and he had missed her while he was away.

Indeed, he could hardly wait to see her again and intended to call as soon as they reached London. He hoped that she would be at home to receive him, for he had bought her a gift, which he believed she would like.

Chapter Eight

To his disappointment, Jack discovered that Charlotte had gone out with her mama for a dressmaker's appointment, but would return for luncheon. Smothering a slight sense of annoyance that she had not waited at home to see him, he took himself off to his club to see some friends and then called in at his London agent's office and signed some papers.

He was congratulated by a few friends on his forthcoming marriage, but noticed a few strange looks directed his way from gentlemen with whom he was acquainted, but not particularly close. It was Phipps who finally told him that a few unkind souls were whispering that Charlotte was not all she ought to be.

'I couldn't get to the bottom of it, Jack,' Phipps said. 'Indeed, no one seems to know what she is supposed to have done, but I believe George Patterson was heard sniggering about you getting the shock of your life one of these days. It was something to do with your marriage, but that is all I know.'

'Well, thank you for telling me. I sensed something, but I am glad to know who my enemies are. Please tell me if you hear anything more definite, Phipps.'

Damn Patterson for his impertinence! Had he dared to hint to Jack's face, he would have gladly given him a thrashing for it.

'Where are you going? You won't do anything foolish?' Phipps looked at him uncertainly. 'Patterson and Harding…they cannot really do much harm whispering in corners, but they are both nasty devils. I wouldn't trust either of them not to pay someone to stick a knife in your back.'

'Thank you for the warning,' Jack said. 'I know what they are, my friend, but I shall not allow either of them to besmirch the name of my future wife.'

'Certainly not. She is a dear sweet girl,' Phipps said stoutly. 'Call him out myself for you, if you wish.'

'Thank you, Phipps, but I think I know the root

of the trouble and I shall deal with it in my own way. However, if you have nothing better to do this evening, I should be grateful if you would bear me company. I intend to visit Lady Deakin's gaming house.'

'But you never play in houses like that… Ahh, I see.' Phipps nodded as the penny dropped. 'It is one of Harding's haunts.'

Jack smiled unpleasantly. 'Exactly. Lady Deakin and her cousin run a gambling club that is on the borderline of respectable. If one wished to make a scene, one would not choose one's club or the house of a friend.'

'I shall be delighted to join you and I'll ask Brock if he feels like accompanying us.'

'An excellent notion,' Jack said. 'I may well need a couple of witnesses.'

Phipps nodded, looked serious and then smiled. 'It sounds as if we have an interesting evening in prospect, my friend.'

'One would hope so,' Jack said and glanced at his watch. 'I must pay an afternoon call. I shall call for you this evening.'

Having parted from his friend, Jack summoned a cab and returned to the fashionable square. He was fortunate to discover that his fiancée was at home this time and was ushered into a charming sitting room, where Charlotte was sitting with an open book in her hand, though she did not appear to be reading it.

She looked up as he was announced, then got to her feet and offered him a shy smile, holding her hand out to him. Jack took and kissed it, then looked into her face, seeing the anxious expression and the shadows beneath her eyes.

'Did you have a good journey, sir?' she asked.

'Tolerable,' he murmured. 'Please do not retreat from me, Charlotte. I have a fair idea of what you are wondering whether or not you should tell me, but there's no need. I intend to silence Harding and his friend for good.'

'He—he has accused me of being a thief.' Charlotte hung her head. 'Unless I pay what he demands, he says he will tell your grandfather that you are marrying a girl of dubious character.'

Jack swore beneath his breath. 'He goes too far! Damn him for upsetting you this way.'

'Perhaps I deserve it.'

'Enough of this foolishness! The man is a cheat and a liar. Hardly anyone will receive him these days. He may be invited to some houses, but those who know of his reputation will not tolerate his company. When I have finished with him, he will wish he had—'

'Please be careful,' Charlotte begged. 'If any harm came to you, I could not forgive myself.'

'Do you think I would let a rogue like that besmirch the good name of the lady I intend to marry?' Jack looked down into her eyes and colour flooded her cheeks.

Of course he would not want the reputation of the woman he intended to marry besmirched!

'I—I would understand if you wished to withdraw.'

'Do you wish me to?'

'Of course not, but—' Jack took hold of her by the shoulders, drew her close and kissed her soundly. His object was to cut off the flow of foolish words, but once his lips touched hers, he found himself liking the warmth, softness and the sweet taste of her breath. His kiss deepened, flaring into passion, and he was not sure how it would have ended had the door not opened to admit her brother.

'Oh, sorry—' Matt said lamely. 'Didn't think to knock… Mama sent me to say that she has ordered tea in the large parlour and will you please both join her there.' He hesitated, then, 'Shall I tell her I couldn't find you?'

'No, of course not,' Jack said and sighed. 'I shall not stop for tea. I came only to speak to Charlotte and to make arrangements for the theatre tomorrow evening.'

'Mama thought you might dine with us this evening. We are entertaining a few close friends.'

'Give my regrets to your mama, but I have a prior engagement for this evening. I should like you to join our party for the theatre and supper tomorrow, Matt. I think you should avoid meeting certain people for a few days—and perhaps an evening in will not hurt you.'

'I was intending to visit some friends after dinner, but they are not given to gambling and it will be just a quiet evening at their home.'

'A perfect solution,' Jack agreed. 'After this evening things should be in a way to being settled.' As Matt went away, Jack looked down at his fiancée and smiled. 'We have some unfinished business, Charlotte, but for the moment I must leave you.'

'You will take care? Forgive me for bringing all this bother to you, Jack.'

'What bother?' he drawled, his mouth slightly

lifted at the corners. 'Civilian life can be tedious when one has been accustomed to the army and campaigning, but it certainly has not been dull since I bumped into a certain urchin.'

Charlotte dimpled up at him. 'I can only be glad that you did,' she murmured. 'I shall look forward to tomorrow evening, Jack.'

'As shall I,' Jack said and took her hand, but rather than the formal air kiss he normally bestowed on her, he turned it over and dropped a kiss in the palm. 'Hold that for now, Charlotte. I shall reclaim it one of these days.'

Leaving her standing there, Jack walked from the house and across the pretty greens that separated her house from his own. He was frowning as he thought of the trap that he intended to set for Harding that evening. What he'd intended at the start was to complete the rogue's ruin, but now he wondered if it might not be better to silence the man's vicious tongue for good.

Jack was an excellent shot and a skilled swordsman. Harding was said to be a decent shot and would no doubt choose pistols if given the choice. It was easier to severely wound a man with a sword while still not ending his life, but a ball through the head or the heart would finish him.

Duelling was frowned on, though seldom pun-ished—unless a death occurred. It would not suit Jack to be forced to flee the country, even for a few months, but if it was the only way to bring Harding down...

Yet perhaps he was letting his anger rule him. He must keep cool and see what chances the eve-ning brought.

'The man is a cheat and a liar,' Brock said when apprised of Jack's intentions. 'I know of at least one young man who took his own life after being ruined by Harding and his cronies. I should be delighted to call him out for you, old fellow.'

'I know of no braver soldier and your skill with the sword is unparalleled,' Jack murmured and grinned, 'but with pistols at fifteen paces I doubt you could hit him.'

Brock's eyebrows rose. 'Are you calling me a poor shot?'

'With a rifle you are excellent, but pistols? I think you should leave them to me, don't you?'

'Perhaps, but if I killed him and had to make a run for it, I should merely spend the next few months in France enjoying myself, whilst you would be frustrated and impatient to return.'

'I'm better than either of you with the pistols,' Phipps claimed extravagantly. 'I should be the one to call him a cheat.'

His friends laughed and mocked him, for they all knew that he could not shoot a pistol half as well as either of them, but he was a devil with the sword and had been a crack shot with a rifle. Phipps was also deadly with a knife, which he threw faster than most men could shoot and his skill had been useful at times against the enemy in Spain, when sometimes you could not be sure who was your friend and who your enemy.

'It is my problem and I'll do the accusing,' Jack said in a tone that allowed no argument. 'What I require of you is that you bear witness to what happens.'

'That is if Harding is obliging enough to visit Lady D.'s house,' Phipps said. 'One never knows where the fellow might be.'

'I was informed he would be there this evening,' Jack said. 'And if my information is correct, he needs to win rather urgently, because he is badly dipped.'

'Close to ruin,' Brock said. 'He has run through the fortune his cousin left him in a matter of years. The man has expensive tastes.'

'Yes, I know,' Jack agreed. 'We must hope that he is just desperate enough to risk cheating this evening.'

Jack saw his quarry the moment they entered the gambling club. Harding was sitting at a table with three hardened gamblers and drinking heavily. Glancing round the thronged rooms, Jack noted that most of the guests were the worst of the scum that hung around at the edge of society, preying on young men who had money to burn, men of little reputation and small fortune. It looked as if there was little prey for Harding and his friends that evening.

Perhaps that was the reason that when they sat down at a table near a window and called for wine and a new pack of cards, it took only a few minutes before Harding rose and came across to them, followed by Patterson.

'Good evening, gentlemen,' he said, glancing at Jack from beneath hooded lids. 'I do not think I've seen you here before.'

'We're out for a laugh,' Phipps said and slurred his words slightly, as if he'd had a little too much to drink. 'Where is that damned waiter? Can a man not get a drink in this place?'

'Allow me, I am known here,' Harding said pompously and signalled to the waiter who came at once. 'Wine for my friends—bring a bottle of the best claret and one of burgundy for starters. You will allow me to join you, gentlemen?'

'Why not?' Brock asked. 'I'm celebrating. Won a packet at Newmarket, fifty-to-one odds and I had a hundred on it.'

'You must have the luck of the devil,' Harding said and looked a bit sick, almost as if he was wondering whether he'd chosen the wrong pigeons to pluck.

'Only with the horses,' Brock said. 'I have the devil's own luck at the cards, but I'm determined to come about...'

'Well, I should be delighted to oblige you. What stakes will you play, gentlemen?'

'Oh, a hundred guineas a game and a side stake of another fifty for each trick,' Brock said. 'No good playing for peanuts.'

'I couldn't agree more,' Harding replied jovially. 'What about you others?'

Patterson and Phipps agreed to the terms, but Jack shook his head and stood up. 'I've seen someone I wish to speak to,' he claimed. 'I'll join you later.'

Harding frowned as he walked across the room and spoke to one of the waiters, but Brock was opening the new pack of cards and his attention was drawn from Jack, who had left the room. When he returned the game was already begun and Jack paused by the E.O. table to place a counter on the table. He stayed there for some time, losing most of the time, but betting constantly on red, while keeping an eye on the card table.

His friends seemed to be holding their own. Phipps had won three hands, Brock one, Patterson one and Harding was losing steadily. Jack moved about the crowded room, speaking briefly with men he knew slightly, and hazarding a few bets at Faro, then, as he saw that Brock had lost again, while Phipps and Patterson had gone out, he wandered back towards them. Standing behind Brock and watching the play with narrowed eyes, he noted each card that his friend discarded, also those that the other two players had thrown in, memorising each one.

Gradually, Harding was accumulating a large amount of gold on the table before him and Jack began to see the pattern of his play. If Patterson stayed in, Harding folded early, but now Patterson was going out early every time, as was Phipps, and Harding was winning every hand. Brock was going down to the tune of two thousand or more.

He threw down his hand at the end of the fourth consecutive winning hand and reached towards the pot, the shock on his face complete as Jack's hand snaked out and caught his arm.

'What are you doing?' he demanded, his colour rising.

'Just this…' Jack said and removed the ace of spades from the cuff of his coat sleeve. 'I saw you tuck this away when you took your last card and then discarded. You knew that with the ace removed from the game no one else could beat your hand.'

'Liar!' Harding blustered. 'How could I have hidden it? I'm sure Patterson discarded that card earlier, didn't you?' He looked demandingly at his crony, but Patterson had gone white and did not answer him. 'You planted this on me, Delsey. It was all a plot to trap me!'

'You are a cheat and a liar,' Jack said calmly. 'You were blackballed at the Nonesuch. White's will not admit you and I shall make it my business to see that no decent house will accept you.'

'Jack couldn't have planted that card,' Phipps said, 'I discarded it earlier and Patterson picked it up and then discarded it himself. I noticed the corner was nicked—you can see it...' He leaned forward and flicked through the discarded cards, revealing that there was no other ace of spades. However, the one that Jack had pulled from Harding's cuff was indeed spoiled. 'I had folded, but I intended to call for a fresh pack before we continued...'

'Damn you!' Harding was on his feet, his neck red with rage. 'I am not a cheat—and I demand satisfaction. Patterson, tell them that card did not come from me!'

'I saw Delsey take it from your sleeve,' Patterson said and swallowed hard. 'You took two thousand off me last week. I wondered why your luck had suddenly changed.'

'You rotten swine,' Brock said. 'You've cheated me all evening!' He rose to his full six-foot-two height and glowered down at the man, whose neck resembled the shade of a boiled beetroot.

'Damn you—and you, Delsey. You will meet me for this!'

'Delighted,' Jack murmured smoothly. 'Name your seconds.'

Harding stared at him furiously, a dark red tide sweeping up his neck and into his cheeks. His eyes goggled, he gave a queer strangled sound and his mouth worked, but no sound came out. His face seemed to fall on one side and then he seemed to buckle at the knees before falling back and crashing into his chair, which went flying. He lay on the floor jerking for a while and one of the waiters came rushing over to see what was happening. He knelt beside the fallen man, loosening his neckcloth.

'Is he dead?' Brock asked conversationally.

'No, sir. He's had some sort of a fit,' the waiter said. 'I'll have him taken upstairs and send for a doctor. The gentleman is still breathing and with good fortune we may save him.'

'Pity,' Brock murmured. 'He is a cheat and a liar—and we don't need his sort.' He picked up the money from the pot, leaving what Harding had won earlier on the table. 'You should take what is necessary to pay for the doctor.'

'I wasn't a part of this,' Patterson said suddenly, looking sick as he gazed at Jack. 'He's cheated me, too.'

'I suggest you take what he owes you now,' Jack said, and as Patterson reached for the pot, he gripped his wrist. 'Let this be a warning, Patterson. Don't talk about what you don't know.'

The other man swallowed hard, then, 'I have no idea what you mean. It was all Harding's idea.'

'Just remember I'm the wrong man to cross and if I have a score to settle I can be ruthless,' Jack said and watched as four burly waiters carried Harding from the room. He looked at his friends and grimaced as they walked away together. 'We can do no more here. I'm sorry it had to end like this, Brock. Allow me to reimburse your for your losses.'

'Keep your money,' Brock said and grinned. 'It was worth it to bring that rogue to justice. If there *is* such a thing as true justice, he won't be troubling you again, Jack.'

'It would seem not,' Jack agreed, but he did not smile. He would have preferred a different outcome, for it felt as if he had unfinished business with Lord Harding.

The friends departed, walking back through quiet streets to Jack's home, where they shared a decanter of brandy and talked over the events of the evening.

'It was fortunate that you managed to nick the corner of that card,' Jack said. 'Without it, the proof would not have been so complete.'

'I'd spotted what he was doing a couple of hands earlier, but it was truly an accident. I intended to have the pack changed the next hand. It was fortunate you struck when you did.'

'Yes, well, he responded as we hoped, but I'm sorry for the rest of it—I would have preferred to meet him as we discussed.'

'It may be better this way,' Brock said. 'At least you won't have to flee the country for six months.'

'If only I could be certain it was the finish of him,' Jack mused.

'He looked pretty queer to me,' Phipps said. 'I've seen the results of a seizure like that—even if he should recover he may have some paralysis or a speech impediment.'

'Harding will be no more trouble to you,' Brock said confidently. 'The man is finished in society and when this gets out nobody will believe anything he says—and Patterson is terrified of being tarred with the same brush.'

'Yes, I think you're right. It was all Harding's

idea. I believe we can forget about this unpleasant incident and I can look forward to my wedding with an easy heart.'

Chapter Nine

Charlotte twirled before her mirror, admiring the gown of pale rose-pink silk that Mama had had made for her dance that evening. She was looking her best and the smile on her face was free of shadows, because the news of Lord Harding's sudden collapse after being accused of cheating at cards had swept through London society. He had been taken out of London by his servants and was still unwell, though he had not died and no one was quite certain what harm the seizure had done him. Indeed, after the first buzz of gossip few people were interested. He had never been a popular man and now he was seen as being beyond the pale.

Mr Patterson had also left London for his own estates, which meant that Charlotte was no longer frightened of being imminently ruined by scandal. Whatever gossip there had been had effectively been quashed, because no one wished to be associated with a man who had been caught cheating. Now that his perfidy had been revealed there were many ready to come forward and accuse him of having cheated them; they had always suspected him, it seemed, and the general opinion was that Jack had done society a good turn by unmasking the rogue.

Some ladies spoke sympathetically of his having suffered a seizure, but most were inclined to think it was his own fault for having behaved so badly. Charlotte could only be glad that the threat of scandal had been lifted, though she was not so hard hearted as to wish the man dead or indeed permanently disabled. She was merely thankful that he was no longer in town.

Since that night, Jack had spent most of his time escorting her and her mama to balls, soirées, drives and picnics while the weather kept fine, also visits to Vauxhall Gardens and the theatre. The day of their wedding had been announced as the first Thursday of September, and once Charlotte's dance was over, Jack had promised to take her down to his grandfather's estate for a few weeks.

'Grandfather is looking forward to meeting you, as is Mama, of course,' Jack told her. 'We shall hold a ball at Ellingham for all our neighbours and friends, but where would you prefer the wedding to be—at your home or at Grandfather's estate?'

'I think Papa would like to hold the wedding at home,' Charlotte said. 'But it will be smaller than a wedding your family might host. I do not mind, for I have only a few friends and relatives to ask.'

'And I have too many.' Jack smiled ruefully. 'However, if we invite them to the ball and entertain them for a few weeks, we may be forgiven for having a smaller affair at your home, my love.'

Papa was consulted, but thought it might be better if the wedding was held at Ellingham after all and so it was agreed. Charlotte would stay at the estate for a month to meet Jack's family, but after the ball she would go home and they would entertain her family's friends, before returning a few days prior to the wedding.

On the evening of her dance, Jack presented Charlotte with a parure of diamonds consisting of a necklace with a magnificent drop pendant, earrings, bracelet, tiara and brooch. He had also given her another beautiful ring for her own and she wore the ruby-and-diamond ring on her right hand.

'You will spoil me,' she said when dazzled by the wonderful engagement gift. 'I feel like a princess.'

'I want you to have all the beautiful things you desire,' he told her and kissed her lightly on the mouth.

Charlotte had blushed and smiled, wondering if he might take her in his arms and kiss her with passion, as he had that day in the parlour, but since then his kisses had been chaste. She regretted that her brother had interrupted them that afternoon, for Jack did not seem minded to repeat his passionate embrace. She could not deceive herself that he was in love with her, for had it been the case he would surely have taken every opportunity to make love to her. Yet his behaviour was everything that a lady could expect of a gentleman with standards of honour.

'We shall not anticipate our vows,' he said once when they were briefly alone and he had taken her into his arms to kiss her softly on the mouth. 'Impatient as I am, the world is too uncertain and

I would not do anything that might harm you, Charlotte.'

'Why should anything you do harm me?' She'd looked at him, feeling puzzled.

'If anything were to happen to prevent the marriage,' he said and frowned. 'I am foolish, I know, for it is not like, but—' He'd shaken his head as she looked at him questioningly. 'No, there is nothing to fear, dearest Charlotte.'

Yet despite all the parties, the drives and the shopping trips, despite the congratulations of friends, the wonderful presents of silver, jewels and china, and the whirl of pleasure, Charlotte detected a shadow hanging over them. Jack was concerned about something. She could not guess what and he would not tell her, but she sensed something…a guardedness in his manner, as if he were waiting for something to happen. It made her a little afraid, though she did not know why.

She did not think his anxiety concerned her for she had heard nothing more from either Lord Harding or Mr Patterson. Indeed, neither had returned to town, though Julia had heard that Lord Harding was recovering rather more easily than had been expected. Yet surely he could no longer be a threat to her; he had been discredited and Mr Patterson was staying clear of London for the moment.

No, she did not think a scandal was imminent, for no one would believe anything Lord Harding said now that Jack had unmasked him as a cheat. Yet there was something troubling her fiancé— though he had not mentioned anything of consequence to her. Indeed, his mind seemed bent only on making her happy.

Her dance was a great success. Charlotte stood with Jack to receive their guests, wearing her diamonds and a beautiful green-silk gown and smiling until her face ached. By her side Jack looked elegant in a blue coat and pale-buff pantaloons that clung to his strong muscles like a second skin. Later, they danced together, and then with others, the evening a pleasant occasion and declared a success by everyone who attended.

'We shall leave town together in four days' time,' Jack told her when he took his leave in the early hours of the morning. 'I have one or two things to do before then, so if I do not call you will forgive me. It is merely business, you understand, but it may take me out of town.'

'Yes, of course,' Charlotte said and reached up

to kiss his cheek. 'You must do exactly as you wish, Jack. I am perfectly content to visit friends with Mama and take my books back to the library, for we shall not return to town this Season.'

'No.' Jack smiled at her. 'I believe you capable of amusing yourself, Charlotte. I would prefer not to leave you, but I…well, it is nothing for you to be concerned over.'

'Are you sure?' she asked. 'I've noticed that you are concerned about something. Is it about me…about what happened?'

'Not directly,' Jack said. 'I received a letter, Charlotte. It was delivered after that incident at the club and it concerns something that happened some years ago. Someone thought I ought to know…' He shook his head. 'As yet I have no proof, but I intend to discover what I can and that may mean a short trip north.'

Charlotte felt coldness at the nape of her spine and her sense of imminent danger increased, but her fears were for him rather than herself. 'Be careful, Jack. If it concerns Lord Harding…he is a vengeful man. He will not lightly forgive what you did.'

'He is confined to his bed for the moment. Besides, I do not fear him, Charlotte—if what I discover is true, it is he who should fear me.'

His tone was such that she looked at him intently, searching his face for a clue, but he merely smiled and touched her cheek with one finger. Even his lightest touch had Charlotte longing for more, but she knew she must not show how very much she was affected. Charlotte's feelings for him ran deeper than she dared show, for she was not foolish enough to imagine that his for her were more than liking or affection. His kiss had been passionate, but he was a young and healthy man and that should not mislead her into thinking passion was love.

'I want this finished and done before the wedding,' he said and frowned. 'I have suspected that something was being hidden from me for a long time, but I never had proof. That night there was someone at the club when Harding was accused of cheating. He witnessed what happened and he wrote to me afterwards, but I am not sure I can trust his word and so I must discover the truth for myself.'

Jack took his leave of her, and Charlotte resigned herself to the idea that she would see little of him until they left for the country. She was uneasy and wished that he had told her more, but clearly he did not wish to confide in her. Perhaps he had not wanted to make her anxious, but her unease would not be banished and she could only pray that she was being foolish to think he might be in some danger.

'We are due to leave in the morning,' Lady Stevens said to Charlotte some days later. 'It is very odd that we have heard nothing from Viscount Delsey, is it not?'

'Jack told me that he might have to leave town,' Charlotte said. 'Perhaps his business has taken him longer than he expected.'

'It is most inconsiderate,' her mama said, looking annoyed. 'Everyone expects us to leave town for the marquis's estate, but how can we go down alone? He should be here, Charlotte. Everyone is expecting an invitation to the ball and we know nothing of it.'

'Perhaps he will be here by this evening,' Charlotte said. 'I wish Matt were here. I do not know how to contact Jack, or where he went.'

'Do you think his particular friends would know?' Lady Stevens was on edge. 'It seems so odd. Almost as if he had changed his mind and gone off leaving you in the lurch.'

'Mama!' Charlotte cried, shocked. 'Jack would never do such a thing.'

'Then where is he?' Mama asked and looked cross. 'If he should call it off now, we shall look such fools and Papa will insist on returning the money. And then I do not know what we shall do. I cannot afford to give you another chance, Charlotte.'

'Jack would never break his promise to me,' Charlotte said, but her throat felt tight and she was close to tears. Jack would not let her down— but Mama was right, it did seem very odd that he'd gone away hours after their dance.

The letter arrived that evening, delivered by one of Jack's grooms. It was addressed to Charlotte, but written in a formal manner designed so that her parents could read it. Jack apologised for the delay, saying that it was unavoidable, and asking them to proceed without him.

Grandfather and Mama are expecting you at Ellingham. Please go on ahead and I shall join you as soon as I am able. I regret this unfortunate delay to our plans, but I have discovered something important that I must investigate.

I am sure Grandfather will be pleased to have you all at Ellingham and I shall be no longer than necessary. I have written to let them know you are coming. Once again, my apologies.
Yours devotedly, Delsey

Mama had been inclined to be doubtful, but Papa had said they would take Jack at his word and leave for the country in the morning. The London house had been given up and their only alternative was to return home. He was travelling with them so there was no need for any other escort, other than the various grooms and servants, most of whom followed in the lumbering baggage coach. Mama had not liked it, but she did not know what else to do and so they left at the appointed time.

Mama complained to Charlotte most of the time for the whole journey, leaving her in no doubt that she had never wanted her daughter to marry a rake and regretted that Papa had allowed it.

'Had you encouraged Sir Percival I am certain he would have made you an offer—and this would never have happened. It was really so unobliging of you, Charlotte.'

'Sir Percival is very kind, but I prefer Jack, Mama.'

'Your father should have asked him to wait for a while so that you could be certain of him.'

'Mama, my father had little choice,' Charlotte reminded her. 'Had Jack not paid the outstanding debt to the bank, Papa must have sold the estate and we should have had only the estate manager's cottage in the village left to us.'

'And might still if Delsey lets you down.'

'He will not,' Charlotte said, but her chest felt as if it had a stone in it rather than a living beating heart. She did not know the viscount very well and could not be sure that he was not regretting his impulsive proposal. Where was Jack and why had he needed to go away now, when all the plans for their wedding were in train? 'Jack would not hurt me like that, Mama.'

'Gentlemen are not always to be trusted, especially men of Viscount Delsey's cut.'

'You must not doubt him, Mama. I am sure he is merely detained on business.'

Charlotte could not help a niggling doubt in her mind that Jack had regretted asking her to be his wife, but she resolutely defended him to her mama. Whatever had taken Jack away from her must be important. She wished she knew just what was going on, and whether he was in danger, but he had not fully confided in her and she worried that something might have happened to him.

She could not bear to lose him now!

Charlotte suspected that Lord Harding had something to do with Jack's sudden need to go off on business, but surely the man was still too ill to be a danger?

Common sense told her that Jack would come to no harm, and yet she was anxious. What was it that had made him seem so strange, almost haunted, as if something played on his mind? Yet no matter how often she tried to solve the puzzle, she came up with a blank. Clearly there was something in the past, something Jack had to sort out—but why now? Why could he not have put it off until after the wedding?

Jack looked about him as he reined in and looked down at the isolated inn. He had been told that he could learn something to his advantage concerning his father's death if he came here alone to meet a man named Jeb Scott. The name meant nothing to him; he was certain he'd never heard it before, but the writer had hinted that his father's death was not an accident due to an obstruction in the road.

Jack had always suspected it. The nagging doubt had been there at the back of his mind for years, festering like a thorn in his flesh, lying like a shadow over his life. He'd almost succeeded in persuading himself that it was nonsense until the letter came after the showdown with Harding. Someone had been a witness of the incident—a witness who claimed to have evidence that would prove Harding was a murderer…as well as all the other things.

Jack realised then that he'd always suspected it. Over the years Harding had made remarks that he could take two ways, but when he'd challenged him, he'd always backed off and claimed that Jack had misheard him. Yet it made sense. Harding's cousin had left him a fortune, which he had wasted at the tables and races—but the man had closer relatives who had inherited the estate and title. Why had Harding been left the private fortune—unless he'd done the man a favour? The Marquis of Rockingham had a young wife he'd suspected of taking a lover—Jack's father. Too old and sick to do anything about it himself, had he pledged most of his fortune to a man who would be capable of any action to gain that fortune?

Harding had always been a harsh, brutal man and he'd shown his dislike of Jack many times in the past—even going so far as to bribe Jack's mistress to tell him about their relationship. Lucy had admitted it to him when he'd finished their affair.

'He didn't want me,' she'd protested. 'All he cared about was hearing me talk of you. He hates you, Jack. I do not know why—but I believe he wants to destroy you and he would use any means to do so.'

'You told him intimate details of our relationship?'

'No,' she vowed, but he saw that she lied. 'I wish I'd never met him, never allowed him to visit me. Jack, please do not leave me. I still care for you.'

'If that is true, then I am sorry, but our affair is over. I intend to marry and I will not deceive my wife.'

'Surely you will need somewhere to come when she begins to bore you?'

'I do not think that will ever happen,' Jack murmured silkily. 'Whereas you bore me, Lucy. I find cheats and liars wearisome and even had I still cared for you I would have finished the affair once you took up with Harding. Of all the men you could have chosen, he was the one I would never tolerate.'

'Why do you hate him so much?'

Because I believe he had a part in killing my father.

The words were only in Jack's mind, but they had been there for a long time, unspoken, unrecognised, but lurking in the recesses of his subconscious. Now he was certain of it.

He rode down to the inn, dismounted and tied the reins of his horse to a post, then went into the inn. It was dark inside and smelled of stale beer and other less pleasant odours. A man with a white apron that was stained with splashes of brown and red wine tied about his waist looked at him through narrowed eyes.

'You be a stranger to these parts, sir?'

'Yes, I am travelling north,' Jack replied, glancing about him. The room was almost empty. In one corner a man sat alone, slouched in his seat, a soft shapeless hat pulled over his eyes. At another table sat two farm workers dressed in smocks and loose breeches, their unkempt hair sticking out from beneath hats that had seen too many summers and winters. 'I was hoping to meet someone here—a Mr Scott.'

'Aye, that be him in the corner,' the innkeeper said with a nod of his head. 'Will I bring you a tankard of beer, sir?'

'Yes, and another for Mr Scott,' Jack agreed.

He walked across to the man, who appeared to be sleeping, but looked up as Jack approached. The farm workers stared to see a London gentleman, but then finished their drinks and got up to leave.

'Mr Jeb Scott?' Jack asked and sat down as he nodded. 'I believe you wrote to me?'

'Aye…' The man was looking at him now, his eyes a startling blue and more intelligent than Jack had expected from his appearance. 'I thought there was something you might wish to know…something concerning your late father.'

Jack's eyes went over his face. 'Have we met, sir?'

'No, for you would not have noticed me the

night you challenged Lord Harding to a duel. I was there with some friends for a certain purpose, but we need not go into that.'

'Are you a military man?' Jack asked, his curiosity aroused, for there was something in him that suggested Jeb Scott had once been a man used to commanding others.

'I was once, but I was involved in some shady business that I afterwards regretted, and I was dishonourably discharged.'

'You are very frank, sir.'

'If you are to trust my word, you must know the worst of me.'

'I judge a man by what I see in him, not by what society may know of him.'

'And do you think me a man to trust?'

'Perhaps—' Jack was interrupted by the arrival of the tankards of beer, which he paid for with a half-sovereign, telling the landlord to keep the change. 'Please see we are not disturbed for a while, sir.'

'Right you are, milord,' the man said and went off.

'What news do you have for me?' Jack asked. 'It concerns Lord Harding—some information, you said.'

'I find it difficult to gain decent employment these days. What I have is worth money.'

'And you shall have it when we're done.'

Jeb Scott leaned forward. 'Just under six years ago, after I was cashiered from the army, I was in a desperate state. I had nothing—money, home or name. My father was ashamed of me—and I was reduced to begging for work...'

'Until someone offered you work?'

'Yes.' Scott inclined his head. 'I was set to follow a gentleman, discover whom he met and report where they met and what they did. That gentleman was your own father, sir. He had formed a...liaison with a woman. I believe they were fond of one another...'

'Yes, I know about her. My father loved her and they should have married, but she had a temper and they quarrelled, but then they met again. Who employed you, the marquis?'

'No, it was his cousin. Lord Harding. He was working for the marquis, but I never met that gentleman. I was employed to discover where they met and that was all. But then my orders changed. I was told that your father had to die. No, it wasn't I,' Scott said as Jack's jaw hardened. 'I refused and was thrown out of Harding's employ. I'm not a murderer, sir—but there are plenty out there who are not so nice. Harding soon found others to do his bidding.'

'You saw what happened that night?'

'Yes. I decided that I would keep an eye on your father, Captain Delsey. I did try to warn him that he might be in danger, but it was my word against Harding's. Your father wouldn't listen to me—or perhaps he thought he could take care of himself. He was determined to discover what had happened to the lady. She died in a riding accident, but he was not convinced it was truly an accident.'

'His coach was held up, was it not?'

'Aye, sir, it was. There were six of them, all with masks and pistols, and they jumped out into the road, firing shots into the air. I'm not sure what they intended to do, but one of them injured a horse and the poor beast reared up in fright. It seems one of the coach wheels was loose and it gave way, then the whole thing lurched over the side of the ravine: coach, horses, passenger and grooms.

'Harding raved at them and they dragged a boulder from the side of the road and rolled it across to where the coach had been, to make it look like an accident. It was so swift that I could have done nothing to prevent it.

'After they had gone, I climbed down to look, but they were all dead. I shot one of the horses that was still alive and in agony. There was nothing I could do for your father and so I rode off.'

'And kept quiet about what you'd seen.' Jack glared at him. 'Why did you not come forward when I sent investigators to make enquiries?'

'Because I went abroad and took work as a mercenary. I returned to England only a few months ago and found work as a keeper on an estate in the north. By chance I visited London on business. My father died and left me his estate, and the lawyer's clerk insisted on taking me out that evening to show me something of life in town. It appears my father relented at the last, though he never asked for me…or perhaps he could not find me.'

'Is your estate in the north?'

'No, in East Anglia. I am here because I have work and my sister and her husband are living at the estate. I visited the lawyers in London to sign to allow them to continue as tenants of the farm. I have friends here in Yorkshire and I intend to buy land myself, but I need five hundred guineas more than I can raise.'

'You expect me to pay you five hundred guineas for this information?'

'No, my lord—for my testimony. I was a witness to your father's murder and that of his servants. If you wish to bring him to justice, I am willing to testify to his guilt.'

Jack stared at him in silence. 'You realise that you might be charged with perverting the due process of the law by keeping silent all these years—and if you were not believed, you would make Harding your enemy?'

'Aye, I'm prepared to take the chance…for my wife and son's future.' Scott looked him in the eyes. 'I've known what it's like to starve, to beg on the streets and to sleep rough. I want security for my family, my lord. If you agreed to pay me, you would see them right whatever happens to me.'

'You would trust me—why?'

'Because I heard what was said that night at that gambling hell. Not one man in that place doubted you, sir. They all spoke of you as being honest and just, and that's why I wrote to you.'

Jack nodded, a glimmer of appreciation in his

eyes. 'Then we have a bargain. I have always suspected that my father's death was not an accident and I believed Harding had a hand in it. Knowing it is so is a relief in itself, but, if he lives and is fit enough to stand trial, I shall expect you to testify. In the meantime, accept this with my thanks.' He took a bag of gold from his coat pocket. 'You'll find three hundred guineas in here. It is all I have with me, apart from travelling money. Put it somewhere safe and then come to me for the rest at Ellingham. I shall be there for a few weeks.'

'But I have not yet kept my part of the bargain.'

'I believe I may trust you, Mr Scott,' Jack said. 'You've given me what I wanted, which is proof that my suspicions were well founded. I'm not sure yet how best to use this knowledge. If I decide to go to court I shall call on you—but there are other ways of dealing with scum.'

A slow smile dawned in the other man's eyes. 'Aye, well, I'll wish you good luck, sir. This will buy me a nice farm I've my eye on and the rest of the money I shall invest for the future. Thank you for believing me. Not everyone would.'

'I'm a decent judge of a man's character,' Jack said. 'I think you would have made a good officer—it's a pity you got mixed up in whatever it was that brought you down.'

'I was a young fool and I trusted an officer I should not,' Scott replied with a smile. 'I regretted it and I've learned to know better.'

Jack nodded, stood up and left. He was conscious of the piercing blue eyes following him as he went out of the inn.

He mounted his horse and rode away from the inn. Jack's thoughts were far away and he was completely unaware that he was being followed. The shot that sent him tumbling to the ground came from nowhere and he yelled in surprise and pain as the ball buried itself in his shoulder. Lying on the ground, blood trickling from his wound, he closed his eyes as the blackness took his mind.

Charlotte, I'm sorry...

It was the last thought he was conscious of before he lost the ability to think and began to slip into the abyss that beckoned.

Chapter Ten

Charlotte gazed out of the carriage window as the long drive unfolded and she saw the imposing edifice that awaited them. The marquis's home was truly magnificent, a long main structure with a facade of gleaming white marble with pillars and a large front door under an arch. The windows were long and criss-crossed with lead so that the diamond-shaped panes gleamed in the sunlight like jewels. There were two wings, one at either end, both of which looked to have been added at different times. Also, a sweep of magnificent lawn with formal beds of roses and shrubs, pathways leading through them to a park, beyond which Charlotte knew was a lake, having glimpsed it through the trees as they drove past.

'Are we here at last?' Mama asked in a plaintive

voice that spoke volumes. 'I thought we should never arrive.'

'Yes, we are here,' Charlotte said. 'It seems ages since we drove through the gates, does it not? The estate is very large, Mama.'

'Yes, well, we knew that,' her mother said, looking determined not to be impressed. 'Where is your papa? He was fortunate that he rode here. So much more comfortable than a closed carriage.'

Charlotte forbore to reply, for a footman resplendent in a scarlet-and-silver uniform had come out and was about to open the door for them. She smiled and gave him her hand, and saw the flicker of a smile in his eyes, though he managed to keep his face suitably grave.

'Miss Stevens,' he said. 'Welcome to Ellingham. His lordship and Lady Delsey are in the morning parlour, miss, and Sir Mordred is with them. Everyone is anxious to meet you—'

'Johnson!' a harsh voice interrupted the friendly footman, and Charlotte saw the black-coated butler waiting to greet them at the head of a veritable army of servants, dressed in either black or grey.

Mama was being helped from the carriage in silence, the footman having been silenced. Charlotte proceeded to the butler, who bowed in a stately fashion.

'Miss Stevens, we are delighted to welcome you to Ellingham,' he said in a formal tone with none of the footman's warmth. 'It is my privilege to introduce you to the staff here. I am Evans, the marquis's butler at Ellingham, and this is the housekeeper, Mrs Moore, Mrs Harlow, her ladyship's dresser, Miss Robinson, better known as Nurse, his lordship's valet, Beedle, the upper parlour maid...'

Charlotte was led down a long line of servants, including the cook, a plump smiling lady in her middle years, various maids, footmen and the marquis's secretary, besides numerous underlings who were not named. She knew it was impossible to remember all their names and faces, but her own maid, Betty, would get to know the others and remind her when she needed to know. It was the first time Charlotte had had her own maid, having shared Mama's, but Papa had insisted she have one now that she was to marry and the girl had been hired three days before they left town.

'If you will come this way, Miss Stevens, ma'am.'

Charlotte followed the imposing butler through

the house to what was obviously the morning parlour at the back. Immediately, she was aware of sunshine flooding into a pretty room, which was furnished in shades of green and cream. The furniture was dainty; she thought it might have come from the master craftsman Sheraton, the satinwood inlaid with dark stringing; cabinets, half-moon tables set against the walls, delicate chairs, a small sofa, and an elegant desk standing near the window gave the room an air of elegance and comfort.

Charlotte's father was standing by the fireplace, at his left hand an elderly gentleman with white hair, fierce grey eyes and a determined chin sat in a wing chair. A little way off on a small sofa perched a lady, who when she stood up was taller than Charlotte, but looked delicate and fine-boned.

The marquis had risen to his feet and now her father was introducing his wife and then Charlotte. As the piercing gaze came to rest on Charlotte, she made a deep curtsy, her manner demure as she lowered her eyes.

'Well, then, young lady, let me look at you,' the marquis said as she straightened up and met his gaze, which had softened. 'So you are the clever miss who has at last made my grandson see the wisdom of marriage. Hmm. I believe I can see why. You are very welcome, m'dear. Daisy, come here and meet your future daughter-in-law. Lady Daisy, Miss Charlotte Stevens.'

'Sir,' Charlotte murmured, a dimple in her cheek as she sensed that behind the gruff manner was a kind-hearted man. 'I am delighted to meet you—and only sorry Viscount Delsey was unable to come with us.'

'Yes, that is a mystery. What do you suppose the young scamp is up to now?' He glanced at Lady Daisy, who had now come forward. 'What have you to say to our young lady?'

'You are very welcome, as Papa says.' Jack's mother spoke in a die-away air, her voice so faint it was hard to hear what she said. 'I dare say you are exhausted. The roads are so terrible and it always gives me a headache to travel far.'

'I am quite well, ma'am,' Charlotte said, 'though a little tired. I believe the journey was harder for Mama than for me.'

'Yes, I am sure. You must be wanting to rest, Lady Stevens,' Jack's mother said with a look of sympathy. 'Do you have your vinaigrette with you? I always carry mine for if I do not I shall be prostrate for hours on arrival.'

'I have had the headache this past age,' Mama replied. 'I shall indeed be glad to lie down on my bed for an hour or so.'

'You will take some refreshment first?' the marquis asked with a slight frown.

'Really, you must excuse me,' Mama said. 'If your housekeeper could show me the way?'

'I shall do that myself,' Lady Daisy affirmed. 'Miss Stevens, will you come?'

'If I may, I should like to take some tea with Lord Ellington,' Charlotte replied. 'Unless you need me, Mama?'

'No, no, my maid will attend me,' her mother replied, waving a lavender-scented handkerchief at her.

She went out with Lady Daisy, talking of the rigours of travel to someone who was able and willing to share every bump in the road and every hurt suffered.

The marquis looked at Charlotte with approval and motioned to her to sit down, then rang the bell for refreshments. He gave Charlotte a moment to settle herself, then fixed her with his disconcerting stare.

'So how long have you known my grandson, Miss Stevens?'

'A few weeks, sir. Papa took a house for the Season across the square to Jack's town house and he came to call on us.'

'Love at first sight, then.' The Marquis made a sound of satisfaction deep in his throat. 'I have been waiting for this day for a long time, girl. I must say it is shabby of Jack to let you come down alone, but I dare say he has his reasons?'

'I cannot help you, sir. He told me it was important, but I know he had intended to escort us here— perhaps his business took longer than he expected.'

'No doubt, no doubt.' The marquis nodded. 'Tell me, Charlotte—you will allow me to call you that, I hope? Tell me, do you ride? Is your first love the country or are you a society miss and will you pine for town within a fortnight?'

'I do not think I shall pine for London,' Charlotte answered honestly. 'I have very much enjoyed my first Season, sir—but until then I had been only as far as Bath and that not often. I enjoy riding and walking, especially with dogs. I have a spaniel called Mister Chops that I would like to bring here, if that will be convenient to you?'

'Naturally, you must bring your dogs and your horses—but I'm sure we can mount you while you are here, my dear. Have you sisters or brothers?'

'I have one brother. Matt has recently joined a cavalry regiment.'

'Good, good, nothing like a spell in the army to help a man know what he wants of life. Jack was never happier, but I had to ask him to come back last year, you know. Had a nasty attack. That damned fool of a doctor of mine sent for him, they all thought I was going to die. I dare say I shan't for a while—but I'd like to see my first great-grandson before I do.' He chuckled as Charlotte's cheeks flushed pink. 'I've always spoken my mind. You mustn't let me embarrass you, girl.'

'No, sir, of course not. Jack… We have spoken of your need and I hope to give you what you wish for if I can.'

'There's a good sensible girl. None of this nonsense about waiting. Jack has chosen well. I'm pleased, Charlotte. His mother is a good sort of woman, but sometimes foolish. I can see you've got a head on your shoulders. I might have known you were exceptional or Jack wouldn't have asked for you.'

'Charlotte has always been a credit to us,' her father said, beaming at the marquis's praise. 'I do not think you will have anything to regret in this marriage, my lord.'

Charlotte felt herself squirming, for she felt she was being held up for scrutiny almost as if she were a brood mare. She wished that Jack had been with her, for she was certain he would have protested to save her blushes. He had shown no sign of being violently in love with her, but he was always a gentleman and gallant to a fault.

At that moment the servants brought in trays of tea, wine for the gentlemen and some almond comfits for Charlotte to nibble.

After they had been served and were once more alone, the marquis looked at her over his glass of Madeira. 'I will ask Mrs Moore to show you over the house tomorrow. You'll need to know your way to the dining room before that, of course, but I imagine you will want to rest this afternoon.'

'I should like to take a walk about the gardens and park,' Charlotte said. 'I shall, of course, change first, but before tea—a walk in the fresh air is so refreshing.'

'And gives one an appetite. I enjoy a walk in the mornings myself. Perhaps you will allow me to accompany you sometimes?'

'I should be honoured, sir. I should enjoy becoming acquainted with you.'

'As I shall with you,' the marquis said and nodded. 'Well. I suppose I must let you go up and change—and see if your mama needs anything. I shall spend an hour or two in my room before dinner. The needs of age, Charlotte. I resent it, especially as I feel it a waste of time when such a lively girl is my guest—but if I am to dine with you, I have no choice.'

'I shall look forward to this evening.'

He rang the bell; the housekeeper appeared and Charlotte followed her from the parlour. The stairs were wide, bordered by magnificent mahogany banisters and the hall ceiling was very high with a glass dome that let the light flood in. The landing above was carpeted in a rich red-and-blue Persian design, small tables ranged against the walls at intervals. Several doors led off from the hall, but they ascended another small flight of stairs at the end of the landing to the floor above, and it was there that the housekeeper opened a door for her.

'This is the guestroom I was asked to prepare for you, Miss Stevens. Your mama has the room two doors down. You have a sitting room, dressing room and bedchamber. I hope you will find everything to your taste, miss.'

'I'm sure I shall, thank you.'

Charlotte went inside and exclaimed over the tasteful decor of various shades of blue, with a thread of cream and silver running through the fabrics at the windows and the covers on the four-poster bed.

'This is charming,' she said as she stood in the doorway of her bedchamber. The sitting room to the left was also decorated in blue, green and cream, the dressing room mostly cabinets of dark wood that would hold clothes and linens. 'And those flowers are gorgeous.'

'Lady Daisy asked for those,' Mrs Moore said. 'We all hope that you will be happy here, miss. Of course these are guest chambers. Viscount Delsey's apartments are on the other side of the house—and your rooms will be there when you are married. You might like to see them tomorrow?'

'Yes, I should, thank you,' Charlotte said, and

the housekeeper smiled and left her to do as she pleased.

She wandered about the apartments, which were furnished with dark wood, unlike the salon where she'd taken tea. However, the window let in sufficient light to make the rooms warm and appealing. She could see that Betty had already laid out an afternoon gown for her and just as she was thinking about changing, her maid came through the dressing room.

'I was told you had come up, Miss Charlotte. Would you like me to help you change?'

'Yes, please,' Charlotte said and turned so that she could unhook her at the back. 'What do you think of it here? Are the maids friendly?'

'Yes, miss. It all seems very comfortable. I have a room to myself.'

'Oh, good. If there is anything extra you need, you must ask me.'

'I shall be quite comfortable, miss. This is a better place than I had before—and I like working for you.'

'I'm glad that you're happy,' Charlotte said. 'I'm relying on you to help me. I don't know everybody yet, and you will soon know the names of all the servants.'

'Yes, miss. I expect so. I'll be glad to help you whenever I can.'

'Thank you,' Charlotte said as she was helped into a pretty pale-blue gown. 'It's warm out, but I had best put on my bonnet and shawl.'

'Are you going out, miss?'

'Yes, for a walk in the garden.' Charlotte turned to her impulsively. 'Have you a lot of work to do—or would you like to walk with me? I want to explore and it might be best if I was not alone.'

'Oh, miss, I should like that,' Betty said. 'I can press your gown for this evening when you're having tea downstairs.'

'Then let us go—you may borrow my shawl if you like, the dark yellow one. Yes, that looks well with your dark hair.'

'Thank you, miss.'

Betty followed her from the apartment and they went downstairs, through the hall and out of a side door into a rose garden. The bushes were heavy with buds, some of which were almost ready to open. They walked through the formal garden at the front of the house, as far as the park. Ancient trees, their branches sweeping down to touch the earth, provided shade and the open patches of ground were bathed in warm sunlight. Overhead the sound of birds singing gave the wood a timeless, peaceful feel and Charlotte caught sight of a rabbit bounding ahead of them.

'This is lovely, isn't it, miss?'

'Yes, beautiful. We have pleasant grounds at home, but nowhere near as large. I should like to walk as far as the lake, but I feel we ought not. It will not be long before tea and it would be rude of me to miss it on my first day.'

They turned and began to retrace their steps. Somewhere not far off the sound of a gun suddenly shattered the peace of the afternoon and both young ladies spun round, looking in alarm as though they expected to see someone charging at them.

'It must be a keeper shooting a rabbit,' Charlotte said. 'What a shame. I suppose it must be done, but I do not care for the thought.'

'No, miss, nor I,' Betty said and frowned. 'You'd think they'd shoot them early in the morning—it could be dangerous when folk are walking in the park.'

'Perhaps.' Charlotte shook her head and dismissed the thought. 'Never mind, no doubt the keepers will realise that I like to walk here in future and we shall not get a fright.' She would mention it to Jack's grandfather later, but for the moment she needed to get back before her mother was awake and demanding to know where she was.

He awoke to the awareness of a pain in his arm and a feeling of not quite knowing where he was, of being disorientated. As he tried sitting up in bed the soreness at the back of his head made him wince and a wave of dizziness swept over him. Sinking back against the pillows with a groan, he opened his eyes again when the door opened and a young woman entered the room. She was dressed plainly, but somehow he did not think her a servant for she had an air of confidence about her, and her smile was warm as she looked at him.

'So you are awake at last, Captain Delsey,' she said. 'My Jeb said he was sure the doctor was right and you would come through with no more than a sore head—but I shan't deny you gave me a fright. When the fever was at its worst I thought we should lose you.'

'Captain Delsey?' He stared at her for a moment. 'Is that my name? Thank you for telling me. Who are you—and where are we, please?'

'Why, I'm Mrs Scott, sir, and this is my home. You came north to talk to my husband and he told you what you wanted to know…and then after you left the inn you were shot. The doctor said the wound to your arm was slight, but you hit your head as you fell and you were ill of a fever for almost a week. Jeb found you, for he had followed you from the inn. He got you to a local inn, sought the advice of a doctor, then hired a wagon and brought you home to me so that I could nurse you.'

'That was kind of you. I've been here for a week?' he said wonderingly.

'Yes, Captain. It took Jeb two days to get you here so I suppose it's nine days since you were hurt. He said you were conscious for part of the time, but rambling in your mind…'

'I fear I remember nothing of what happened,' he said apologetically. 'Perhaps your husband can tell me more. Is he here, Mrs Scott?'

'He is at work, sir, but he will be back soon. I'm sure he will be glad to tell you what he knows, though it may not be as much as you might hope.'

'Do you know what my first name is, ma'am?'

'I believe it is Jack, sir. My Jeb said you were

the grandson of a marquis, but I know little else, except that most people call you Captain Delsey.'

'Thank you for your kindness. I suppose I must have been robbed. Did they take everything?'

'Jeb says he thinks he disturbed them for he saw two men ride away as he arrived. You have a gold watch and chain, which is there on the chest by the bed, sir—and there's a signet ring on your finger…but only a few coins in your pocket.'

She placed a jug of cold drink beside his bed and poured some into a glass. 'It's lemon barley, sir. My granny always swore it was the best thing after a fever. Would you like me to help you sit up?'

'I think I can manage if you would just give me the glass.' He smiled at her as she plumped up the pillows. 'Thank you. They feel much better. I was fortunate that your husband found me in time.'

'Yes, sir. If Jeb hadn't taken it into his head to follow you, you might have died on that lonely road. Not many people pass that way unless it is market day.'

Jack was thoughtful as his kind nurse left the room. He sipped the cool lemon drink and found it pleasant, nicer than the drink Nanny had insisted on giving him in the nursery... Where had that thought come from? Until Mrs Scott had told him, he hadn't even known his own name so how could he recall a sour drink his nanny had made him drink when he was a child? Mrs Scott had sweetened it somehow so that it was pleasant; Nanny had not believed in spoiling the child.

He struggled to find other memories, but there was nothing more than the vague picture of a large house in the country, probably where he'd grown up as a child. Of his life prior to the shooting he could recall nothing, though if he was Captain Delsey he must have served in the army.

Captain Jack Delsey. Frowning, Jack wondered what kind of a man he was and whether he was content in his life. If that were the case, why would he forget? Was it the blow to the head or had he deliberately blocked everything from his mind, because he did not wish to remember? Amnesia was something even the most eminent doctors knew little about, but Jack believed it could be caused by a blow to the head...now, why did he know that? Something to do with his army days?

Clearly he was a man who did not panic easily, because he was able to face the blankness in his mind without fear. He was, he supposed, fortunate in that Mr Scott knew his identity and could supply some of the missing links.

Could he trust the couple? There was nothing to prove their statement that he was the grandson of a marquis, yet it should be easy enough to prove. Studying the signet ring on his left hand, he saw a crest and the letters *JD* entwined. At least the initials fitted and something about Mrs Scott's honest way of speaking made him feel he could trust her.

Managing to reach his watch and chain, he studied the small seal of gold and amber that hung from the chain. It, too, bore the letters *JD* entwined with a crest, and the watch also had a crest but one letter was different—*MD*. Who was MD? Obviously it had not always been his watch. Perhaps it had belonged to his grandfather or his father? Were they both alive?

Jack sighed with frustration. It felt as if he were lost in a thick mist. In the distance he could see glimpses of things that might be his home or people he knew, but the mist was too deep to be penetrated. He could only wait until Jeb Scott came home and hope that he could tell him more.

Chapter Eleven

'Really, I consider this to be too bad,' Charlotte's mama complained when they sat together in Charlotte's private sitting room, partaking of tea and coffee, with soft rolls and honey, that morning. 'We have been here almost two weeks and no word has come from Delsey. It is more than impolite, it is downright rude.'

'I am sure he must have been detained somehow,' Charlotte said, but looked at her mother anxiously. 'I am worried, Mama. I do not think Jack would have left it so long had he been able to let us know how he is. I fear something has happened to him.'

'Your papa said as much,' her mother replied. 'I believe he intends to speak to Ellington this morning. We really cannot go on like this, Charlotte. Unless Jack either writes to explain or arrives soon, I think we should go home. It is awkward to be staying here without any idea of when the ball is to be held or when he will finally decide to return.'

'I am sure Grandfather Ellington will set Papa's mind at rest,' Charlotte said.

When they went downstairs later to join the marquis and her Papa for luncheon, however, she discovered that her optimism was ill founded.

'Your father has raised my awareness,' the marquis said to her. 'I cannot understand why Jack has behaved so badly. It is not at all like him. If he tells us he is coming to stay, then he comes. I could understand a slight delay if he had some important business of which I know nothing—but two weeks is beyond all bounds. Therefore, I think I shall send someone to look for him. I shall send my agent to London to discover where he was bound when he was last heard of.'

'Do you think it necessary?' Charlotte asked doubtfully. 'Do you not think he might feel annoyed that we were prying into his affairs?' Despite her own fears, she felt that the man she knew would not take kindly to having his affairs investigated.

'I shall not take such minor considerations into account,' the marquis said, his thick brows meeting in the middle. 'Jack has either behaved totally out of character or something is the matter with him…he may have met with an accident.'

'Oh, no!' Charlotte gasped and turned pale. 'Surely he would not… It could not be…'

The marquis stared at her, his eyes fierce as they met hers. 'Do you know something we do not, Charlotte?'

'I know there was a quarrel before my dance… someone Jack disliked and I believe he accused him of cheating over a card game…'

'And why have you not spoken of this before?'

Charlotte's cheeks were warm. How could she explain that she believed Jack had forced the quarrel on Lord Harding because he had threatened her? Everyone had been so kind to her here, but if they knew the truth it would be very different. She could not bring herself to reply with her parents watching and shook her head.

'I am certain it could have nothing to do with the quarrel, sir. I know there was to have been a duel—but the other man collapsed and was very ill…a seizure, I believe.'

'And was the business that took Jack away from town connected with this person?'

'I cannot tell you, sir, for I do not know. I dare say I should not have known any of it if...' She drew a deep breath for she could not go on. 'Truly, I do not know anything more, except that Jack meant to avenge an insult to me...'

'At last it begins to make sense,' the marquis growled. 'Very well, I shall not press you now, but I wish you had told me this before. I shall set my agent on to it at once.'

'Forgive me. At first I thought it merely some business, but I have been worried of late.'

'Charlotte, what was this insult and who was it?' Mama's tone was sharp. 'I demand that you tell me at once.'

'I cannot,' Charlotte whispered. 'Please do not be angry. I did not think anything more would happen after...' She choked back the words and would not continue despite the displeasure in her mother's eyes.

'I shall speak to you later, alone,' Mama said sternly.

The marquis summoned his agent and the rest of the company moved into the dining room. Because Lady Daisy was present, Mama contented herself with giving Charlotte black looks, but after lunch she compelled her to go upstairs to her sitting room.

'I insist you tell me everything,' Mama said in her sternest voice.

Charlotte had never defied her before, but this time she remained stubborn and would not confess it all.

'I told the marquis all I know, Mama.'

'What was the insult made you?' Mama asked.

'It was just… A gentleman tried to…' Charlotte shook her head. 'I cannot speak of it, please do not ask me. Jack knew and was angry. He said it would not happen again. I believe he forced the quarrel and there would have been a duel, but… the gentleman in question was taken ill.'

'Lord Harding!' Mama frowned. 'I remember hearing something about a quarrel and a man being taken ill…was that it, Charlotte?'

'Yes,' she replied, but would not look at her mother. 'He was confined to his bed—how could he have done anything to Jack?'

'No doubt he has men that he employs, men who might do anything he bid them. You should have at least told Ellington the name of this man, Charlotte. Why did you not do so?'

'Because I wasn't sure if…' Charlotte turned away as the tears stung her eyes. 'If anything has happened to Jack it will be because of me.'

'That is nonsense. You cannot be held to blame for gentlemen's quarrels. However, you must tell Ellington the name of this man, for Jack's sake.'

'Yes, Mama. I shall do so—' Charlotte broke off as the door of the sitting room was thrown open and her father walked in. Something in his manner told her he had important news. 'Papa— what has happened?'

'We have this minute had word of Delsey,' her father said. 'His messenger arrived just after luncheon and has been closeted with the marquis. Apparently, Delsey went north on business and was injured. Someone shot him.'

Charlotte's hand went to her mouth. 'Is he dead?' she whispered and began to tremble as her mind conjured horrendous pictures.

'No, he was not severely injured by the ball,' he said looking at her in concern. 'Sit down, my dear child. You are shaking like a leaf.'

'Jack…' Charlotte said faintly, but sank back in her chair.

'As I was saying, his wound was not serious, but you must brace yourself, my love—Jack may not remember you just at first. It appears that a blow to the head robbed him of his memory, though he was with an acquaintance. That person saved his life and was able to tell him who he was and where he lived. They are returning together, since Jack was ill of a fever, which weakened him, and does not care to travel alone just yet.'

'He may not remember me?' Charlotte stared at him, feeling numb with shock. 'How can that be? I do not understand.'

'I have heard of the condition. I believe it is called amnesia, but I do not know how long it may last—or if it could be permanent.'

'Amnesia?' Charlotte echoed the words. 'Permanent…but if Jack does not know me…' She could not put her thoughts into words for they were private to her and Jack. She remembered so clearly the proposal he'd made her.

Jack was not in love with her, but he liked her spirit and he thought she would make him a good wife—one who would not complain if he were to spend some time in London without her…or if he decided to take a mistress… She *would* mind if he left her alone for long periods and it would hurt terribly if she knew he had a mistress. But she'd accepted the bargain, because she loved

Jack, and because she hoped he might come to love her in time. Besides, she'd felt that she could not bear to marry anyone else. If he could never love her, to be with him and bear his children must be enough.

'He will remember when he sees you,' Papa said comfortingly. 'A man in love cannot fail to know the woman he loves. There will be a bond between you that will bring him back, Charlie.'

Charlotte blinked hard. Her father seldom spoke to her so lovingly. He had always left her to her mother's care, only stepping in when he could see that she was in some distress. For him to be so considerate must mean he feared for her future happiness.

'We must be glad that the settlement was signed in London,' Mama said in a tone that brought back the harsh reality. 'Otherwise Delsey might not feel it his duty to pay Papa's debts. We must hope that he does recall his memory before too long. The wedding should not be postponed or it may never take place.'

'No, ma'am,' Papa spoke decisively. 'The young people will need time to come to terms with each other. I shall not have Charlotte thrust into a union with a man she may not know. We cannot know what this has done to Delsey's character.'

'Surely he cannot have changed enough to make the marriage contract null and void?'

'I am concerned with my daughter's happiness, not with financial details.'

'Papa, I wish to marry Jack no matter what,' Charlotte said into the silence that fell between her parents. 'If he still wishes to wed me, then I shall not withdraw—no matter if he is a little changed. If this…illness…has made some difference, it is surely my duty to help him through it?'

'Do you love him, Charlie? I thought you were merely obliging your mama and me.'

Her cheeks were warm, but she met his questing gaze honestly. 'Yes, Papa. I love him and it would break my heart to lose him.'

'Then I shall say no more. We must simply hope for the best.'

Charlotte agreed, excused herself to her parents and left them to talk privately. Taking her shawl from where it lay over a chair, she went out into the formal gardens. The sun was warm, but there was a chill wind and she held the shawl tightly about her shoulders. She was feeling emotional, having been to the brink of despair and back only to learn that Jack might not recognise her when they met.

Supposing he was much changed! He might no longer find her amusing or admire her...for all his memories of their first meeting would be gone.

Tears were burning behind her eyes as she walked in the park. If Jack did not care for her... the years ahead could be very empty, but she would keep to the bargain she'd made with him. All she could hope was that he would gradually regain some of the memories he'd lost, both for his own sake and for hers.

It was not until she had been walking for some time that Charlotte had the feeling that she was being watched. She turned and looked about her, at first seeing no one and then catching sight of something white—a man's shirt, perhaps. She thought whoever it was had moved behind the large oak a little to her left and halted. She wondered whether to challenge him, but then decided to be cautious.

She recalled hearing a gunshot in the woods the first afternoon that she'd walked here with her maid, and thought that perhaps it had been a poacher. Charlotte had meant to speak to the marquis about it, but somehow she had forgotten and now wondered if the person spying on her might also be a poacher. If she challenged him, he might do her some injury. It would be much better to return the way she had come and mention the incident to the marquis later.

Jack reined in as they approached the house, glancing at the man who had insisted on accompanying him all this way. Jeb had very reasonably argued that the person who had tried to kill him previously might well try again and that two men travelling together were safer than one.

'It is a big house, my lord,' Jeb said. 'Your house in London was large, but nothing like this.'

'Yes. I had vague memories, but no clear vision of the place. I was hoping my first sight of it might bring everything flooding back.'

'I take it you remember nothing more?'

'I fear not,' Jack said and grimaced, a mocking look in his eyes. 'Shall we face them? It's a damnable thing, Jeb. I cannot even recall the young lady I am pledged to marry.'

'Damnable,' Jed agreed. 'I regret that I cannot

help you, sir. I have told you what I know—but I've never met Miss Stevens.'

They had not stayed to visit his house in London, even though Jeb knew its direction. Jack did not wish the news of his loss of memory to sweep through society, as it must if he'd returned and cut every acquaintance he had simply because he did not recognise them. In the country he would have more time to accustom himself to everything that seemed so alien and strange. He must relearn faces and names, and there must be someone amongst his friends or servants who could help him to recover some of his memories.

'Well, I do no good sitting here,' Jack said and urged the horse forward. As they dismounted at the front of the house two men came running to take the horses. Neither of their faces registered, though he saw that one of them looked him in the eyes, as if expecting some recognition.

'Hillsborough, my lord,' he said at last. 'I was with you through the war as your batman and am now your head groom.'

'Thank you and forgive me,' Jack said. 'I am glad to see you here. You may be able to help me. I shall visit the stables later—but first I must see my…grandfather.'

'They are waiting for you anxiously, my lord. We were all relieved when your message came.'

'Yes, I imagine so.' He turned to Jeb. 'Go with Hillsborough, Jeb, and tell him what you can of my stay in the north.'

'Yes, my lord.'

'And then ask for me. You are my guest. I owe you my life and you will stay here as a guest.'

Jeb inclined his head, then walked off with the groom.

Jack entered the house, looking about him. He felt there was something familiar about his surroundings, something that seemed to welcome him, was a part of him, and yet still he could not claim to remember. A distinguished man who could only be the butler came up to him and inclined his head.

'Welcome home, my lord. Your grandfather is waiting in his private sitting room. He would like to see you before the others greet you.'

'Yes, if you would conduct me… Forgive me, I feel I know you but your name eludes me.'

'Evans, my lord. The housekeeper is Mrs Moore, and of course, there is Nanny and your grandfather's valet, Beedle…'

'Yes, thank you,' Jack said and nodded grimly.

He had so much to learn if he was to take up the reins of his life again—and he must if he were to have any chance of a normal life. As for his enemy…well, he must trust Jeb to help him there. In the former soldier he had found a good friend and the bond between them had grown stronger on the journey here. 'Perhaps tomorrow you will present all the staff to me, Evans. I must get to grips with this affliction as swiftly as possible.'

'Of course, sir. Nothing has ever stopped you before, sir. I am certain it will not be long before you have conquered this.'

The butler led the way upstairs and along the landing to a large double door at the end. He knocked and opened it, announcing Jack to the occupant of the comfortable room. Looking across to the window where an elderly man was sitting in a wing chair, he saw a man of some sixty or seventy years with a shock of white hair, bright fierce eyes and bushy brows. Having become acquainted with his own face in a slightly spotty mirror supplied by Mrs Scott, Jack saw that there was a strong resemblance.

'Sir,' he said, offering his hand as he strode across the floor to greet him. 'Forgive me for causing you so much distress. I ought to have sent word sooner, but it was not easy.'

'There is another you must make your apologies to,' the marquis said gruffly and wrung his hand. 'Charlotte's mother was most distressed. I believe she thought you had deserted the girl. Though Charlotte remained calm herself, as well behaved as the lady you have chosen for your future wife ought to be.'

'Charlotte...' Jack said the name with a kind of wonder. Had he fallen desperately in love with this young woman? It seemed that he must have, since he'd proposed within a few weeks of meeting her. Jeb had known that much for the gossips had been full of it. 'Yes, I must certainly apologise...but you say she took it calmly? Was she not distressed?'

Perhaps it was not a love match on her side? How awkward it was not to know the truth of the situation.

'She confessed to being anxious when pressed, but thought it wrong to pry into your private affairs.' The older man's right hand came out to grasp Jack's and he grasped his shoulder with the other. 'It was so unlike you to break a promise, Jack. I confess I have been anxious from the start.'

'I am sorry to have worried you, sir. It was most unfortunate and the consequences are worse than they might have been. With the wedding looming, I must learn to know people's faces and what they are to me. Have I many friends in the district, sir?'

'You have friends everywhere. From the time you could walk and talk, you made friends with anyone that came your way, including all the tenants. The first thing you do when you visit is to go off on a tour of the estate and talk to everyone, ask about the land, their families and inspect the state of the cottages.'

'Then I take an interest in the estate?'

'When you are here. We have an agent, of course, and a bailiff to run it from day to day, but you always have such good ideas for improvements—that's why you're so wealthy. Your own estates that your maternal grandfather left you have prospered, as have your many investments—though it's no use to ask me about them. You must send for Ellis Simpson—he lives in London and is both your secretary and your agent. Your lawyer is his father, Mr Herbert Simpson.'

'Thank you. I shall of course ask them both to come down as soon as it may prove convenient for them.' Jack heaved a sigh of frustration and ran his fingers through his thick hair. 'There is so much to learn and I hardly know where to begin.'

'Perhaps when you've been here and begun to feel better in yourself the memories will return.'

'Yes.' Jack smiled oddly. 'I have flashes sometimes… I saw this place as through a mist before I even knew my name. I was fortunate that Jeb knew so much of my life or I might have been lost for much longer.'

'He is the man you spoke of.' The marquis frowned. 'Can you be sure he was not concerned in the attack on you?'

'He was not responsible for it, but may well have contributed to it happening…not intentionally. It was Mr Scott I went to meet, sir. He had important news for me—something it seems I had suspected for a long time…'

'You do not wish to tell me?'

'It is a delicate matter and one that would undoubtedly cause you pain, sir. I shall not trouble you with it until I am certain of the outcome.'

'Are you still in danger?'

'Yes, I imagine whoever attacked me will try again. I know too much and so does Jeb. What he told me could hang a man, and others, I suppose—though they acted under his direction.'

'Then you must take great care. I could not bear to lose you, too, Jack.' The marquis's gaze narrowed. 'Tell me, does this mystery concern your father?'

'It might,' Jack admitted, then shook his head. 'Forgive me, sir, I must seek out my betrothed, for she will think I am ignoring her.'

'Yes, of course,' his grandfather agreed in a gruff tone. 'But promise me you will be careful in future?'

'Of course. I have no wish to die just yet.' Jack's smile flashed out, bringing an answering smile from the older man, for it was the first he'd seen of the young man he'd loved all his life. 'And now, sir, you must excuse me.'

Jack hesitated outside the small parlour at the back of the house, to which Evans directed him after telling him that Miss Charlotte was to be found there in the mornings.

'Lady Stevens and Sir Mordred are in the green

drawing room, but Miss Charlotte asked if she might have tea in the small parlour. I believe she often walks in the gardens and the French windows lead out into the walled garden.'

'Thank you, Evans,' Jack said. His butler seemed determined to give as much information at every opportunity and he could only be grateful for the loyalty of his grandfather's people. Much of the feeling of being lost had left Jack since they rode on to the estate, for he felt he belonged here even if he could not remember his childhood.

Breathing deeply to calm the strangely erratic beating of his heart, he opened the door and went in to the small parlour. It was furnished in soft shades of green and cream, and the furniture looked as if it had been well used and loved.

This had been his grandmother's room...

The thought came unbidden to his mind, but was lost as the diminutive figure by the window turned to look at him. Her hair was dark, but the light from the sun touched it with fire; her pale face had an enchanting elfin appeal and her eyes were large and deep. She stared at him with an eagerness that was tempered with uncertainty and something of her vulnerability touched his heart. Jack wished with all his heart that he could recall her, could go to her and take her hands and tell her that he loved her and had been lost without her, but the words would not come. He did not know her. He moved towards her, offering his hand in a formal way that irked him even as he struggled to break down the barrier his mind had erected.

'Miss Charlotte. How can I beg your pardon for what has happened? I know that I was called away on business and that has been explained to me—but how I came to desert you when I should have escorted you here I cannot explain.'

'You intended to return in good time,' Charlotte replied, smiling up at him. 'I am so happy to see you safely returned, Jack. I suppose you cannot tell me why someone shot you— Was it because of me? Because of that quarrel in town?'

'You mean when I accused Harding of cheating at cards?' Jack frowned, for all he knew of the affair was what Jeb Scott could tell him. 'Why should it have concerned you?'

'Because he threatened me and you were determined to punish him…to make certain that I was safe.' Her eyes clouded as she realised that he knew nothing of what she would tell him. 'I fear your trouble is my fault, sir.'

'Why? I beg you will tell me, because I have no idea. I am sorry, Charlotte. I know it must pain you, but I can remember nothing of our meeting or anything that happened.'

'Nothing at all?' Her eyes lowered and he saw a single tear slide down her cheek. 'I fear you will hate me if I tell you it all.'

Jack reached out and caught her hand, leading her to the open window. 'Come, the day is warm, let us walk in the garden. You may find it easier to tell me away from the house…somewhere we shall not be overheard.'

'There is a little summerhouse. Grandfather Ellington says you often went there with your grandmother when she was alive.'

'Show me the way,' Jack suggested and smiled down at her. She was lovely to look at and he thought her honest and charming, yet he sensed unease in her and knew that what she had to tell him would be revealing and perhaps distress her, too. 'My promise is made to you, Charlotte. I shall not withdraw. I do not wish to—but there must be no secrets between us.'

'There were none on my side.' Her wide eyes

looked up at him then. 'You asked me to marry you because Grandfather needs an heir,' she said softly. 'I promised I would be a good wife and give you children and you said you would make me happy—but you never said you loved me, though I believe you felt some warmth towards me.'

'Did I not speak of love?' Jack frowned over the information. 'I think I must be hard to please if my heart was not your own, Charlotte.'

'Matt—my brother, for whom you purchased colours—calls me Charlie and you do it some-times.'

'Charlie?' He nodded and saw the dimple at the corner of her mouth. 'Yes, I see why. Please continue, Charlotte. Tell me, if you will, how we met.'

'I was dressed as a youth in some of Matt's outgrown clothes and I was escaping from two men who were pursuing me. One of them was Mr Patterson and he is a friend of Lord Harding—'

'Good grief!' Jack was astonished and laughed out loud. 'What on earth were you doing dressed like that? Was it for a masquerade?'

'No, it was very early in the morning and in

London. I…' She swallowed hard and he saw real fear in her eyes.

'Please do not be afraid of me, Charlie. Whatever it is cannot be so bad—or why would I have asked you to marry me?'

'At the time you were inclined to think it amusing and yet you were cross with me, too, for risking my reputation and more. If those men had caught me, I should have been ruined.'

'It was a foolish masquerade. But there was more?'

Charlotte dutifully told him the whole of what had happened. When she had finished, she lifted her head, half-defiant, half-ashamed. 'If you no longer wish to marry me, I understand.'

'I knew this in London—before I asked you to marry me?'

'Yes, of course. You guessed it from the start—but you made me confess it to you and scolded me. You said that if I ever stole from a friend of yours, you would beat me.'

'Did I indeed? How very unchivalrous of me,' Jack said, but his mouth quivered. 'I seem to have been harsh to you. I wonder that you accepted my offer.'

'Oh, no, you were never harsh. I assure you that

Matt was furious with me—and if Mama ever knew she would disown me.'

'Then we must make certain she never discovers your little secret.'

'I was afraid that Lord Harding intended to inform your grandfather. He threatened me with exposure if I did not pay him the four thousand pounds Matt owed him.'

'You will not do so,' Jack said sternly. 'Not one penny. As far as you are concerned, none of it ever happened. I shall deal with Harding. I have a personal score to settle with him.'

'Do you think it was his men who tried to kill you?' Charlotte looked pale and shaken.

'I am certain of it,' he told her. 'However, it has little to do with you, Charlotte. Harding's hatred of me and my family goes back much further.'

'Oh…I had thought it all my fault that you were hurt.'

'No, certainly not,' he replied and led her to the seat in the white marble folly. The small summerhouse was in the midst of a riot of climbing roses and beds of sweet-scented flowers, the heady mix filling the air with a soft perfume. 'You are not to blame. What you did was foolish, but far from being a crime. You recovered a worthless necklace but Harding could never prove it was you that took it. He is a cruel, vindictive man and I shall settle with him in good time.'

'You must be careful. If he tried to have you murdered once, he will do so again.'

'I was not expecting him to strike against me. He was, I believed, ill and close to death, but clearly that was not the case. His seizure could not have been as severe as I was led to believe at the time, for I imagine I thought he would die. I have learned since that he is recovering.'

Charlotte reached out to touch his hand, gazing up at him. 'It must seem so strange, to know only what people tell you…so many pieces of the puzzle must be lost to you.'

'Yes…' Jack felt the nerve jumping in his throat. 'People are helpful. Grandfather, the servants… and you, Charlotte. Everyone has something to tell me and in time I believe the rest will come back. I must try to live with what I have and be grateful that I am alive.'

'Amen to that. I am very grateful for I could not have borne it had you died,' she said simply and looked as if she meant it. Jack felt something stir inside him. This girl was like an open book to him, the pages his for the turning; he could see her feelings in her eyes, sense her hurt and her hope. He did not believe he flattered himself by thinking that she loved him…was deeply in love with him.

Jack was not certain what kind of a man he had been, but he knew that something in this girl's eyes touched his heart. He felt warmth spreading through him, pushing back the mist and the loneliness that had pervaded him when he first realised that his memories were lost. He'd had no name, no home, but now he had both—and, he believed, there was love for the taking. His heart was responding to her and instinctively he reached for her and drew her into his arms. His kiss was soft, enquiring, and he felt the instant response even though she drew back after a few moments and looked at him uncertainly.

'You must never be afraid of me, Charlie,' he said softly. 'I promise I shall not hurt you…at least not intentionally.'

She nodded and smiled, but he knew she was trying to hold back. He believed that she cared for him, but she was afraid to show it— Why? What had he done or said to make her unsure of him?

Jack trailed a finger down her cheek. 'What are you thinking?'

'That I am very fortunate,' she replied, 'if you still wish to marry me?'

'Forget that foolish escapade. We shall never speak of it again,' he said. 'I see that you do not quite trust me, Charlotte. Perhaps that is not surprising since I must seem different. You see, I do not know myself as yet. I can only know how I feel at this moment—and I want to make you happy, my love. I think we should marry soon. I must deal with this other business first, but after that...' He took her hand and carried it to his lips, kissing the tips one by one. 'I shall court you, Charlotte, teach you to trust me and to love me.'

Her eyes seemed deeper than the ocean as she gazed up at him and he wanted to drown himself in their cool depths, to forget this business of Harding—but knew he could not. His father's death must be avenged.

'I do not think it would be hard to love you, Jack—but first you must know yourself and be sure that you love me.'

Chapter Twelve

Alone in her room as she changed for tea that afternoon, Charlotte thought of her walk with Jack and the interlude in the summerhouse when he'd kissed her. His kisses had been light as a butterfly's touch, without passion or demand, teasing, encouraging a response from her, which she had not been slow to give. It seemed that her determination to keep a little aloof from him had gone flying the moment his lips touched hers.

In London he'd seemed so much at home, a man of fashion and of the world, an invisible barrier keeping her and the world at bay. He'd offered her everything but love...but this new Jack was different. There was a look of steel in his eyes when he spoke of his enemy, but otherwise he seemed softer, more ready to love and to be loved. She was not certain what to make of it, though she knew that when she was in his arms she longed for more. She'd wished that they could have gone somewhere even more secluded than the shaded summerhouse…a room where they could close the curtains and lock the door and she could melt into the warmth of his embrace…and that was a scandalous thought for a young unmarried girl.

Charlotte had been determined to keep something of herself back, but when he'd caressed her cheek and kissed her, asking her to trust him, she'd wanted to give all that was her— her very soul. She'd wanted to, but something held her back. Once he recovered his memory, would he remember that he had a mistress in London and that marriage to Charlotte had been merely a means of giving the marquis the heir he craved? That he had not been in love with her, but merely considered her a suitable wife? Would he become the charming but slightly distant man she'd known in London? She was not sure how she would feel if he shut her out after this time of sweet togetherness.

Charlotte had been prepared to accept what he gave, for she knew the alternative was to marry where she could not love. But if she believed in this new Jack, gave her heart to him completely, only to have this new warm and loving man snatched from her, how could she bear it?

And if he never recovered his memory, would she ever be certain that he was wholly hers? Would he be the man she had fallen so desperately in love with? Perversely, she wanted the man she'd known, but she wanted him to look at her in the way the new Jack looked at her. A smile of derision touched her mouth, for she knew she asked too much.

She'd told him the truth about how they had come to meet, even though she had feared he might turn from her in disgust, but he'd laughed at her fears—and she'd seen the man she'd fallen in love with. Jack was in all essentials but one the man she'd known in London—yet there was something different and she did not know what it was.

Charlotte almost thought that this Jack might truly be in love with her. Something in his smile, in the caress of his voice, made her feel he was genuinely attached to her and yet it was difficult to give everything without fear of hurt. Jack had given her all the material things that she could ever desire—but there was one thing she feared might elude her, one thing she craved. She wanted his heart, the very essence of him, to know that he was truly hers, as she was his. But perhaps it was never possible to have complete love.

She'd given her word that she would never cling or demand that he dance attendance on her and she was too proud to break it, so although she responded to his kisses, she did not initiate them.

Lady Daisy wept when she first saw her son and threw herself into his arms, begging him to tell her that he still knew and loved her, but was gently put away.

'Dearest Mama, of course I love you,' he replied in a gentle, yet repressive tone. 'I simply cannot recall it for the moment. I beg you to accept my apologies and to forgive me if I cannot share your memories of my childhood—but I know I am your son and shall not forget my duty to you, or my affection. I am always at your service.'

She mopped at her eyes, stared at him as if he were a stranger and retired to her seat to sniff into her handkerchief, sending the occasional resentful look at Charlotte. Feeling uncomfortable but not knowing what to say, Charlotte contrived to keep a smile in place. She knew that in some odd way Jack's mother blamed her for his manner, which she later told her was so unlike him for he was the most considerate of sons.

Charlotte wondered what she considered inconsiderate in his behaviour towards her, for surely he could not be blamed for losing his memory.

Perhaps it was her ladyship's habit to blame others when she was distressed over some imagined slight? It was no wonder that Jack did not care for clinging ladies.

Jack had chosen to sit by the window with Charlotte that afternoon some days after his return and was engaged in flirting with her and making her laugh. He had spent the past few days between meetings with his grandfather's agents, the tenants, various neighbours and the library, where he had been renewing his love affair with the volumes of poetry on the shelves.

'I had no idea there was such a wealth of treasure on Grandfather's shelves,' he told Charlotte. 'I believe it must be your influence, my love, for I am told I hardly touched them before this.'

'You mock me,' she retorted giving him a wicked look. 'I swear you must have known of

Byron and of Shakespeare's sonnets, Keats, Shelley and Wordsworth, to say nothing of Captain Lovelace's wonderful verses…'

'Byron must be known to everyone, for fashion decrees it,' Jack declared, his eyes bright with mischief. 'Though I do not think I was an admirer of his until you made me see the glory of his scenes of valour and grandeur.'

'Nor are you greatly now,' Charlotte murmured. 'Do not think you deceive me, sir. You will gain nothing by this mockery, for I am devoted to his verses and shall not be swayed however much you jest.'

'Then walk with me, Charlie—or shall we ride? I could take you for a drive…we could visit some friends that have come down this week from town.'

'Friends of yours?'

'Yes, Phipps has come down to stay with his cousins for a couple of weeks. In his letter informing me of his arrival, he seemed a little put out that I had not contacted him.' Jack frowned and Charlotte's hand reached towards his, touching it briefly.

'You were the best of friends,' she said. 'You told me how much you cared for those friends that were in the army with you. Do not doubt yourself, Jack. I am sure the feeling of brotherhood will come back when you are with them again.'

'Are you?' he said and the laughter was gone. For a moment she saw such a bleak look in his eyes that her heart sank. With her, Jack was almost his old self, though he was warmer, more eager to please than she recalled. He seemed at ease with his grandfather, but with his mother he was not sure how to behave. Her parents, of course, saw little difference for they did not know him, but Charlotte sensed that he was uneasy with himself at times. It was as if he was searching for what the old Jack would have done or said, rather than relying on instinct. She knew that certain things came into his mind, prompted by a word or a scene, or even a line of poetry, but for the most part his past was still lost to him.

'Will you wait while I go up and put on my bonnet and shawl?'

'Of course,' he said and leaped to his feet. 'I will have my phaeton made ready. It is time I taught you to drive it, though perhaps my team is too strong for you?'

'Indeed, I do not think so if I do as you bid me,'

she retorted. 'I may be small, but I am strong enough.'

'Horses respect command,' Jack replied. 'It is not a matter of strength if you treat them properly and teach them to respect you—as you must respect them.'

Charlotte nodded, smiling as she sped away to put on her bonnet and place a shawl about her shoulders. She was dressed in a walking gown of green silk, but did not stay to put on a more formal carriage gown. Surely in the country one did not need to be a model of fashion when out for a visit to one's friends?

She had noticed that Jack's knowledge of horses was instinctive; driving was not one of the things he'd had to relearn. It was putting names to faces that he found difficult, but his opinions on literature and music had all been there in his mind, waiting to spill out when he was animated. Often now he spoke of things with confidence; she'd even heard him say that he'd been happier in the army than ever before in his life, but when questioned could not explain such a remark. He only knew that it had been a good time for him, though he could not tell her why.

It was as if all the knowledge of his life was

there, all the facets of his character had remained, but the structure of his days was missing. He did not know who he was in the habit of playing cards with, though the servants who knew him had supplied the names of many friends. Yet still he was unable to put faces to the names and, though he had begun to recognise neighbours and to greet them as if he'd known them all his life, Charlotte sensed he was still uneasy. His baggage and horses had been sent for from the inn in the north, where, in his ignorance, he'd been forced to leave them; the groom had been dispatched to bring his possessions back with all speed and instructed to pay whatever was owed.

Jack smiled at her approvingly as she joined him in the hall a few minutes later. 'I swear you are a refreshing change, Charlie. Most ladies I've known keep one waiting an age.'

She looked at him enquiringly but made no comment. It was the kind of remark Jack made without knowing where it came from, so she merely smiled.

'Papa says that Mama is always late when he is ready to set out on a journey, and that half the time is spent repacking because she fears something has been forgotten. He finds it annoying.'

Jack nodded, but did not reply, merely giving her an odd look as they went out to the waiting phaeton. She guessed that his own mama was of a similar disposition, for she had heard the ladies talking together and wondered if her chance remark had stirred old memories. Sometimes it might be that the irritating memories might be more firmly fixed than pleasurable ones.

They went out to where the stylish high-perch phaeton was waiting behind a team of mettlesome black horses. Charlotte admired their noble heads, clean lines and spirited manner as they pawed at the ground, clearly impatient to be off. Remembering something her father had taught her as a child, she went up to the horses and stroked their soft noses, whispering a greeting. She would have liked to feed them a sugar lump, but thought Jack might not appreciate it, though had she thought to bring a piece of apple he could not have objected.

'Come, Charlotte,' he commanded and held out his hand. 'I trust you did not feed them sugar? They are fresh and will be difficult enough to handle as it is.'

'Would I dare?' she asked, dimpling up at him. 'I always give my own darling a lump of sugar.

She expects it and would be most disgruntled if I forgot.'

'Your *Brown Velvet?* I remember I thought you spoiled her when you told me that before.'

'You remember the name of my horse?' Charlotte stared at him hopefully. 'Has it all come back, just like that?'

Jack wrinkled his brow in thought. 'I seem to recall we had been riding together in the park that morning. You wore a blue habit...and you gave your horse sugar and told me that your own mare expected it. I thought the name unusual.'

'Oh, Jack,' Charlotte said, turning to him eagerly as he climbed up beside her on the driving box. 'I *was* wearing a blue habit and I *did* give the horse you hired for me a lump of sugar... Does this mean...*is* your memory coming back?'

'Some things...just vague wisps...' He shook his head as he took up the reins. 'Do not look so anxious, Charlie. I am sure it will happen... At least bits seem to come when I least expect it, but I am resigned to the fact that it may never be a complete return.'

He gave a little flick of the reins and the magnificent horses set off. His steady hand kept them to a modest trot until they reached the main road and then gradually let them have their way, so for a while Charlotte felt like clinging to the side of the seat, half-fearing they would bolt and she would be thrown. However, having given the horses a chance to use up some of their restless energy, he slowed the pace and then turned to her with a lift of his brow.

'Do you want to try them?'

'Yes, please,' she said, responding instantly to the challenge she saw in his eyes. 'Just tell me how I should hold the reins, for I do not want to damage their mouths.'

'I should not let you,' he said. 'Just remember to be steady and not jab at them. A firm gentle hand is all they need, because once they know you mean to be obeyed they will accept your mastery of them.'

Charlotte listened as he explained what she ought to do, then took the reins into her own hands. The horses immediately pulled, as if they sensed the change and meant to test her, but she held them firmly without jabbing and they responded to the voice of command.

'They have beautiful manners,' Jack murmured softly. 'I broke them to it myself.'

Charlotte was concentrating on driving the

spirited team and did not respond to his remark—
after all, it was as Jack said, things came to him
like tiny wisps of mist that he plucked from nowhere. It was best to ignore it and behave as if it
were natural, for to be always calling attention to
a chance remark might harm his chance of making a full recovery.

It was such a beautiful afternoon and Charlotte
was conscious of feeling happy as they bowled
along the exceptionally good country road, which
unlike many was smooth rather than plagued
with deep ruts. It was as they approached the
entrance to what was clearly a large estate that
Jack took them back in hand and they turned in
through a pair of magnificent wrought-iron gates.

At first there were open fields to either side,
some with sheep grazing, others with horses who
stood watching as they cropped the rich grass,
but then they entered a tree-lined avenue and at
the end she saw a large country house built of
faded red brick. Not as large or magnificent as
the marquis's residence, it had a gentle elegance
that she found very appealing.

Jack brought the horses to a halt outside the
front door and within seconds two grooms came
running to attend them. One helped Charlotte

down and the other spoke with Jack for a moment before leading the horses away. A shout from the house alerted Charlotte and she looked round. Seeing that two men of about Jack's age were coming to meet them, she told him that his friend Phipps was the man on the left dressed in a blue coat.

'Forgive me, I do not know the other gentleman,' she whispered as they came up to greet the new arrivals.

'Miss Stevens,' Phipps said and took the hand she offered, bowing over it. He turned to Jack with a mock scowl. 'Where the hell have you been? I was expecting an invitation to join you at Ellingham.'

'Forgive me, old friend,' Jack murmured and clapped him on the shoulder. 'Things have been difficult. I shall explain later…' He hesitated, looking at the second gentleman uncertainly.

'Oh, of course, you don't know my second cousin Harold Peckham do you? He's in the Third Rifles and on leave. Pecks, this is Jack Delsey, of whom you've heard me speak often—and his betrothed, Miss Charlotte Stevens.'

'Sir, Miss Stevens, delighted to meet you,' the young man replied, looking slightly hesitant and a little in awe of a man he had no doubt heard much about. 'Phipps was concerned that you did not return to town as arranged.'

Jack inclined his head, nothing in his manner giving away the dismay he felt on realising that he had clearly broken a promise to an old friend. Clearly, he must tell Phipps at least a part of the truth.

'I met with an accident,' he said. 'Someone took a pot shot at me and I might have died had not a good friend come along and helped me. I dare say my promise to you went out of my head, Phipps. Indeed, the knock on my head has made me a little forgetful. You must forgive me if I seem not to remember things... I am sure this condition will clear soon enough, but bear with me if I seem slow in certain areas.'

Jack did not wish to offend his friend by letting him guess that he had no memory of their long acquaintance and hoped a slight loss of memory might account for any lapses on his part.

'Good grief!' Phipps was clearly concerned. 'Well, you may rely on me to fill in any gaps, dear fellow. Do you know who it was that shot at you—not Harding? Pecks has been telling me something you might be interested to know, concerning a young officer. The poor fellow was tricked into signing away his estate and ended up putting a ball through his brain...' Seeing Charlotte's look of distress, Phipps apologised. 'Forgive me—not suitable conversation for a lady. Please, both of you, come in and I shall send for refreshments.'

An hour later, they took their leave, having secured a promise from the young men that they would dine at Ellingham on the following evening. Charlotte had been taken upstairs to refresh herself before joining the gentlemen in the parlour for tea, so she did not know just what Jack had told his friend or the full story concerning Lieutenant Peckham's friend who had been driven to suicide because of a card game.

They had been driving in silence for a while before Jack turned to her, looking thoughtful. 'I did not tell Phipps that I had completely lost my memory, for it might have made him awkward with me. We touched briefly on old times, but I had only to agree with him. As you said, I felt at home with him and it will become easier as time passes.'

'You do not think that he could help you to remember so much more?'

'Perhaps…yet it seems as if…'

Charlotte was never to learn what was on Jack's mind for the peace of the afternoon was shattered by a gunshot. The ball whistled past her and nestled in Jack's shoulder, making him cry out and for a moment the reins went lax as he slumped against her.

'Jack!' she cried, but the horses had been spooked and she had no time to worry about his injury for it was imperative that she take over the driving before they bolted. 'Steady, steady—' she said in as firm a voice as she could manage.

The reins in her hands, she was fully occupied by holding the spirited pair, but did not attempt to bring them to a hasty halt, doing as she was sure Jack would if he were conscious and letting them run until the worst of their panic was over. She must in any case avoid coming to an immediate halt lest the assassin was still close by. Only when she judged enough time and distance had been covered did she bring the horses to a gradual halt and turn to look at Jack. He was bleeding copiously, but when she touched his face, his eyes flickered open; it seemed that he was holding on if only by a thread.

'Jack!' she cried, uncertain of what to do for the best. 'You've been hit!'

'Get me home, Charlie,' he murmured. 'Just get me home…'

Charlotte pulled off her shawl and hurriedly tied it around his shoulder as tight as she could, then took up the reins again. It took all her will not to give into tears, but she could only think that she must do as he'd told her and get Jack home as quickly as she could.

Driving at a sensible pace, she set the horses off again, conscious that Jack was leaning against her, barely conscious and still bleeding. Her heart was beating fast and she felt numb with fright, but something kept her going as they covered the remaining distance. She must get him home because otherwise he could bleed to death.

She screamed for help as soon as they stopped at the front of the house and within seconds several men had come rushing to help her. A groom held and calmed the horses, while servants from the house reached out for Jack and bore him inside. Charlotte jumped down without waiting for assistance and ran after them, her throat choking on the tears she'd held back all this time.

'He was shot as he drove home,' she cried. 'I held the horses, but could do little for him. Please, you must fetch the doctor. Someone...quickly!'

'Don't you worry, miss,' a footman said comfortingly. 'Beedle will look after him. This isn't the first time Master Jack has come home with a ball in him.'

'Charlotte, where do you think you are going?' Her mama's voice stopped her as she started up the stairs after them.

'Jack has been shot. I must help him.'

'Come back here this instant,' Mama said. 'Look at you—your gown is soaked with blood. You must change immediately and then you may come to the parlour and tell us what has happened.'

'But, Mama, Jack is hurt. I must go to him.'

'Charlotte, do as your mother bids you.' Her father had come out into the hall and lent his voice to Mama's. 'Delsey's people will look after him. Come and drink a glass of brandy, it will settle your nerves.'

Faced with her parents' combined opposition, Charlotte was forced to follow him to the parlour. He poured a small measure of brandy into a glass and bade her drink it. She sipped it twice and put the glass down, but he pushed it back into her hand and made her swallow it all.

'Now,' he said when the glass was empty. 'Take a moment and tell us what happened, my dear.'

'We visited Jack's friends and were coming home…' she said, tucking trembling hands into the folds of her skirt. 'On the way there Jack let me drive so when the horses took fright at the shot and I saw he was hurt, I took over and let them go until they calmed, then I stopped and bound my shawl around Jack's shoulder. He told me to get him home and so I did.'

'You were a good, brave girl,' her father said. 'I'm proud of you, Charlie. Most young women would have gone into hysterics.'

'What I ask is what Delsey has done to make someone so determined to kill him?' Mama said coldly. 'I am not at all sure that you should continue with this engagement.'

'How could you, Mama?' Charlotte stared at her in distress. 'Even now he may be dying…' She gave a sob and tears welled in her eyes again.

'Do not fear, my love,' her father said and touched a hand to her shoulder. 'I think Delsey has been through worse on the battlefield. You should go and change your gown now. I will discover how he is and come and tell you.'

Charlotte could only obey, though she was close to rebelling. Had it not been that she feared she might get in the way, she would have defied both her parents and gone to his room. What did propriety matter when Jack might be dying?

Chapter Thirteen

Charlotte had changed into a simple afternoon dress of pale-blue silk when her father knocked at the door and asked if he might enter. She gave permission and her maid curtsied as he entered, leaving them together. Charlotte moved towards him urgently.

'How is he, Papa?'

'Sleeping, I imagine. Beedle said the ball scraped his flesh, but did not penetrate the muscle and must have passed right through the thick seam at the shoulder of his coat. Although he bled a great deal, and will doubtless feel under the weather for a few days, he is in no danger of dying—providing he does not contract a fever, of course.'

'Has a doctor been sent for?'

'At once, but Beedle knows his job and I doubt

the physician will do more than nod his head and offer some foul healing draught.' Papa smiled at her. 'Of course, had it not been for your cool head, it might have been much worse, Charlie. This is the second time our assassin has tried to dispose of Jack. We must assume that given the chance of a second shot he would have made sure of him this time.'

Charlotte shivered, her hands twisting in her lap. 'That is why I did not dare to stop for more than a few moments to tie my shawl about his shoulder. I could not bear that...' She shook her head and could not continue.

'You cannot tell me why this is happening?' Papa gave her a look of interrogation.

'No, Papa. Jack has told me that the attempt on his life had nothing to do with what happened in London. He says it is an old story that is rooted in the past, but he will not tell me anything more.'

'It is all very well, but you were with him this time, and you might have been badly hurt—or even killed. Your mama thinks we should go home at once and postpone both the ball and the wedding.'

'No!' Charlotte cried. 'I shall not desert Jack. You cannot expect me to leave him when he needs me the most. I will not do it. Mama must stay. Please persuade her. She is in no danger and nor am I—it is Jack this wicked man wants to kill.'

'I have told her this, but she is severely displeased.' Papa sighed. 'I shall do what I can to appease her, Charlie—but this must stop. I cannot allow you to be exposed to constant danger.'

'I am sure I am in no danger,' she replied, as calmly as she could, though her nerves were stretched. 'Please, Papa. I love Jack and I need to be with him.'

'Well, we shall not run away this time, but if it happens again…'

'God forbid! Jack will do something about it when he is well enough,' Charlotte said.

'Yes, I dare say. Well, I have calmed Mama down for now, but please think twice before leaving the estate in an open carriage again, my dear. I really do not want to lose my daughter.'

Charlotte went to him and kissed his cheek. 'Thank you, Father. I do love you very much.'

'And I you, my child.'

He went away and left her. Charlotte waited for a few minutes and then walked down the landing and into the wing where Jack's apartments were housed. She felt guilty as she approached the door of his room, but surely no harm could come from simply asking.

Beedle answered her knock. He smiled broadly as he saw her and opened the door wider, admitting her to the small sitting room that fronted the connecting bedchamber.

'Come in, miss. I expected you would come. Captain Delsey is sleeping at the moment, but I shall tell him when he wakes that you came to enquire.'

'Is there anything I can do to help?'

'Why, bless your sweet face, miss. There's nothing he needs just now, though he'll be pleased to see you when he's allowed up in a chair, I dare say.'

'Yes. He will get better, won't he?'

'The captain has seen worse than this, miss. I recall after the Battle of Waterloo, he was in a lot of pain with his leg then. We thought he might lose it, but he came through. He'll see this off and be as right as rain.'

Charlotte cried, a sob in her voice, 'But he was wounded only a few weeks ago. He was only just recovering.'

'Aye, but he's a strong man, miss. Don't you go

worrying. He'll be up and ready for the ball next week, you see if I'm not right.'

Charlotte thanked him and left, going back to her own part of the house and then to the top of the main staircase. Her mother was coming along the landing and called to her. She waited obediently for Mama to come up to her.

'I went to your room, Charlotte. You were not there?'

'I enquired of Mr Beedle if Jack was all right.'

'Surely your father had told you so?'

'Yes, but I wanted to ask.'

Her mother made a tutting noise, then, 'I shall not have you visiting him in his room. You must wait until he is able to come down. I am relying on you to behave properly, Charlotte—otherwise I shall wash my hands of you.'

Charlotte was tempted, but the unkind words remained unuttered. Her mama was quite right to remind her of what was proper, even though she longed to be with Jack this moment, sitting by his bed...waiting for him to open his eyes and look at her.

She must, however, behave as her mother expected of her. Perhaps Jack would not care for it if she made a show of fussing over him. Gentlemen did not always want a lady hanging over them, even if they were in love—and Charlotte could not be certain of Jack's feelings towards her.

'I shall do nothing that would cause you shame, Mama,' she said with dignity.

Blinking back her tears, she walked downstairs to the parlour that the family used when there was no company. Fortunately, they were not expecting guests that evening and the marquis had sent his regrets but did not feel like dining with them that evening. He did, however, request that Charlotte would visit him in his sitting room after she had dined.

Charlotte refused to look at her mother and replied that she would be delighted to spend some time with him that evening. Surely there could be no impropriety in sitting with a gentleman old enough to be her grandfather?

Glancing at Mama's face moments later, she saw the look of disapproval she'd expected, but nothing was said. Her father was nodding at her and seemed to be happy with the arrangement. Since Jack was ill and the marquis had chosen to dine upstairs, there were just the four of them, and, as Lady Daisy seemed to have little to say other than to fret over her son's injury, it was almost as if they had been at home, except that there were more servants to wait on them.

Mama rose from the table after they had finished eating their puddings and led the way back to the parlour they had used earlier. She frowned at Charlotte.

'I shall go up to my room as soon as I've had tea. Do not sit long with the marquis. I cannot say I approve of your visiting him in his private apartments, but your father sees no harm in it.'

Making her escape as soon as she could, Charlotte went straight up to the marquis's rooms and found him sitting by a fire, a blanket wrapped about his legs.

His eyes sought hers and he smiled a little stiffly, 'Forgive me if I do not rise, my dear, I feel a little shaken after your dramatic arrival this afternoon...'

'Of course you do, sir.' Charlotte went over to him, kneeling by his chair to look up at him. 'I am so sorry to have upset you. It was very shocking for us all.'

'Most of all for you,' he said and laid a blue-veined hand on her head. 'I am distressed that this should be happening. I wish I could be certain why it is happening now. Jack would not wish to worry me, but I think I shall insist on being told. I wanted you to know that instructions have been given to double the keepers patrolling the grounds—and in future an armed groom will follow you wherever you go.'

'Yes, that would help to settle Mama's fears,' Charlotte agreed. 'I believed at first it was my fault—but now I think something else may be behind these wicked attacks.'

'Why did you think it might be your fault?'

'If I tell you, you may think less of me, sir.'

'Nothing could make me do that,' he murmured and touched her head as she continued to kneel at his feet. 'Please trust me, Charlotte. I need to protect you—and my grandson.'

Haltingly, and with her cheeks on fire, she told him how she'd met Jack and what she'd done that night—and of the threats that Harding had made her.

'Well, miss, I confess you have surprised me.' The marquis was silent for a few moments, then nodded. 'I can see why you would think you were to blame for what happened to my grandson, but somehow I think there is more to it. I am certain, though, that Lord Harding is behind these attacks—but there may be another reason.'

'You are not angry with me, sir?'

'Your actions were shocking, but understandable. You did something reckless to protect your brother—he was not as honest as he might have been, for had he asked rather than taken the necklace without permission it need not have happened.'

'It was very wrong of me to steal it back, was it not?'

'To steal something that does not belong to you can never be right. But the question of ownership is a grey area here, for it was not your brother's property to give away. The necklace had no real value and you meant only to protect your brother. I might have done the same at your age. I was a high-spirited young fool in those days and would in similar circumstances have tried to protect my youngest brother. Silas was inclined to be reckless...unfortunately, he died before he reached maturity. As you know I have a married granddaughter—the child of my daughter, now unfortunately deceased—but I fear I have not been lucky with those dearest to me and lost my only son to an accident some years back.'

Charlotte saw the grave look in his eyes. He shook his head, seeming distressed. 'What is it, sir?'

'I think… I believe I know what is the cause of all this.' He sat forward, a grey, bloodless look about his mouth. 'You were not the cause, child—an added factor only. I always felt that Jack thought as I did…that his father's death was not truly an accident.'

'You think your son was murdered?'

'Yes.' The marquis was silent for a moment, then, 'I cannot tell you more for I do not know it all, but I believe it concerns a lady…the woman my son should have married. His love for her ruined his marriage. Jack's mother never stood a chance of capturing his heart.'

'You do not think she killed him?'

'No, it would have been her husband…or more likely his cousin arranged it for him.'

'Lord Harding?'

'Yes, of course. It fits perfectly. If Jack discovered something suspicious, he would not let it rest.'

'But Lord Harding is confined to bed…or we believed he was.'

'Yes, but presumably he can speak and think.'

The marquis looked thoughtful. 'I doubt he would have done the deed himself.'

'Mr Patterson…' Charlotte cried, looking up at him with sudden inspiration. 'They were always together in London. Do you think he was one of the assassins? That perhaps he is afraid that Jack will go after him next?'

'Patterson…' The marquis seemed to be turning the name over in his mind. 'I have not heard of him, but if he was involved you could have hit upon the answer. I shall set my agents to finding the man and, if he is in the vicinity, he shall be watched. If he is our man, he will not shoot Jack so easily again, for my men will put a ball through him if he dares to venture here.'

Charlotte looked up at the proud, fierce face and laughed. 'You sound just like Jack when he is angry,' she said. 'I do hope I have solved the mystery, though it may all be my imagination.'

'I hope this nonsense has not given you a dislike for the marriage, child?'

'No, sir. Mama thought we should go home, but I would never desert Jack while he needed me.'

'You love him, do you not?'

'Yes, sir.'

'I thought so from the first. I am glad of it,

for his father's marriage was not a love match. I wanted more than that for my grandson.'

'I wish you will not tell him so, sir,' she said. 'Jack asked me because he wished to please you and hoped we might give you an heir. He likes me and I make him laugh, but I am not sure he is in love with me.'

'Nonsense! He adores you, Charlotte.'

'If that is so, I am glad of it—but he has not said it, at least only in jest.'

'Well, well, I dare say he will tell you in his own good time. Once I thought he would never wed, for I was sure he would not unless he could give his heart—but then I saw you and I understood why he had decided to oblige me.'

Charlotte smiled and did not disagree. Jack had always been charming, amusing and good company. But how could she know that beneath the enigmatic face she saw there was a heart that beat for her?

The following morning, Charlotte was up and dressed before her mama had risen. She went quickly to Jack's apartments and knocked; Beedle answered the door as before and his smiling face gave her her answer.

'The captain is much recovered this morning and there is no fever,' he told her cheerfully. 'He is perhaps a little tired, for he lost a deal of blood, as you know, and is not ready for visitors, but perhaps this afternoon...'

Charlotte hesitated, then made up her mind. She would risk Mama's displeasure for she could not allow Jack to think she did not care enough to visit him.

'After tea, when I go up for a rest before I change?' she suggested and was given a wink by the valet.

She left the family wing and returned to her own room to collect a shawl and bonnet, then went downstairs. It was such a lovely day and now that she was reassured that Jack was recovering she thought she would go for a walk about the estate. Because of what had happened, she would not go beyond the gardens or into the park, but instead walk as far as the folly and sit there amongst the roses and flowering shrubs.

As she walked through the formal gardens, she caught sight of at least three gardeners bending over their barrows, but something in the way she was observed told Charlotte that these were some of the marquis's special keepers and their job was to keep watch over her rather than weed the immaculate beds.

One of the men straightened as she approached and touched his hat. 'Lovely mornin', miss.'

'Yes, lovely,' she agreed, giving him a mischievous look. 'I am going to the summerhouse.'

He inclined his head, but made no reply. Charlotte walked on, a smile on her lips, because she was glad that there was no need to be nervous. She thought that one of the so-called gardeners might be following her at a distance, but did not glance round for there was no reason. Nothing could happen to her when she was being so closely watched.

She reached the marble folly, sat down on the bench with its elaborate scrolled legs and thought of sitting here with Jack. He'd kissed her here and it had made her heart beat so very fast. It was the first time that she'd thought he might truly care for her—but could she be sure that he was not just playing the part he believed was expected of him? How could she ever know unless he recovered his memory?

Lost in her thoughts she did not immediately take much notice of a rustling sound in the bushes behind her. Why should she after all? If anyone was there, it would only be the keepers the marquis had set on to patrol the grounds.

Getting up, she wandered over to the rose bushes, which were full of buds. She would like to pick some for Jack's room, but wondered if the gardeners would object, though this part of the garden had been left to overgrow and was a pretty wilderness by design rather than accident.

Perhaps if she went back to one of the gardeners they would give her some shears to cut the stems. She bent her head to smell a rather lovely red rose; then, hearing a sound behind her, glanced round. A man—one of the new keepers, she thought—was approaching her. He wore a wide-brimmed hat pulled down over his face so that she could not see his features clearly.

'I should like to cut some roses,' she said. 'Would you fetch me some shears, please?'

Bending down to admire a particularly beautiful bloom, she was thinking of her visit to Jack later. A shadow loomed over her and, becoming aware that the man she'd asked to fetch some shears had not obeyed her, she attempted to turn, but the silk of her gown caught on a thorn and, intent on freeing it without tearing the delicate material, she was taken by surprise when the man suddenly lunged at her from behind, placing a pad over her mouth.

'Scream and you're dead,' a voice said gruffly close to her ear.

'Help!' she cried and kicked out at his shin in desperation. One of the men she'd thought a new keeper was not what he'd seemed. How could he have managed to approach her without the alarm being raised? She'd believed herself so safe, but she'd been misled, as others must in thinking him one of the marquis's new employees.

Charlotte tried to struggle, kicking out and trying to thrust him off, but he grabbed her about the throat, cutting off her flow of air, and then she realised that she was feeling faint. There was a substance on the pad over her nose and mouth; its strong odour overpowered her and was robbing her of the strength to fight against her kidnapper.

'No…please…' she tried to say and then her knees went and she collapsed into the arms of the man who had attacked her. As he swept her up, her gown tore, leaving a jagged piece of silk on the rose bush. Charlotte knew nothing of the damage to her gown or anything more as she was hoisted over the man's shoulder and carried away.

* * *

'Where is Charlotte?' Mama demanded when her husband walked into the parlour where a cold nuncheon had been set out. 'I have looked right through the house for her. I thought she might have gone riding with you?'

'No, I haven't seen her since last evening. She may be with Ellington. I'll speak to Evans—someone will have seen her.'

'If she is with Delsey, I shall have something to say to her. Unless she is in his apartments she must have gone out. I spoke to Evans only a few minutes ago. She was not with the marquis then.'

'I will ask Jack if he's seen her.'

'Really, this is the outside of enough,' Lady Stevens said and would have followed her husband had it not been that he turned and frowned at her in such a way that she desisted. 'Very well, but find her. I cannot think where she has gone.'

Sir Mordred spoke to the indoor servants first, but, as his wife had told him, no one recalled seeing her that morning. Deciding that Lady Stevens must be right, he made his way to Captain Delsey's room. He was admitted, but the valet told him at once that they had not seen Charlotte since she asked how Captain Delsey was early that morning.

'She was wearing a shawl, sir. Perhaps she meant to go out for a walk.'

'Ask Sir Mordred to come in, please,' Jack's voice from the other room made them both start forward. When they entered, it was to find that Jack was on his feet, wearing his breeches, but no shirt; his face looked deathly white and his stance was unsteady, as though he might have to sit down hurriedly. 'What is this about Charlotte? Has she gone missing?'

'I'm sure there's no need to worry,' Sir Mordred said hastily. 'My wife was anxious, but I dare say she went for a long walk and forgot the time.'

'Charlie isn't foolish enough to leave the estate after what happened yesterday,' Jack said. 'You must call out the men, Beedle—set up a search party for her—and send Jeb to me. She may be in danger...' He cursed and sat down on the edge of the bed abruptly. 'Damn it! I'm as weak as a kitten.'

'You should not try to get up, sir,' the valet said. 'You lost a lot of blood yesterday.'

'And should have lost more had it not been for Charlie,' Jack said harshly. 'If anything happens to her, I shall not forgive myself.'

'God forbid,' Sir Mordred muttered. 'My wife said we should go home until you had sorted out this unpleasant business.'

'It is a pity you did not heed her,' Jack said, a trace of bitterness in his voice. 'I do not wish to part with her, but if we cannot keep her safe… For God's sake, did no one think to set more keepers on?'

'Ellington assured us that he had doubled the normal patrols,' Sir Mordred said and moved forward as Jack groaned. 'Are you in pain, Delsey? Please lie down. I am sure we shall find her.'

'I wish I could be as sure. I need help. Please send word to Phipps immediately. He and Jeb are to come and see me the instant they arrive—and send Hillsborough to me now.'

Sir Mordred hesitated, but felt as if he were a subaltern being given orders by his superior officer and found himself obeying. Once downstairs, he gave Evans Captain Delsey's instructions, and then, rather than confront his wife, decided to go out and join the search for his daughter.

After Sir Mordred had left, Jack allowed himself to rest against his pillows whilst his mind wrestled with the wild thoughts that fought for supremacy. His memory seemed to be returning in leaps and bounds, and had been since he recovered his senses that morning, but scenes and snatches of conversations were jumbled in his head, like the clamouring of a hundred voices all seeking attention. He had to concentrate on the present problem, not give in to these other voices demanding to be heard. For the moment it did not matter which club he was accustomed to attending nor how very many acquaintances he had in London—he must concentrate on finding Charlie, because he was sure she had been snatched as a warning to him.

How could anyone have infiltrated the security laid on to guard Charlotte? And yet, amongst so many new men brought in to patrol the grounds, one more stranger might not have been remarked, especially if that man had assumed the garb of a keeper. Whoever it was had used cunning and disguise to achieve his evil purpose.

Surely that devil would not harm her? What good could come of murdering the girl to whom Jack was engaged? The abduction might serve as a warning to him, but the attempts on his life were sufficient if he'd been open to intimidation; Harding must know by now that he was not to be scared off. And yet was it Harding? The man might have lived, but was surely not up to planning these acts of revenge—especially the kidnap of his fiancée.

Jack frowned, as his thoughts circled like a puppy after its own tail. Who else might want him dead—or silenced? Was the price for Charlotte's life to be his silence? Had she been taken as some kind of surety or for a ransom? Harding was a hothead, but was he capable of a plot of this nature? Especially after being taken violently ill at the gambling hell? Yet who else could it be?

Jack was no nearer to finding a way through the maze in his mind when a knock at the door heralded the arrival of Jeb Scott. He entered somewhat awkwardly and stood looking towards the bed in an uncertain manner.

'Have you been told?' Jack demanded. 'Miss Stevens has gone missing. You have not seen her?'

'She went walking this morning, sir. I saw her stop and speak to one of the gardeners—well, properly speaking he was one of the men set on to watch over her. I heard her tell him she was only going as far as the folly.'

'Has anyone been to look for her there?'

'I spoke to your butler and he said the men would search the gardens and park, so I imagine they will go to the folly, sir.'

'Yes.' Jack looked thoughtful. 'She would think it safe there with so many of our men about—but it is almost a wilderness and possible for a man to stay hidden there. We have to find her, Jeb. I fear what he might do to her.'

'It can't be Lord Harding, sir. Word came only this morning—he passed away ten days ago. He was thought to be recovering, but then something happened—your agent wasn't exactly sure, but he understands Harding had a visitor who may have upset him. Sounds of a quarrel were heard which led to a further violent seizure and his death.'

A frown creased Jack's brow. 'Yes, that fits the picture I had begun to build. Harding may have paid someone to make another attempt on my life, but…Charlie's abduction was carefully planned. Whoever it was has been watching and waiting for his moment.'

'Why would he take her, sir? Do you think it is a warning to you—or for a ransom?'

'Would that it were merely the ransom,' Jack said, a nerve twitching in his throat. 'If anything happens to her, I shall not forgive myself. I should have seen this coming. I should have sent her home until I knew this was over.'

'I doubt he'll harm her, sir. What benefit would it be to him?'

Jack nodded, eyes narrowed in thought. 'The night my father died, did you see the faces of any of those rogues?'

'They were all masked, sir,' Jeb replied, 'but one of them pulled his muffler down to answer Harding when he gave the instructions for the coach to be sent over the edge…and, yes, I saw his face clear.' Jeb frowned, then, 'He had the look of a gentleman. Perhaps one of Harding's friends?'

'Yes, I think you may have hit upon it,' Jack said and pressed the heel of his hand to his temple as he tried to pluck a thought from his jumbled memory. 'There was someone in London…a man who was always with him. I remember that I confronted him over something.' He shook his head and sighed, closing his eyes for a moment in pain. 'Never mind, it will come to me.'

'Harding must have had many acquaintances, my lord—but I do not recall the man I saw that night being at the club when you challenged him.

Though to be honest I did not look at anyone else much.'

'Perhaps he was not…' Jack sighed and then a knock sounded and the next moment someone poked his head round the door.

'May I come in?' Phipps asked. 'I rode over to visit with me cousin and was told of your injury. I understand you wish to speak with me?'

'I'll go and join in the search,' Jeb said. 'If you require anything more, my lord?'

'No, go and join the search. I'll speak to you later.'

'Well,' Phipps said, approaching the bed after Jeb had gone. 'I do not like the sound of this, Jack. Someone wants you dead, or out of the way at least—and what's this about a search?'

'Charlotte may be missing,' Jack said. 'The damnable thing is that I'm stuck here and cannot look for her myself.'

'Yes, that must irk you,' Phipps agreed. 'I'm more than willing to assist in any way. I'll ride round the villages and ask if anyone has seen anything of her, if you wish?'

'She would not have left the estate after what happened yesterday,' Jack said. He rubbed at his shoulder and cursed. 'Do you recall in London—

there was a man always at Harding's side, the pair of them went most places together. I'm damned if I can remember his name.'

'Do you mean Patterson? Thickset fellow, not ill looking, but sails close to the wind. I heard that he left town in a hurry after Harding had that seizure and only just ahead of his creditors.'

Jack's frown cleared and he grinned. 'Thanks, Phipps, it had slipped my mind for a moment, but it was him. In debt, was he? I hadn't heard that.'

'You were too busy with other things,' Phipps said and gave him a hard look. 'Do you not think it is time you took me into your confidence, old fellow? I'd swear there's more going on here than I yet know.'

Jack hesitated, then nodded and beckoned him closer. 'Yes, well, I do not wish everyone to know, but there is an old mystery and one I am determined to solve...'

Despite the advice of the physician, who called to see how he was the next morning, Jack was shaved and dressed when Phipps arrived. He'd brought his cousin and some of his grooms with him, for they were going to spread the search out beyond the estate. Every inch of it had been searched the previous afternoon and evening, but apart from a small scrap of silk on a rose bush, no further trace of Charlotte had been found.

'We'll find her,' Phipps assured him. 'He won't harm her, Jack. The man isn't a fool. He must know that you would not rest until he was caught and punished. No, he wants something from you and he's taken her as his surety for payment.'

'I hope you're right,' Jack said, grimacing as he felt the pain in his shoulder.

'Are you sure you should be up?'

'It's merely soreness from the wound itself,' Jack stated firmly. 'Yesterday I could hardly stand, but I'm all right to join the search now.'

'Would it not be better if you waited here? In case there is a ransom note?'

'I can't ride, but Hillsborough will drive me,' Jack said. 'There are places I know…secret hidden places that others might not think to look. I can't just stay here not knowing whether she is—' He choked off the words. 'If anything happens to her…'

'You really care for her.' Phipps looked at him in surprise. 'In town I wasn't sure. You've never been one for romance. I thought you were a confirmed bachelor for a long time, though I knew you'd have to marry for an heir. I thought that was it— She was the kind of girl who would give you an heir without being too much of the clinging wife, content with what you could give her...'

Jack's gaze narrowed. 'You thought she accepted me for the title and fortune?'

His memory was still hazy, still jumbled. Charlotte herself had told him that it was to be a marriage of convenience and perhaps that was all it had been. Yet he'd felt that she cared for him deeply and he...these past few days he'd felt something stronger than mere liking.

'It was the impression you gave me, Jack. No offence. I did not think it a love match then, for neither of you gave any sign of it.'

'I'm not offended,' Jack said, but was thoughtful. 'Perhaps it may have started that way, but I find it almost impossible to think of a future without her.'

Jack spoke instinctively, yet Phipps had raised a tiny seed of doubt in his mind. He did not truly know Charlotte and she was a self-confessed adventuress in that she had been willing to take that necklace by stealth. Could he be certain that she was the charming innocent girl he'd thought her and not a scheming adventuress? Had she taken him just for his fortune?

'She is the woman I intended to marry.' His inner instinct told him that he must continue with his plans. 'If she has been abducted, I shall not rest until I find her.'

'Then I wish you much happiness for the future, and I give you my word we'll find her—and we'll get to the bottom of your father's death as well. You have a lot of friends, Jack, there isn't one of us that wouldn't answer your call. All you have to do is make it.'

'Thank you.' Jack's smile was grateful and yet a little wistful. 'I just pray that we find her alive and unharmed. The rest seems hardly to matter at the moment.'

Chapter Fourteen

When Charlotte opened her eyes it was to pitch-blackness. She was instantly aware of a dull headache and a nasty taste in her mouth. She moved cautiously and realised that she was lying on the ground on a blanket and what she thought might be a bundle of straw, which pricked her flesh.

Where on earth was she? She sat up in sudden fear and hit her head on something hard. Smothering the cry that rose to her lips, she tried to remember what had happened to her. She'd been thinking of picking some roses for Jack's room when…someone came up behind her. She'd been rendered unconscious by something foul…strong, like ether, she thought. Whoever had put that filthy stuff over her nose and mouth must have brought her here—wherever she was.

Now that her first panic was over, Charlotte

began to think and take note of what she could smell and hear. It was impossible to see, but she could move and feel, and she guessed that she was lying on boards of some kind, a heap of straw covered by a blanket was the only bed she had. No wonder she ached everywhere. She must have been lying here for hours. Her sense of smell was acute and she thought she must be in a barn, because as well as the smell of straw she could smell stronger odours…horses and their waste. As if to confirm her suspicions, she heard a soft nicker, and then a faint shaft of light came through a crack above her and she realised that she was in the loft of a stable.

Thank goodness she had not tried to find her way in the dark for she could easily have fallen over the edge. She moved her legs and arms, discovering that thick ropes bound her. Her wrists and ankles felt sore for whoever had captured her had tied her securely. She'd been heavily drugged and her captor had left her here, where he thought she must be safe for a few hours. Where was he—here in the stable?

'Are you there?' she whispered in a croaking voice that sounded nothing like her own. Her throat was dry and sore and she was aware of a strong desire for water. 'I need a drink of water...'

No reply came and the small amount of light disappeared as swiftly as it had come. Charlotte was afraid to move lest she slip over the edge, but whatever was providing the light obliged her by coming back and stronger than before. She thought it must be the moon, sliding in and out behind the clouds.

She must take her chance now, because everyone would be worried about her. She was worried for Jack. He would think she did not wish to visit him... No, of course he wouldn't; they would not tell him while he was ill. The thought comforted her. She did not want him to lie there and worry about her, because she was going to get out of here herself.

The safest way to explore her prison was to edge herself forward on her bottom, Charlotte decided, for with her ankles bound she could not stand. She didn't think the loft was high enough for her to stand in any case. Somehow she must find a way of getting free of these ropes. She tried to pull her wrists apart and found they gave a little, but no matter how hard she tugged they would not come free. Inching forward on her bottom, she sat on something hard and gave a cry as a sharp point pricked her flesh.

It must be some kind of instrument used in the stables. Wriggling off it, she leaned over to see and discovered that someone had carelessly left a long blade after using it to cut string from the bales of straw used for bedding. Had her hands been bound behind her, she did not think she could have managed to pick up the long curved blade, but because they were tied before her, she was able to get the handle, secure it with her knees and position the blade against the ropes.

The only way she could hope to cut them was to rub the rope against the sharp edge and each time she did so, she felt the sting of the hemp cutting into her flesh, but slowly, painfully, she felt the threads of the rope give way and after an age had passed, it gave way sufficiently for her to slip first one hand and then the other free. She felt the stickiness of blood and knew that she'd cut herself while slicing through the rope, but her fingers found only a small graze and, though it stung terribly, she did not think she would come to harm, for the blade had been well sharpened and was not rusty.

Once her hands were free it was the work of

moments to cut the rope binding her ankles. As the last strand fell away, she drew a sigh of relief. Her captor must believe her well and truly secured or he would not have left her alone in the stable, but at any moment he might come to make sure she was still drugged.

She must get out of here! If only the light were better, for in the dark she could easily fall and break a limb or even her neck. How to descend to the stable itself? There must have been a ladder, she reasoned, for her abductor could not have got her up here without one.

There were sacks of what felt like grain or some kind of feed for the horses. By crawling cautiously on her hands and knees, she discovered that the piles were high at the back of her, and lower towards the front, so she reasoned that must mean the lower piles were nearer the edge. It wasn't possible to see the edge of the loft floor, and every now and then she had to stop because the moon went behind another cloud and the loft became pitch-black. Eventually, she found the edge; reaching very carefully in front of her and moving slowly, she crawled from one side of the large stable block to the other. The ladder had been taken away. Of course it had. If she was fool enough to jump, she could break her leg or even her neck.

Damn him! Charlotte felt the anger rising inside her. What kind of a man would abduct a defenceless woman and leave her in a barn alone, knowing that if she stumbled in the dark she could fall to her death? Clearly he did not care what happened to her. Or perhaps he'd thought she would stay drugged for ages and meant to return in the morning?

Well, she wasn't still unconscious and she was damned if she was going to stay here and wait for him to decide what to do with her. Her head might ache and she might feel sick, but somehow she was going to get out of this place.

Suddenly, Charlotte laughed. She wasn't a defenceless woman and if she could climb up wisteria clinging to the wall of a house, she could almost certainly get down from this stupid loft. It was a wooden floor and therefore it had to be supported by struts, vertical as well as horizontal. As the moon lit up her prison again, she hung over the edge and looked down; there was a wooden post just a little to her right, and, of course, a wooden structure separating the horses' stalls one from the other.

Moving cautiously to her right, she pulled up her skirts and tucked them into her sash so that her legs were free, then she cautiously put one leg over the edge, moving it until she felt the wooden post. She slid her foot down and then kicked out until she felt the wooden structure of the partition. Lowering her other leg, she curled it round the post as she let go, and caught at it with her hands, sliding her body down. It was rough and she felt the splinters enter her flesh and gave a cry of pain. The horse in the nearest stall nickered at her and she made soothing noises. For a moment as she let go of the post she teetered and then fell across the soft warm back of the unfortunate horse. It snorted uneasily and moved as if startled, but she soothed it and, sliding down to the straw at its feet, stroked the long back and then its nose. The horse quietened, nickering again as if welcoming the company.

Charlotte felt her way to the front of the stall and found the door. Both the top and bottom half were closed and bolted from the inside, but it was the work of a moment to pull them back. As soon as she opened the top half, the moonlight showed her there were three horses in the stables and she noticed the tack hanging on one wall near a side door that was used as the entrance to the stable. It was a secure way of keeping the horses, for one must enter that way to gain access rather than through the individual stalls. What her captor had not considered was that she was already inside.

An idea came: if she let the other horses go free it would serve to delay any attempt to follow her. She took a bridle and saddle, and slipped them onto the horse that had seemed to welcome her. Then she walked along the stables and unbolted all the doors before leading her horse out into what appeared to be a farmyard, though a much-neglected one, with no sign of any other beasts. She mounted her horse and then watched as the other horses emerged from their stables. Surprised at their sudden freedom, they did not move until she suddenly sent them scattering as she kicked her mount's flanks and dashed past on her way to the meadow she could see beyond the open gate.

She heard a shout as she cantered through the stable yard, realising that someone had roused and discovered her escape. Bending over her horse's neck instinctively, Charlotte flinched as a shot whistled past her head. She kicked lightly at the horse's flanks, urging it forward towards the open meadow and started across it; the two loose horses, startled by the shot, followed close behind her. More loud voices had joined the first and another shot was fired. Her own horse was panicked and rushed on without encouragement from her, Charlotte hanging on for dear life, the loose horses keeping pace as they fled across the wide meadow. Charlotte hoped that they would follow the instinct of their kind and keep up with her for as long as possible, because her captors might try to follow. They could not hope to catch her on foot, but once the horses were caught would surely scour the countryside looking for her.

Her elation kept her going for some minutes. She saw a gate looming ahead of her and looked for some other way of leaving the meadow, but decided that it was her only exit. Gritting her teeth, she rode at the gate and to her relief her horse soared over it, one of the loose horses following her. Charlotte's stomach seemed to fall away from her at some point. She felt slightly sick and dizzy by the time all four feet were on the ground again, but ahead of her was a wide expanse of open ground and she bent over her horse, urging it on. One loose horse kept pace for several minutes, though the other must be still in the meadow. One of the men might try to follow, but she had a head start and he would first need to catch the horse.

She had no idea of where she was and in the moonlight the countryside looked ghostly and vast. Charlotte was not even sure she was riding in the right direction, but she needed to get as far away as she could. In the morning she would find someone who could tell her the way to Ellingham. For now all she needed to do was to put as much distance as she could between her and anyone who might pursue her.

'No luck?' Jack asked as Sir Mordred entered the dining room. He had just returned himself. Had his shoulder not pained him damnably, he would still have been out looking. Hillsborough had seen that his colour was ghastly and insisted on bringing him home.

'You must rest for a while, eat something, and then we'll try again, my lord.'

'Yes, of course.' Had Jack been able to drive himself he might have told his faithful groom to go to hell, but the man deserved something to eat and Jack knew that if he did not drink a brandy he would probably collapse. Now he frowned as his future father-in-law shook his head and looked grim. 'Do not give up, sir. We'll find her. I promise you.'

'Yes, I hope to God you are right.'

'There are still a few places left to search. I thought of somewhere, but I'm afraid I havn't the strength to go on. I shall go out again now—and you must rest, sir. Charlie won't forgive me if she discovers her father is ill.'

'Why do we not go together?' Sir Mordred asked. 'I do not know the area well. It seems useless to waste time on the villages, for she would not have gone that far herself. If she were abducted, he would have taken her somewhere isolated.' He hesitated as the butler entered. 'Yes, have you news?'

'A note has arrived for Captain Delsey.'

Jack moved towards him, snatching up the sealed paper and breaking the wedge of wax. He read swiftly and swore, then handed it to Charlotte's father.

'Good grief! The man must be a lunatic,' Sir Mordred cried. 'Fifty thousand! Who would pay such a sum? Even a tenth of it would be impossible for me.'

'But not for me,' Jack said. 'It would take time, but it could be done.'

'You would not consider it, even with your wealth—'

'If it is the only way to have her safely back,' Jack said grimly, 'it must and shall be done.'

'Surely you will go on looking for her? To give in to such blackmail would go much against the grain with me, Delsey.'

'What is money against her life?' Jack smiled grimly. 'I would gladly sacrifice my estates in the north for Charlie's sake. It is my duty to protect her, for this abduction was meant to punish me. Even if I did not care for her I would be bound to do all I could for her, and as it is I am deeply concerned for her safety.'

'Yes, but...' Sir Mordred was clearly distressed at the idea of Jack being pushed into such a sacrifice, but even as he paused there was a commotion in the house and then one of the footmen burst in, looking wild-eyed and excited. 'What is it, man? My daughter—'

'My lord,' Johnson said, 'it's your lady. She rode into the courtyard not a moment ago, exhausted and near to fainting, but she's here—and alive.'

'My God!' Jack took a step forward, swallowing convulsively as the emotion swept over him. 'Where is she, Johnson?'

'Mr Scott took her. He carried her up to her room.Her mother and Mrs Moore went with her. We've sent for the doctor, my lord.'

'Yes, that was right.' Jack felt suddenly faint and sat down on the nearest chair. 'Good grief, I'm shaking like a leaf. Was she alone? How did she get away? Does anyone know what happened?'

'No, my lord. We saw her and Mr Scott reached her just as she fell from the horse. Somehow she'd held on, but she must have been riding for a long time for the horse was sweating and she... Well, she looked close to death, sir.'

'I must see her.' Jack's strength came back. He strode from the room, taking the stairs two at a time in his haste. Sir Mordred was running to keep up with him. They reached Charlotte's apartments at the same time and Jack entered, closely followed by her father.

'How dare you come in here?' Charlotte's mother rounded on them, her voice thick with fury. 'This is my daughter's room for the duration of her stay here and I will thank you to remember it. As soon as she is recovered I am taking her home—where she will be safe, which she is not thanks to you, sir.'

'My dear,' Sir Mordred said, 'please consider whom you are speaking to. We must consider Charlotte's happiness. She cares deeply for Captain Delsey and it must be for her to decide whether or not—'

'No,' Jack said clearly, his voice carrying further than he realised in the sudden silence. 'I agree with Lady Stevens, sir. As soon as Charlotte is well enough, you must take her home with you. We shall postpone the wedding until such time as I know she will be safe here— If that can be achieved, which for the moment I doubt since only carelessness could have led to her abduction. It might be better if she were no longer connected with this family if we cannot guarantee her safety.'

Lying in clean fresh sheets, having her forehead bathed with cool water, Charlotte heard his voice as if from a distance. She wanted to call out, to tell him that she would never leave him, but her throat hurt and she could not speak. Whatever that wicked man had given her had made her throat very sore and she had not stopped to drink or rest until she'd reached the safety of Ellingham. She'd been on the verge of collapse when she arrived, but with her head upon the cool pillows she was fully aware of what she'd just heard.

Jack was saying that she must go home. He wanted to postpone the wedding, to call it off. He no longer wanted to marry her. Clearly, he no longer considered his bargain worthwhile. It had never been more than a marriage of convenience on his side—and now he wished he had never offered for her. He wanted to send her home…away from him, for her safety, but also because she'd caused him so much trouble. She could not bear it that he should send her away, but her mother would not allow her to stay here unless Jack insisted. And he had agreed with Mama.

Realising that she had finally tried his patience too hard, Charlotte closed her eyes, letting the tears trickle down her cheeks. She was too weak to protest, though the knowledge that Jack didn't truly love her was breaking her heart. It had seemed the last few days that he might truly care for her, but had he done so, he would not send her away.

He had thought she would make him a conformable wife, but she was just too much trouble. It was her fault that Jack had been shot… because she'd stolen that necklace and he'd quarrelled with Lord Harding…over her. Tears trickled down her cheeks because she knew that her wonderful dream was over. She would have to release Jack from his promise.

'It's all right, my dear,' Mrs Moore said, stroking her forehead. 'You have a nice sleep and when you wake up everything will be fine.'

Charlotte found that she was too tired to do anything but sleep, but she knew that nothing would ever be right for her again, because Jack no longer wanted to marry her.

'Are you feeling better, Charlotte?' Mama looked at her when she entered her private sitting room and found her dressed the next morning. 'The doctor said that you should stay quietly in bed for a few days.'

'I am quite recovered, Mama,' Charlotte said. 'It was just that I had been drugged and I had to ride for such a long time before I found anyone to direct me—and then I realised that I must have ridden at least ten miles in the wrong direction, so I had to turn back. I got lost twice and seemed to wander for ages, and my head started to ache.

I could barely speak loudly enough to ask the way, then I saw a sign and I knew where I was.'

'Why did you not ask for help at an inn? Someone could have sent word and your papa would have come for you in the carriage. There was no need to ride all over the countryside like a harum scarum.'

'Do not scold the child,' Sir Mordred said, entering the room at that moment. He bent to kiss Charlotte's cheek. 'I see that you are feeling better, my dear.'

'Yes, Papa,' she said. 'It was merely the aftermath of that foul drug and tiredness. I dare say Mama is right, but I had no money and I must have looked such a sight. All I could think of was that I must get home before you all went out of your minds with worry.'

'You were very brave,' her father said and sat down next to her, taking her hand in his. 'Do you feel able to tell us what happened now?'

'As much as I know,' Charlotte said. 'I was near the folly. I was thinking of picking roses for Jack... How is he, Papa? Is he recovered?'

'Yes, much better today. Yesterday he was in a deal of pain and it was made worse because he insisted on helping in the search for you.'

'Yes, of course. He would feel responsible,' Charlotte said. 'I meant to give him some roses to cheer him, but someone put a rag over my mouth and it rendered me senseless and then…I woke up in the loft of a stable. I was bound, but was able to break free of the ropes. But then I realised the ladder had been taken away…'

'How frightened you must have been!' Mama exclaimed.

'At first,' Charlotte said hesitantly. 'Then I managed to find the uprights and the dividing structures of the horses' stalls and realised I could climb down—'

'It is a wonder you did not break your neck,' her mother interrupted.

'No, Mama, I am good at climbing,' Charlotte said. 'I got some splinters in my hand and they are a little sore still, but I scrambled down and fell over the horse. It is a lovely little horse, Papa. I should like to keep it, for it did not try to throw me off or bite me—and I was able to ride away, after letting the two other horses free.'

'That was clever of you,' her father said. 'It must have hampered their pursuit—for it sounds as if there were three men who captured you.'

'Yes, I suppose there must have been,' Charlotte said. 'Though I only remember one voice as he grabbed me. He said that if I screamed he would...' She shook her head. 'I do not quite remember, but I should like to speak to Jack. There is something he should know.'

'I am sure Captain Delsey has plenty to do without listening to you, Charlotte,' her mama said harshly. 'They are still trying to find where you were taken and the culprits.'

'Don't you see, that is why I must speak to him.' Charlotte appealed to her father with a look that spoke volumes. 'If he may not come to me, then I shall come down. I must speak to him.'

'Don't fret, my love,' Papa said. 'Be damned to propriety, he shall come up to you. Lady Stevens, I should like a word with you later. Please leave me with my daughter. I have something to say to her.'

If Charlotte had not been feeling so sad she would have laughed at her mother's outraged expression, but she could not forget that Jack wanted her to go home, because he wished to postpone the wedding—perhaps for ever. There was a dull ache in her chest and she felt as if a dark shadow lay over her world.

'Well, I have acted only in my daughter's interests,' Mama said, but got up and left the room without further protest.

'Now, then, Charlie,' Papa said and took her hand in his. 'Your mama thinks you should go home and postpone the wedding, but I do not agree. It was hardly Delsey's fault that you were kidnapped. He was ill and could not oversee the arrangements. We believe that whoever abducted you was mistakenly accepted as one of the new keepers and thus able to move freely about the estate. Delsey has been reading the riot act and I imagine the men will be more alert in future. I have been taken into the marquis's confidence and I realise that some further measures must be taken to protect you both—but I cannot think you would wish to leave at this time?'

'No, Papa, I do not,' Charlotte said, then bit her lip. 'But if Jack no longer wishes to marry me...'

'Is that more of your mother's meddling?' Papa looked grave. 'I am very certain that Delsey thinks only of your safety, but I think you safer here where you can be protected. After all, what is to stop that devil snatching you from us at home?'

'I agree with you, sir,' Jack's voice spoke from the doorway. 'In my first distress at Charlotte's abduction I thought as her mama so clearly does—that she might be safer away from me. But I have since given it much thought and think we should marry as soon as possible. I have taken steps to make certain that she will be properly protected in future. I am distressed that she should have been subjected to such an ordeal.'

'Then there is no more to be said.' Papa rose and touched Charlotte's head in passing. 'I shall leave you together. I think Charlotte has much to tell you, Delsey.'

'Thank you, sir.' Jack walked to the door with him, then returned to take the seat next to her. His gaze was soft and yet grave as he looked at her. 'Forgive me, my dearest. I would not have had you suffer as you have these past few days for all the world.'

'It was not your fault. I should have been aware. Besides, I was more afraid when you were shot than when I awoke in that stable...'

'You were taken to a stable? Do you know where?'

'I'm not sure, but I think the nearest village was signposted as Wintersmere...' She faltered as his eyes narrowed. 'I cannot be certain for I was riding so fast at first, and then I saw no one or even a house for miles. Mama thought I should have gone to an inn, but indeed I did not pass one for such ages and by then I was nearly home, Jack.'

'You would not have seen an inn out that way, at least none that would be safe for you to frequent. I believe I know the village—it is but a hamlet in truth, with few houses in the district, and they are mainly farmhouses and set back off the road.'

'I'm sure it was a farmyard that the stables led into,' Charlotte said and nodded, 'but disused. I saw no sign of stock or even a few hens, though it was night when I escaped and the moon would keep disappearing behind the clouds.'

Jack touched her wrists, which had been bound with clean linen. 'You were hurt. He shall pay for that, whoever he is,' he vowed. 'When I find him, I shall thrash him to an inch of his life and he will spend what is left of it in prison—if I have my way it will not be long before he pays the ultimate price.'

'Oh, Jack,' she said brokenly. 'You said it was not my fault you were attacked—but it was indeed. You see, I know who abducted me. He only spoke a few words, but I could never forget those sneering tones—it was Mr Patterson. The man who chased me through the park. Lord Harding must have sent him to be revenged on us.'

'No, my dearest Charlie. Lord Harding is dead.' She gasped and felt the chill touch her neck. 'Do not blame yourself or me, for the blame is another's. It appears Harding had a visitor the night he died and that person distressed him so much that he had a severe attack and this time died of it. I believe that person may have been Patterson. I dare say Harding had been his banker for some time and he feared losing his source of income. Very likely he threatened him with exposure if he did not receive more money and that was likely the cause of Harding's seizure and subsequent death.'

'I did not like him, but I did not wish him dead.'

'You might have done for you had cause, but I had more, Charlie. Harding paid to have my father killed…or more accurately his cousin was the paymaster for them both. Harding arranged it and I believe that Patterson was one of the rogues that carried out the foul deed. Indeed, now that you have named him as your abductor, I am certain of it.'

'You know they killed your father?' She looked at him in shock.

'I knew that Harding was involved, but then I realised that he could not be the instigator of what happened to me, and then you. Only a man with a guilty secret to protect would go to such lengths to warn me off. Therefore it must have been one of the assassins—and that man is Patterson.'

'If he wanted you silenced, why did he not kill you—and me?'

'Because he also wanted money and Harding's money was no longer available to him,' Jack said grimly. She was trembling and he held her hand tighter. 'It seems that fifty thousand pounds was the price he put on you.'

'Jack! Oh, no, how could he think you would pay such a ridiculous sum?'

'He must have known that you are more precious to me than my estate, my horses or my very life,' Jack said. 'I would have paid his price and more to have you back.' A slow smile started in his eyes. 'But poor fool that he was, he underestimated you, Charlie. He did not know that you would escape and so save me from falling prey to his greed.'

Charlotte swallowed hard. 'You couldn't really think me worth so much…' she whispered. 'I thought… I thought you were sending me home because you no longer wished to wed me. That I had caused you too much trouble.'

Jack stared and then the penny dropped. 'You heard me speaking to your mama just after you arrived back in a state of exhaustion. I was at my wit's end, Charlie. I could not think straight, as I told your father just now—and I was angry that we had not protected you as we ought. How he got to you with so many men patrolling the grounds I cannot imagine. In the circumstances, I thought perhaps you would be safer at your father's house, but then I realised that Patterson would try again. He is deeply in debt and needs money—to live abroad, I dare say. Nothing will stop him, for he knows that I mean to see him hang if he remains in England. If he had killed me he would have been safe from justice, but without money he was lost—and so he decided to extort money rather than finish me off.'

'What are we to do?' she asked. 'We cannot live in fear of our lives.'

'Nor shall we.' Jack smiled and kissed her hand, holding it firmly. 'This morning I went to see a friend of mine who happens to be the local magistrate. I lodged a complaint against Patterson and gave a good description—and offered a reward for his capture. The result is that there is now a warrant out for his arrest.'

'Jack!' Charlotte stared at him in wonder. 'How could you give a description of Patterson to the magistrate? Do you remember what he looks like?'

'I remember everything,' Jack told her, his finger moving over her hand in a caress. 'There are strangely a few gaps, and some of it is like a jumble of pictures that do not quite make sense, but most things are clear to me. I remember that night in London when that brute was pursuing you, the way he threatened you. Had my memory not been lost I might have realised it was he who shot me the first time, for I caught a glimpse of him riding away just before I lost consciousness, though I could not see his face clearly.'

'How wicked he must be,' Charlotte said and looked at him anxiously. 'I have almost lost you twice, Jack. Please do not let him come near you again, my love.'

'I shall not,' he promised, but he was lying, though she had no sense of it. 'I will visit you again as soon as I can, my love. Stay here and rest today. Promise me you will not venture outside again unless either I or one of my people are with you.'

'Yes, of course,' she gave her word easily. 'I cannot wait for our wedding day, Jack. You will not postpone it, whatever Mama says?'

'Believe me,' he murmured huskily. 'You could not be more eager than I, my dearest one. I shall marry you the moment I can and no one will stop me.'

He bent down to kiss her softly on the mouth, before leaving her.

No one would stop him, Jack vowed silently as he went out of the room, down the stairs and joined his friends waiting for him in the hall below. No one would stop him, because he intended that Patterson and his friends would be dead before nightfall...

Chapter Fifteen

Charlotte was glad enough to rest for the remainder of the morning, but after eating most of the temptingly light lunch that Cook had sent up for her on a tray, she became restless. Rising from her comfortable chair, she walked through to her bedchamber and looked out of the window. It was a beautiful afternoon and the sunshine called her, but she'd promised Jack she would not leave her room that day.

She returned to her sitting room just as someone knocked and called out that they might enter. Seeing the marquis step rather hesitantly into the room, she gave a cry of pleasure and went to greet him.

'How lovely to see you, sir. I was just wishing I could go out, but now I am quite content. Please will you not sit down?'

'Why shouldn't you go out for a little walk if you wish?'

'Jack asked me not to, because he thought I should rest—and I suppose he was anxious lest the assassin should return.'

'I do not fear it,' the marquis said. 'We have guards patrolling every inch of the grounds. Come, my dear, walk with me. You will be quite safe, I promise.' He patted the pocket of his coat. 'I am prepared should the rogue be bold enough to try it. I was counted to be a pretty shot when I was young, you know.'

Charlotte laughed in delight, for his old-fashioned gallantry was so appealing. She retrieved a lacy shawl and placed it around her shoulders, then took his arm, smiling up at him.

'Now I do not fear anything,' she said and twinkled up at him. An answering response lit his faded eyes, making him look young again. 'It is such a beautiful day, much too nice to be cooped up inside.'

'Empty!' Jack growled in disgust as they broke into the farmhouse and discovered their prey had flown. 'I had hoped they might have lingered long enough for us to corner the beast in his den.'

'He must have gone almost at once,' Jeb said after touching the black range in the kitchen. 'It is cold—and you can see the remains of a meal left on the table.'

'I'll take a look upstairs,' Jack said and felt angry that his quarry had outwitted him. He'd banked on the man taking it for granted that he would be too ill to come after Charlotte's abductors.

He went upstairs, searching from room to room. Three had been used, the beds left in a mess and clothes abandoned on the floor. Clearly they had been woken suddenly, perhaps by the noise of the horses stampeding to freedom. When they discovered that the girl they had treated so badly had managed to escape, they had fled in a panic, leaving many of their possessions behind.

'Jack?' He turned as he heard Jeb's voice. 'They've left you a note. I opened it—by God, he's tricked us nicely. You'd better read what it says. I've sent some of the men on ahead.'

'What the hell...?' Jack seized the piece of paper and scanned the few lines, a savage curse leaving his lips as he crushed it into a ball and threw it down. 'By heaven, I'll break the devil's neck for this!'

Jeb picked up the discarded threat and pocketed it, for evidence if needed.

By the time you return she'll be gone and you'll never see her again unless you pay the fifty thousand pounds I asked for.

'He is damned sure of himself. I do not see how he can hope to get to her when the grounds are crawling with armed men. If they see anyone suspicious, they will grab him and if he resists...'

'They've been told to shoot anyone who avoids their challenge.' Jack grunted. 'What if a gentleman calls openly and asks to see me, claiming to be a friend? If he is bold enough for this, he will try anything.'

Jeb nodded, then said, 'Aye, I think he might, sir. Yet surely he cannot reach her room without being challenged.'

'We must get back there,' Jack said and went off at a run to where his groom stood waiting with the horses. 'We need to find the shortest way back, Hillsborough. You know this part of the country best—get us home as swiftly as you can.'

Jack was frowning as he mounted his horse.

Would this nightmare never end? He had hoped to finish it by cornering Patterson, and either thrashing him or putting a ball through his head. The man was clever and had anticipated Jack's revenge. He could only pray that Charlotte was still safe in the house, for surely his servants would not allow the man to get near her there…

'Well, that was quite delightful, my dear. I enjoy our walks together and I shall miss you when Jack takes you off to his own estate.'

'Surely we shall spend much of our time in the country here with you, sir.' Charlotte looked up at him lovingly. 'My grandfather died before I was old enough to know him—may I take you for my own?'

'I should be delighted if you would adopt me,' the marquis said and chuckled as they stepped inside the cool of the hall. 'Now if you will excuse me, my dear, I must speak to Evans about something. Please go into the parlour and Mrs Moore will bring us tea in a few minutes. I shall not keep you waiting long.'

'Yes, Grandfather,' Charlotte said and kissed his cheek. 'I think I will go up and wash my hands before tea.'

They parted and she ran lightly up the stairs to her room. Charlotte was humming one of her favourite tunes as she opened the door and went in, throwing off her shawl and walking through to the bedroom. Hearing the door of the dressing room open, she did not turn, but said, 'I shall not change for tea today, Betty.'

On receiving no answer, she turned quickly and saw that it was not her maid, but a man she remembered only too well, though he had dressed in the garments of a footman and wore a black wig to disguise himself. Anyone seeing him from the rear might not give him a second look. The man was clearly a master of deceit and had managed to evade the guards for a second time.

'So, you escaped me last time,' Patterson said. 'It will not happen again, Miss Stevens.' He gestured with his arm and she saw he was holding a pistol cocked and ready. 'If you try to resist, I shall kill whoever answers your call. I intend to keep you alive until I get my money, but I do not care who else I kill.'

'What makes you think Captain Delsey will pay you anything? Why should he?'

'Because he wants you,' the man snarled. 'Either I get my money or I'll see you dead.'

'You killed Jack's father,' Charlotte said, refusing to panic even though a scream was building inside her. 'You are going to hang, Mr Patterson. Even if I am not alive to see it, it will happen.'

He had taken a few steps towards her, jerking the pistol to make her move towards the door, but she refused to budge and stood stubbornly, uncertain of what to do for the best. If she screamed for help someone would come, but this devil was desperate enough to do as he threatened and kill whoever appeared. No, she must keep calm and let him believe she was cowed by his bullying. She had got away from him once, surely she could do so again.

Charlotte saw that she must do as he ordered. She took three steps towards the door and then froze as it opened.

'No, do not come in,' she cried, but the door was pushed open wide and her mother walked in. 'Mama!' Charlotte cried in dismay. 'Please go while you can!'

'What is this, Charlotte? It is coming to something when I am not permitted to enter—' The words died away as Mama saw the wicked pistol pointing at her, but not for long. Not even an armed man could silence the outraged mother.

'What do you imagine you are doing in my daughter's bedchamber, sir? How dare you come in here! I shall not stand for this. I demand that you leave this instant!'

'Mama, he is the man who abducted me,' Charlotte tried to warn her, but her mother was too angry to listen. Seeing the look of shock in Patterson's eyes at being addressed in such a fashion, Charlotte looked around desperately for something to distract him. The silver paperknife on her dressing table was just within distance of her hand if he did not notice her reaching for it.

'I do not care who he is,' Mama declared, drawing herself up in a picture of outraged propriety. 'I will not have strange gentlemen in my daughter's private rooms. You should be ashamed of yourself, sir!'

She bustled forward, intending Charlotte knew not what, but Patterson's uncertainty when faced with an outraged matron would have been comical had he no pistol in his hand. It seemed that years of polite society manners had temporarily given him pause, for gentlewomen of Lady Stevens's stature had been known to make strong men weep when on the receiving end of their vitriol. In the instant that he was still deciding what to do for the best, Charlotte snatched up the paperknife and darted forward, stabbing him in his arm. He screamed and the pistol dropped from his fingers. Mama dived for it faster than her daughter would have believed possible, snatched it up and then backed away from him, the pistol wavering unsteadily in her hand. Patterson hesitated, snarled with rage and went after her. Charlotte screamed loudly for help as the two closed. Mama was brave, but he must be too strong for her. Charlotte rushed into the attack, ready to stab him again, in the back this time, but before she could strike the pistol went off, the sound of it shattering.

'Mama,' Charlotte screamed just as the door of her room was sent flying open and two of the footmen rushed in. 'Oh, Mama, please! He has shot her!'

However, even as she spoke what she thought the truth, Patterson staggered back, clutching at his stomach, blood trickling through his splayed fingers as he held himself, staring at the woman who had just shot him in disbelief.

'Charlotte, are you all right?' Papa appeared in the doorway, just as his wife gave a little cry and fainted into his arms. The front of her silk gown was spattered with blood. 'Good grief, has he killed her?'

'I think the pistol went off as they fought for it,' Charlotte said. 'Mama picked it up after I stabbed him in the arm and he tried to wrest it from her, but…somehow it just went off—'

Mama was stirring. Her eyelids fluttered. 'Is Charlotte all right?' she whispered through white lips. 'That wicked man was going to take her and I couldn't let him. Have I killed him? I meant to…'

'Hush, my dearest,' Papa said and glanced at the footmen, who, being well trained, looked blank, as if they had heard nothing. 'He was trying to take the pistol from you and it went off by accident. That is what happened, is it not, Charlotte?'

'Yes, Papa. Mama was simply trying to protect me. I shall of course be happy to tell the magistrate what happened.'

'Yes, I thought you would,' he said. 'I am going to take your mama to her room. She is distraught and needs to lie down for a while. Can you manage here, my love?'

'Yes, Papa…' Charlotte heard the sound of running feet and then Jack burst in, followed by Hillsborough, Jeb Scott and two of the grooms.

'What in the world is happening?' Mama whispered faintly. 'This is quite improper...quite improper...'

'Yes, my dearest,' her husband comforted her. 'We shall have to overlook it this once in the circumstances. I'm going to put you to bed and then Mrs Moore will bring you a nice cup of tea. Now that Delsey is here, I am certain we can leave all this business to him.'

He swept his wife from the room and she went, quite overwhelmed by his mastery, and perhaps the shock of realising that had the pistol turned the other way, it might have been her lying on the floor.

'Charlotte...' Jack gave the now very still body of Patterson a cursory look. 'You are unharmed? I cannot apologise enough for what happened. It is damned carelessness! How could he possibly have got into your room?'

'He came through the dressing room...' Charlotte heard a muffled cry. 'Oh, dear, I think perhaps he tied up my poor Betty! And he must have stolen a uniform. We may find that he has overpowered one of the footmen.'

'It was my best uniform he took,' Johnson said. 'When I discovered it had been taken from the laundry room, where it had been steamed and pressed, I spoke to Smith here and we came straight to your room, for I thought it must be him. Though how he managed to get into the house, I don't know.'

'I dare say we shall discover that he forced an entry somewhere below stairs,' Jack said. 'Perhaps Betty may be able to tell us more. She sounds in distress…'

'I'll see to her, miss,' Johnson said and disappeared into the dressing room.

'Get him out of here.' Jack nodded his head at the dead man. 'You cannot stay here, Charlotte. I'll have the maids move you into your new apartments next to mine.'

'Thank you. I do not think I could sleep here after this.'

Charlotte allowed herself to be led away, Jack's arm around her. She leaned against his shoulder, feeling comforted by his strength.

'Mama will not be arrested, will she?' Looking up at him, she saw the grim expression in his eyes. 'I've told everyone it was an accident, but I think… I believe she intended to kill him…'

'Good for her,' Jack said. 'Your mother has more courage than I gave her credit for. I thank

God that she did what she did, for it might otherwise have been too late. No, my darling, she will not be arrested for heroically saving her daughter from a murderer.'

Charlotte laughed a little hysterically until he caught her to him, holding her and stroking her hair, as she started to tremble and then to weep into his shoulder.

'Yes, cry if you want to, my darling. You've had more to put up with than any young girl should.'

'No, it is foolish, for it is all over now, isn't it?' She drew back and gazed into his eyes. 'No one else will try to murder us in our own home?'

'I sincerely hope not,' he replied with a tight smile. 'I believe it is over, Charlie. I cannot imagine how Patterson managed to get into the house, even via the servants' entrance. Be sure that I shall discover it and if anyone was careless...' He left the threat unfinished and Charlotte shook her head at him.

'I think a man as devious as Mr Patterson would get in even if he had to kill to do it,' Charlotte said. 'Perhaps he simply pretended to be one of the new keepers, as before—until he found that uniform and realised it would allow him to use the servants' stairs. If seen from behind, who would think anything wrong in a footman being there? He was desperate…so desperate that he would have done anything.'

'Tell me, how did your mama manage to get the pistol from him?'

Charlotte told him how angry her mother had been to discover the man in her daughter's bedchamber, how she'd demanded he leave and advanced on him—and then how Charlotte had stabbed his arm, causing him to drop the pistol.

'I have never seen Mama move so fast. Indeed, I did not think she could.' Charlotte frowned in thought. 'I am not sure she could have killed him had he done nothing, for her hand wavered, but he tried to wrest the pistol from her and somehow…'

'It went off by accident,' Jack said and smiled into her eyes. 'Better for everyone that we stick to our story. Your mama may have intended it— and if she did I salute her, for not many ladies of her breeding would have had the courage to do it. However, in the eyes of the world, it must and shall be a fortunate accident.'

'Mama was determined to protect me,' Charlotte said and then she was laughing. 'I have always found her strict notions of propriety irritating, but I can only admire her for having the strength to stand up for them in the face of a loaded pistol.'

'Had she not, I might have lost you,' Jack said and his eyes seemed to devour her with their intensity. 'I shall never be able to thank her enough.'

They had been walking as they talked and now they had reached the door to the apartments, which Charlotte knew would be hers when they were married. Jack opened the door and they went into the pretty sitting room, which was decorated in various shades of buttery cream, pale green and silver.

'This is so pretty,' Charlotte said. 'Mrs Moore said you asked for it to be done just before we came down, but it was not finished until last week. I have been longing to see inside.'

'I asked her not to show you until it was ready,' he said. 'Have a look at the rest of it and see if you can be comfortable here.'

'Of course I can, Jack. I can be happy anywhere that you are.'

'The door to the dressing room has a key, which you can lock on your side,' he told her with a rueful look. 'Your mama may not feel it enough to keep me out—but I promise not to come through until we are married,'

'That cannot be soon enough for me,' Charlotte replied and lifted her face for his kiss. 'I love you so much, Jack.'

He held her to him and she felt his arousal through the thin silk of her gown, melting into his arms as they kissed again and again, until Jack drew back and released her with a smile.

'I think we should go down for tea, do you not, my love? I must be able to assure your mama that your innocence has not and will not be violated…that your chastity will remain untouched until our wedding night and if we stay here I am not sure that will remain the truth.'

'Must you really give that promise?' Charlotte asked, looking up at him wickedly. 'Well, if you must, then I think we should bring the wedding forward—don't you?'

'You are a wicked girl,' Jack said with a moan of need and gathered her into his arms, 'but I am very willing to wed you tomorrow, my darling.'

'I think we must wait three weeks, unless you happen to have a special licence?'

Jack chuckled, bending to drop a kiss on her brow. 'It so happens that I had my secretary procure the very thing…and I believe we should hold the ball next week, as arranged, and marry two days later.'

Charlotte's agreement was lost beneath his soft but demanding lips, and it was only some ten minutes later that she remembered the marquis was expecting her for tea.

'Oh, dear,' she said. 'I do believe we shall have to request some more hot water for it will have gone quite cold.'

'We had best go and join Grandfather, he is bound to worry until he sees for himself that you are perfectly well.'

Chapter Sixteen

'Well, Charlotte,' Mama said, looking at her in the beautiful white silk-tulle-and-lace gown that had been made for her in London by a French seamstress. 'I am sure you make a beautiful bride—and though I cannot like the sleeping arrangements Viscount Delsey insisted upon these past two weeks, I believe you are still innocent.'

'Yes, Mama, of course,' Charlotte replied, avoiding her mother's sharp gaze. She was still untouched in the sense her mama meant, but she had learned to respond to Jack's lovemaking, even though he had shown admirable restraint in the face of her willingness to give all that he desired. 'Jack gave his word he would not come through the connecting door until our wedding night—and he is too honourable to break it.'

'And so I should hope. I dare say you do not

need instruction on how to behave once you are married. I should have to be blind not to see the way you react when he so much as touches your hand.'

'I love him, Mama. Is that so very wrong?'

'Not at all. I am glad of it,' Mama said and smiled. 'When you have daughters you will want what is best for them, my love, as I did for you, and if they are lucky enough to find love you will be happy for them. My scolding has always been for your own good.'

'Mama, you may scold me as much as you wish,' Charlotte said and hugged her. 'After what you did... You saved me from that dreadful man. Even had Jack arrived in time, Patterson would not have hesitated to shoot him, or any of the footmen. It was your manner that threw him off balance. The look on his face as you berated him...' She broke into happy laughter. 'Truly, it was so comical!'

'Well, I am glad you can laugh over it,' Mama said and then a look of pure mischief came to her eyes. 'I've eaten far more terrifying men for breakfast, my love. If he thought he could take you away under my nose, he was much mistaken.'

'Oh, Mama, I do love you,' Charlotte said. 'I

never truly understood you until that day, but I do now—and I shall try to follow your example when I have daughters of my own.'

'You must try to give Delsey a son first,' her mama instructed. 'Not that he will mind, for I never saw a man so besotted in my life. I dare say you will twist him round your little finger.'

Charlotte smiled, but made no reply. Jack was not so easy to manage as her mother believed, but she would not have had him any other way.

'You look beautiful,' Papa said as he gave her his arm and they prepared to enter the church. 'I'm so proud of my daughter.'

'I'm not always an angel, Papa.'

He nodded at her, a twinkle in his eyes. 'Do not imagine I do not know what kind of mischief you get into, Daughter. Your brother confessed the whole to me before he left for the army. He asked if I thought he should repay that damned four thousand, but I told him to forget it. Harding and his kind are the scum of the earth—and we shall never mention him again.'

'I was afraid to tell you, for I thought you would be ashamed of me.'

'How could I when all you did was try to protect your brother?'

In saying that she was not an angel, Charlotte had not quite meant what her father thought, but she kept her own counsel, for the secret of the little hidden room at the top of the house was hers and Jack's alone. In his arms there she'd learned to know what loving was all about, though Jack had not taken her maidenhead. He'd kept his word and the door of the dressing room remained locked each night, but no one had made a promise about warm summer afternoons, when they opened the windows of their secret hideaway and listened to the birds sing as they kissed and touched to their heart's content.

If Charlotte had doubted Jack's feelings for her, she no longer had cause, for he had shown her in every possible way that he adored her.

Smiling confidently, Charlotte walked the length of the aisle on her father's arm, her heart singing with joy. Jack and Phipps stood waiting for her and Jack turned to look at her as she came to stand at his side. Her veil was fine and she could see through it well enough to recognise the love in his eyes as he reached for her hand.

His cool fingers curled about hers possessively, holding her lightly, but with a firmness that spoke of his determination. She was his, had been his for longer than either of them had truly recognised and now he was claiming her before the world.

The vicar spoke of love and duty, of the purpose of marriage in the eyes of God, and then asked them to repeat their vows. As Jack slipped a heavy gold ring on her finger, a look that she had come to know and love entered his eyes; it was a look of complete love and of belonging.

After the ceremony and the signing of the register, they walked from the church to the ringing of bells. People from the estate and the villages crowded forward to shower them with rice and rose petals, and then they were running for their carriage, Charlotte clinging to the straw doll she'd been given by a young girl.

'To bless your fertility, Lady Delsey,' the girl said and subsided into giggles as Charlotte blushed.

The reception was lavish, for the marquis had invited more than three hundred guests and they flowed through the rooms and out into the gardens, where a huge marquee had been set up to accommodate them all.

Even the people from the estate were being entertained in another part of the large gardens, and Jack took his bride to visit them and thank them for all their hard work in the days leading up to the wedding. So much delicious food had been prepared that extra cooks had been brought in from London, one of them Jack's own chef, who had created the wonderful wedding cake— four layers of sugared exquisite artistry that had the guests gasping, decorated with delicate flowers, baskets of birds with feathered wings and spun sugar ribbons to cover the bridal couple on top.

Because Jack had decided that they would celebrate their wedding nuptials on the estate, they did not slip away as was often the custom, but danced the night away with a hundred guests in the huge ballroom. The older generation had retired to the various parlours and the drawing room, leaving the younger ones to dance until dawn.

The marquis had gone up to his room after the reception was over, declaring that he was tired but happy. Lady Daisy had kissed the bride and declared herself satisfied.

'I thought Jack would never be himself again,' she'd told Charlotte the day before the wedding, 'and when he lost his memory and seemed not to know me I was willing to hate you. Yet now he is the son he was before his father died—and he tells me it is your doing, because he has found something he'd never thought to know in you. So, if I was ever cold to you, you must forgive me, Charlotte. You've made my son happy and that is all I ever wanted.'

Charlotte told her there was nothing to forgive and they had parted on good terms. Lady Daisy had become firm friends with Charlotte's mother and was to stay with them once the happy pair had returned from their honeymoon.

'It is best that you become accustomed to being the mistress here without her,' Mama had told Charlotte. 'You are the future marchioness and you must greet her as family but also your guest when she comes to stay.'

After they had bid the last of their friends good-night, some departing to their homes, some to the many guest rooms, Jack took her hand and led her upstairs to their own apartments. He left her at the door, reminding her that the connecting door had been unlocked and the key put away, where it would stay for the rest of their lives.

'You are mine now, Charlie,' he murmured against her lips as he opened her door and saw her inside. 'I shall not keep you long. Send your maid away as soon as she has helped you out of that dress.'

Charlotte nodded wordlessly, his hand lingering in hers until she reluctantly let him go and he went out into the hall. Betty was waiting for her in the dressing room and came in when she heard them, looking at Charlotte uncertainly.

'Shall I undress you, my lady?'

'Just help me out of this,' Charlotte said. 'Then you can go to bed. Thank you for sitting up for me—and for making me look beautiful today.'

'You always look lovely, miss,' Betty said, slipping into the old form of address. 'And I like to look after you.'

She undid the long line of pearl buttons at the back of the gorgeous wedding gown and helped Charlotte out of it, then carried it away into the dressing room, and slipped out of the hall door moments before Jack appeared wearing a crimson-and-black-striped dressing robe.

Charlotte turned to welcome him, noting that his feet were bare. He must have stripped quickly, impatient to claim his bride, for she had not finished taking the pins from her hair.

'Sit down and let me do that,' he said, his voice slightly hoarse. 'You have lovely hair, my darling. I like it best when it is loose on your shoulders.' He lifted it, kissing the back of her neck.

Charlotte shivered, feeling the rush of desire that his touch aroused in her. She was glad that he had taught her to respond to his touch without being shy, for it meant that she could be as eager as he for the natural fulfilment of their loving. She arched her neck, enjoying the sensations trickling through her, relishing the feel of the hairbrush as he stroked it over her hair, letting it ripple in shining tresses to fan out on her shoulders. The feeling was so exquisite that she moaned with pleasure, and then she was on her feet, turning to him as he crushed her against him. His need was urgent and she melted into him, the evidence of his fierce desire making her tingle with anticipation. Slipping the straps of her chemise over her shoulders, he sent it slithering to the floor, his eyes seeming to feast on the glory that had been denied him until this moment. As his lips touched the hollow at the base of her throat, she gave a strangled cry and almost swooned into his arms, feeling them surround her strongly, and her body was exultant. Tonight she would be completely his.

Jack swept her up in his strong arms, carrying her to the bed, his eyes deep with love and desire. He placed her carefully amongst the fragrant sheets and then discarded his robe. The sight of his honed, strong masculine body made her catch her breath, for despite the scars that told of past battles and fresh wounds still not completely healed, he was magnificent.

Lying beside her, Jack gathered her into his arms and began to caress her willing body. Charlotte realised that she had previously only glimpsed the pleasure that could now be hers, for their touching and kissing had not set off the fierce hunger that now roared through her as she felt his cool flesh against hers. Silken smooth, his body hard and so masculine, so divinely strong, made her thrill and cry out, her back arching as she reached for him.

Their coming together was swift, for both were

in need, and they were carried to a heady climax that made Jack shout out and Charlotte shed tears as she clung to him. He wiped the tears and apologised for the pain he must have caused as he took her virginity, but she only shook her head.

'You told me how it would be the first time,' she said and touched his cheek, smiling as he looked concerned. 'Next time we shall not be in so much hurry…'

'No, no hurry, at all,' he murmured huskily, and after a short time of holding her pinned against him by his long strong legs, he began to make love to her again, this time with his lips and tongue, and his stroking hands. 'We have all the time in the world. The rest of our lives, my darling.'

Charlotte gave herself up to his caresses, but this time he brought her to a quivering climax without entering her himself and when she asked him why, he told her that he would not have her in pain.

'Tomorrow and all our tomorrows will be time enough to explore the pleasures of love, besides, this gives me pleasure. Touching you, looking at you, exploring all the places I have longed to make my own. I adore you, my Charlotte, and I have all I need right here.'

She smiled and her hands moved over his shoulder, caressing the satin skin of his back. 'To think that I once believed you wanted only a marriage of convenience…for the heirs that I might give you…'

'If we never had a child I should not care for myself, though Grandfather would be disappointed.'

'I shall not disappoint him, for I have promised him he shall have a grandson first,' she said, giving him a look that made him laugh and pull her closer. 'I am so glad that we have found love, Jack.'

'No more than I,' he said and was serious for a time. 'I never expected to and when we first met I liked you, but did not realise that you could come to mean so much to me. Only when we met again did I see how fortunate I had been in my choice. When my father died and I thought it might be because of a woman something closed up in me. I blamed her for taking him from us…and I hated her, because I knew he had never loved my mother or me as much as he loved her… I believed she had hurt him deliberately and thought all women faithless. Only when I had forgot my prejudice did I allow myself to fall in love.'

'Your father must have loved you. You were his son.'

'Perhaps—but *she* was the one who haunted him all his life. I did not understand then, my darling. I did not understand that it was possible to love a woman so much that life would mean nothing without her.'

'Is that how you love me?'

He nodded and stroked his finger round the sensitive part of her ear. 'Yes, though in London I did not know it. You amused me. I liked and admired you, Charlie, but I did not know how to overcome the barrier in my heart—and then I lost my memory. I forgot my distrust of your sex and when you dimpled up at me, when you spoke so honestly, trusted me, and then saved my life, I lost my heart, truly and for ever. When I discovered that you'd been snatched from me, I thought I should die if I could not get you back.'

'Then losing your memory was a blessing in disguise,' she murmured and cuddled up to him, her eyes meeting his wickedly. Stroking one finger down his naked chest, she said, 'Are you sure we have to wait until tomorrow?'

The question went unanswered as his lips found hers in a kiss that was so sweet and tender, yet fiercely demanding, that it took her breath and she had all the reply she needed.

* * * * *

MILLS & BOON®

Why shop at millsandboon.co.uk?

Each year, thousands of romance readers find their perfect read at millsandboon.co.uk. That's because we're passionate about bringing you the very best romantic fiction. Here are some of the advantages of shopping at www.millsandboon.co.uk:

* **Get new books first**—you'll be able to buy your favourite books one month before they hit the shops

* **Get exclusive discounts**—you'll also be able to buy our specially created monthly collections, with up to 50% off the RRP

* **Find your favourite authors**—latest news, interviews and new releases for all your favourite authors and series on our website, plus ideas for what to try next

* **Join in**—once you've bought your favourite books, don't forget to register with us to rate, review and join in the discussions

Visit **www.millsandboon.co.uk**
for all this and more today!